Night Birds off Lifandoy

Nature warden Tim Corn helps to spot a rare seabird, an all-black storm petrel, off the little Isle of Lifandoy. Meanwhile terrible news from a Press source reveals that Lifandoy's ownership has changed, while Tim's eccentric Uncle Wilfred has vanished down a hole and made a historic discovery, which he reveals to Tim and his fiancée Jessica Bull.

But all is overshadowed when a Canadian cult, the People of White, arrive to take over the island. The cult's demands soon shock the islanders as they insist on white food and drink, and ban white clothing and Bibles. Tim's ideological foe Graham Fytts sides with the cult, while Wilfred, Jessica's scheming small sisters Alice and Rosalind, and Darren Stocks with his beery friends all plot to evade its restrictions. The cult's members in return attempt to brainwash or convert the islanders.

But do all the People of White believe in their cause? Why might Wilfred go underground again? How could the cult's control devastate Tim and Jessica's wedding plans? Why are the black petrels at the centre of a likely clash, and who might turn violent? Finally, could anyone break the cult's hold over the island and make Tim and Jessica's wedding possible after all?

The author

George B. Hill is a retired research chemist. He has three grown-up children, Joanna, Peter and Angela and lives with his wife Christine in Sandbach, Cheshire, UK, where they attend a Baptist church. He began writing more seriously in 2012 and writes Christian fiction and on science and faith.

Books self-published by George B. Hill
(on Kindle, other e-books and in print):

Legend Sci-fi:
The Song of Rockall   (Kindle, 2013; others & print, 2014)

Lifandoy stories:
A Nest On Lifandoy   (Kindle, 2013; others & print, 2014)
An Orchid On Lifandoy   (Kindle, 2013; others & print, 2014)
Falcons Over Lifandoy   (Kindle, 2013; others & print, 2014)
Night Birds Off Lifandoy   (Kindle, 2017; others & print, 2017)

Non-fiction traditionally published by George B. Hill:

Alderley Park Discovered: History, Wildlife, Pharmaceuticals (Carnegie Publishing, 2016)

See the author's website at www.hillintheway.co.uk for more details including his other writing.

George B. Hill

NIGHT BIRDS

OFF LIFANDOY

*Very best wishes
to Richard*

George B. Hill

Acknowledgements:
Cover illustration: the sitting bird is not a Swinhoe's Storm Petrel but the closely related Tristram's, kindly made available on Flickr under Creative Commons (attribution license) by Beth Flint who photographed it on Nihoa Island at Midway Atoll. I could not find any good sitting Swinhoe's Petrel close-ups, but the flying birds are Swinhoe's, made available in the same way, and photographed by Geoff Lim per Alvin Wong. [Incidentally, a Swinhoe's is pictured being held by Rev John Stott in his classic of Christian natural history, *The Birds our Teachers; Biblical lessons from a lifelong bird-watcher* (2007).] Also from CC, by Jodipedia, is the boat (an Isles of Scilly launch) and by D. C. Atty are the white-clad figures. I thank all the above for generously making their images available. The main picture of the cove is a reversed image of Telegraph Bay on Alderney.

4

For Edna, who kept me going

Table of Contents

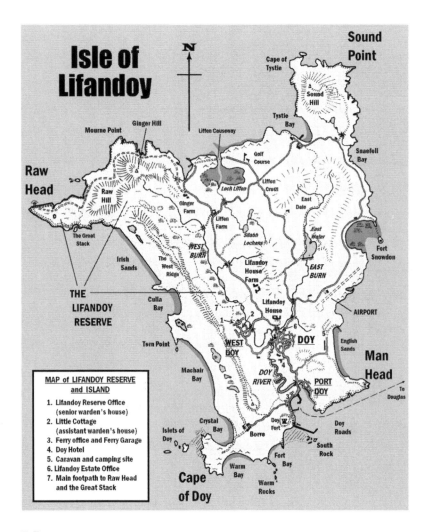

Map: A colour version of the above map appears on the back cover. A large printable colour copy may be downloaded free from the '*My Maps*' page of the author's '*My Writing*' website, at www.hillintheway.co.uk

Lifandoy lies in the Irish Sea south-west of the Isle of Man. However, it is not a real place! - although it is a composite of several real islands. The author invented Lifandoy and began writing stories about it around 1990.

8

1 – Black All Over?

'A plane missing?'

Mesmerised by the endless procession of waves, I was only half listening to Simon. I questioned him without moving my body or turning my head. 'That sounds bad! What did you say, Simon? You have a press report of a light plane lost over the English Channel?'

'Correct.'

I was dimly aware that Simon was reading the screen of his mobile phone. 'Is that a message from your newspaper? This plane – you say that there were passengers en route to Lifandoy on board?'

Simon lowered the phone. 'Er – yes. The report from my office says...'

'Oh! *There's* one. Hey, Keith! *Keith?*' I paused while shouting and rattled off an apology to my informant. 'Sorry, Simon. I'll be with you and your lost plane in a minute. Just let me tell – oh, KEITH ... Keith, there's another one! Do you see it? Too late – it's gone. No, I didn't get a good view. I only had a brief glimpse of the outline. It went out of sight. It should reappear in ten seconds. Just about opposite you, behind that breaking wave crest...'

A wiry, sun-browned figure in a khaki jacket, slightly shorter than me, glanced my way across the sloping deck, sniffed, and turned seaward to follow my pointing finger.

'I see it, Tim. In fact, I see two – there's another one, following it.' Keith's acknowledgement did not sound especially grateful. Nor did he turn his face back toward me as he spoke. This was not, however, from brusqueness. Rather, it was because his eye-sockets were now pressed to the business end of a weathered but useful-looking pair of binoculars.

Below the lenses of the latter, beyond the stanchioned rail where Keith stood, whitened water flowed. The supply of it seemed endless, due to the fact that the creamy carpet was unrolling constantly from a roll of foam under the fast-moving bow of the car ferry *S. S. Bagpipe*, on whose foredeck we stood.

The car ferry's stubby bow pointed across a blue sea, choppy but without whitecaps. To our right, the sea framed a large, presently cloud-laden and shadowed landmass. Otherwise the briny horizon in most directions was nearly clear, with only a cloudy hint of faraway land. Yet in one direction, directly ahead, lay a familiar lumpy outline, that of the approaching grass-green body of our home and workplace, the beautiful and presently sunny Isle of Lifandoy.

'No.' Keith announced his conclusion just as I came to the same one. Keith's voice, as he lowered his binoculars, was resigned. 'Those two are just the same as all the others we've seen. Both have white patches in the usual places. Neither of those two is black all over.'

'*Black all over?*' A different, deep voice spoke behind me. 'I'm sure he is, by now. He's certainly vanished into a black hole, at least!'

All three of us turned in surprise. I addressed the newcomer. 'Hello, Angus. What brings you down here, leaving the ferry to steer itself? You're not here with more news of this vanished plane of Simon's, are you?'

'Not me.' The speaker was Angus Donald, the regular helmsman of the *Bagpipe*. An old friend, he had an odd smile on his face. He wrinkled his brow. 'I know nothing of any missing aeroplane. No, the disappearance I'm talking about is that of your Uncle Wilfred, Tim.'

I stared. 'Uncle Wilfred? How could he disappear? He's far too large-as-life for his whereabouts to be in any doubt.'

'Oh, they know *where* he is. He's certainly present, and unharmed – as far as they know.'

'Unharmed?' I double-took.

Angus nodded. 'I thought I had better come down and tell you myself. The Port Doy harbour office has been on the radio with a message from Jessica. Your Uncle Wilfred has had a slight accident.'

I pursed my lips. '*Slight?* What sort of an accident?'

'He's fallen down a hole.'

'A hole? A deep one? A well, or a mine-shaft, or something?'

'No. It's not a very deep one.'

'Ah. Was this on one of his archaeological digs?'

'No. As far as we can understand, Wilfred appears to be entirely blameless, *this* time.' Uncle Wilfred was notorious for his eccentric activities. 'He has vanished along with his lawnmower.'

Keith spluttered. 'What? In the middle of his lawn?'

'Not in his own garden,' replied Angus. 'It appears he was mowing the lawn outside the chapel at West Doy.'

'That's right. He mows it on Saturdays. Normally he remains visible.'

'Well, this time the grass just opened up and swallowed him. Your Aunt Martha saw it happen and called the emergency services. Sergeant Farquhar came straight up from Doytown to the hole.'

'And the police are now looking into it? Great!'

'Wilfred called up to say that he was unhurt, but that he couldn't climb back up. He asked for a torch, and Sergeant Farquhar tossed him one down. Then the fire crew arrived and lowered a rope sling. But Wilfred wouldn't use it.'

'What? Why not?'

'He says the hole is too interesting. He's refusing to surface again.'

At my shoulder, Keith stifled a laugh. I protested. 'He must come up! He's still down there?'

'So Jessica told me. He has even asked for a thermos of tea to be lowered. And another set of batteries for the torch.'

'As you say, he will be black all over,' Keith responded, 'which is more than can be said for these rare birds we've been watching for.'

Angus looked interested. 'Ah. So *that's* what you've been doing down here. I wondered why you were staying on the draughty deck, instead of coming up into the warm cabin to pay me your usual compliments.'

Simon was puzzled. 'What birds can you see from the *Bagpipe* that are black all over? All the seabirds I've seen have been ordinary white seagulls; mind you, I wasn't watching for blackbirds or crows!'

I sniffed. 'We would not be watching for blackbirds in the middle of the Irish Sea.' I leaned over the ship's rail and gazed out. 'Ah yes, *there* we are. Do you see that little bird flying along the wave-tops over there?'

Just above the white spume, a tiny morsel of life was whizzing towards the ferry's bow, flickering as it followed, on frail wings, the moving surface of the water. In shape and size it was not dissimilar to a large swallow, except for a glaringly white patch of plumage on its rump. Simon blinked at it. 'Isn't that a house martin?'

I laughed. 'A surprisingly common mistake, actually. No, it's a Storm Petrel. Just an ordinary, white-rumped one, though.'

'A petrel? And you're looking for *black*-rumped petrels? Are they very rare?'

'Yes. It's a long story. But if you see one...'

Excitedly, Simon gazed around at the sea. With all the enthusiasm of the hopeless tyro, he stabbed a finger. 'Hey, is that one? Or, no, wait a minute – look at that!'

Both Keith and I sighed audibly and smiled. As wardens on the Isle of Lifandoy's large nature reserve and as nannies to every novice naturalist who arrived there, we both owned patience as a professional tool. We lifted our binoculars. Keith took the second bird, which was coming straight at the ship; automatically, I took the other.

The bird I could see was plainly an immature gull, dirty brown but with no shred of black in its plumage. I had seen that much with the naked eye, but Simon was my friend; I had no reason not to humour him as much as I did many of the novice birdwatchers I dealt with every day.

'It's a young common gull.' I stated the obvious, and then paused for Keith to announce his similarly pedestrian verdict. There was a brief pause. 'And behind it...'

Keith's voice, when it came, was slightly raised. 'Just a minute, Tim – that one *is* a petrel – it almost looks – hey! Get *that!*'

Startled, I fumbled for my binoculars, raised them to the bird as it raced to overtake the ferry, then dropped them instantly as the bird vanished under the ferry's slightly raked bow. I sensed Keith making a galvanic series of bounds across the deck. I followed, just in time to get my binoculars focused on the tiny creature as it shot out from under the *Bagpipe*'s hull. Undoubtedly a petrel, it showed its rump to us perfectly as it departed at right angles to the *Bagpipe*'s steady course. Without doubt, the little bird was black all over.

Keith and I both stared, clenching our binoculars and bracing our legs desperately as the ship rolled, until our eyeballs watered and the bird was a vanishing dot many wave-tops away. At our side, Simon and Angus stood patiently until Keith lowered his binoculars slowly.

'Well, *I'll* be...'

What Keith was about to be was not revealed, for at that moment Simon's mobile phone shrilled in our midst. Simon answered the call tersely.

'Stanley, *Chronicle*. Yes? What? Why?' He frowned at us in puzzlement. 'My office says to hold for a minute while they check an urgent message for me. Hey...' He lowered the phone slightly from his ear and turned to me 'Was that really one of the birds you're looking for? What exactly was it? I don't suppose I could put a story in the newspaper about it, could I?'

Keith and I exchanged thoughtful looks. 'Well ... there are facts we certainly wouldn't want to see printed,' I said. 'But I suppose you could drop in on me tonight if you want to hear more of the story.'

'At your cottage? Would seven o'clock do?' Simon nodded. 'And also – well, about your Uncle Wilfred: I don't suppose he might still be down that hole by the time we get to port, might he?'

Keith looked puzzled. 'Why?'

I grinned. 'I believe Simon thinks he has a story coming on about Uncle Wilfred, too. Uncle Wilfred and his hole are about to be immortalized in tomorrow's *Manx Chronicle*.' Simon reddened slightly at my words. 'Oh, don't worry, Simon. I'm not offended – it's obvious Uncle Wilfred is OK. In fact, you can do what you like with him.'

Simon grinned. Then his grin faded as his phone called his attention again. He answered cheerfully, and then listened intently.

'What? Yes? Oh, it is? That's bad. And the passenger list? Yes?' He listened again, and his face turned suddenly pale. 'What? *Who?* You're sure he was? *And...*' The journalist's eyes lifted as he listened, and he gazed quietly ahead of the ship towards distant Lifandoy. 'Yes, of course. Yes, I see.'

We had all become aware of the change in Simon's demeanour. There was silence as he ended the call and turned to us.

'That light plane has been declared lost,' he said. 'It's not turned up and it can't still be flying – it would have run out of fuel long before now. It was a private aircraft, but its flight plan was a perfectly good one. It disappeared from the radar screens twenty minutes after it took off from France, half way across the English Channel. No wreckage has been reported, but air accident investigators have already been called in.'

The other two had become puzzled by the conversation. Angus raised an eyebrow. 'It's a long way from here,' he said. 'Why are you telling us?' Keith had already lost interest and was scanning the sea with his binoculars once more.

I explained. 'There were passengers en route for Lifandoy on board; although I can't imagine who might fly all the way from France to Lifandoy in a private plane. The only Lifandoy person with enough money to do that would have to be the man who owns the lot, the…'

'The Earl of Lifandoy?'

Suddenly, the name Simon had pronounced seemed to hang in the air. Keith lowered his binoculars again and stared at him.

He nodded. 'Yes, I'm sorry. The passengers who were on board … well, there's no official list of names yet, but the first report is that the plane was definitely carrying the Earl of Lifandoy himself.'

There was a shocked pause. 'I hope nothing has happened to him. That could be seriously bad.' Keith voiced our thoughts. 'I mean, his family would be devastated, of course. But it could be bad local news also, for a lot of people.'

Simon looked at him. 'For you?'

'What?' Keith shook his head. 'No, I'm one of the lucky ones. I have an off-island employer and no relatives on Lifandoy to worry about. Tim and Angus would feel it more, at least through their families.'

'Feel what?' Simon wrinkled his brow. 'I mean, I know the Earl is important to Lifandoy. His fortune oils the island wheels, and his political pull with the Government also provides for development grants and that sort of thing. But Lifandoy has a substantial population and a big tourist trade. It wouldn't wither overnight if he weren't there, would it?'

We glanced at each other. It fell to me to answer. 'It's more than him oiling the wheels, Simon. It's a great deal more than that. The Earl of Lifandoy owns virtually the whole of the island of Lifandoy.'

'Owns? Do you mean, *personally*?'

'Lifandoy was a very late addition to the United Kingdom. It is still almost the equivalent of an independent feudal state, with the Earl as the feudal lord. Oh, he's a good landlord; in fact, we all know very well that Lifandoy would have only half its present population without his influence and, on occasion, his generosity.'

Simon was astonished. 'Are you telling me that most people on the island don't own their own homes?'

'Hardly anyone does. Nearly all homes on Lifandoy are tenanted or leased. The Earl owns the lot, except for a couple of ancient monuments. Even the port and police station and schools and churches are on the Earl's own land. And so are all the employers.'

Angus nodded slowly. 'If ever the island were sold, say to a property company, or carved up and marketed in bits, the tenants could be seriously bought out. There would be a huge demand from mainlanders for holiday cottages. Most of the tenants could never find the capital to pay auction prices for the roofs over their heads. Family homes held for generations would fetch prices their occupiers could only dream of. And a major population drop would put half the island's employers out of business, too. It could be the end of Lifandoy as a community.'

Simon frowned. 'But surely that would not be inevitable? I mean, the Earl's heir or heirs might be as generous as he has been.'

'And they might not. They might sell out to a property company that would asset-strip Lifandoy. It depends on who...' Angus paused and turned to me inquiringly 'Who his estate passed to ...Tim? Has the Earl ever made known the terms of his will?'

'Not to my knowledge. It's always been assumed the island would pass to the Earl's son Vivian.' A sudden, horrible thought gripped me. 'Simon? I don't suppose you have a report on who else...'

He was already on his mobile. We waited grimly as his distant office relayed an answer. When he lowered the phone, his face was still. He looked up. 'I'm sorry. Lady Lifandoy and Vivian were on the plane, too. And I have some more news. Some wreckage has been sighted not far from where the plane vanished, along with an empty inflatable dinghy. There was no sign of any survivors in the water.'

The blanket of shock was growing heavy. As the ferry came level with the Man Head lighthouse, the first point of Lifandoy island, we all lifted our eyes to gaze at the dark cliffs of the Head. Angus spoke. 'All those people. All those homes. All that island. *Now* whose is it? What does the future hold?'

I grimaced. 'I think it just went black all over.'

2 – Another Heir

The anxious debate went on. Except for Angus, who had returned to the bridge, we were still worriedly debating the likely provenance of the claims of the Earl of Lifandoy's nephews, nieces and other relations on his estate, when the *Bagpipe* rounded a low point and came within sight of Port Doy, Lifandoy's only real harbour. Discussion slowed as the ferry sailed through a harbour roads alive with small craft enjoying the fine conditions. We watched a string of sailing dinghies tacking nervously away from the slowing ferry's course. Then the inner haven came into view, with its marina of tall-masted yachts, their hulls iridescent in the sunshine. The *Bagpipe* creamed in and turned tightly across the harbour, frothing the water over a large area as she came to a halt and went noisily astern. A couple of cormorants flew from their roosting places atop a small concrete obelisk whose purpose had long since been forgotten; and a black guillemot that had been fishing peacefully paddled hastily away from the froth. The ferry's captain nudged his grumbling ship up to the wooden pier as smoothly as if it bore fenders made from eggs.

On the partly open car deck below, the drivers settled themselves for a short wait. The foot passengers were less patient and crowded around the gap in the rail, and then surged down the gangway as soon as it had ceased to grate to and fro on the pier.

Keith, Simon and I paused to allow some excited rucksack-clad youngsters to wobble after a harassed-looking youth leader down the steep slope. Then, with a wave up at Angus on the bridge, I walked easily after the other two down onto the pier of my home island. But my attention was not on the other passengers, nor on my companions.

Someone standing quietly on the pier watched me with interest as I approached. It was a young woman of about twenty-three, a year or so younger than I was. She had long, un-fussily arranged blonde hair and a shapely figure whose finer points I was at once able to appreciate. Keith and Simon, who reached her first, behaved in an odd manner. They walked up to her, smiled, gave a soft greeting, then immediately stepped past her and stood with their backs to her just beyond, talking in slightly loud voices about things of no importance.

The young woman looked toward me with an expression that was slightly coy but expectant. I walked straight up to her, with a directness that told any observer she was no stranger to me. She did not move a step; yet her quiet body language was powerful enough to make my knees, still wave-accustomed from the deck, feel distinctly unsteady.

From the top of the gangway my pace had been constant and my momentum unbroken. As she met me, the young woman turned her head slightly, so that the first contact between us was when my lips met firmly at an angle the moist, soft ones of Jessica Bull, my fiancée.

It was a long kiss, even though Jessica's nose was tickling my cheek. We reached around and held each other, pulling our bodies that bit closer than necessary, hugging every trace of warmth and sensation from each other, as we always did nowadays when one of us came back from travelling for any reason over the wine-dark sea.

Although we were young and in love, ours was an embrace not entirely of passion; I felt also, as I knew Jessica did, seriously grateful that we were once more together. Nowadays, we were always careful to keep thankfulness not only as a gift but also as a sort of weapon against the griefs of life. It was not that we feared losing each other. In fact the opposite was true: we had already faced total loss and had been given each other back from beyond our hopes.

Yet since we became engaged we had rarely been without a touch of defiance against the world, as we both remembered events that had so nearly robbed us of each other. So our embrace was not only ecstatic but sharp and bittersweet, and much more sensual because of it. We held as tightly to each other as might be expected in public for a couple shortly to be joined in Christian marriage. And there, surrounded by all the bedlam of a packed car ferry unloading efficiently while the tide fell, we clung, smiling at each other with our eyes.

■　■　■　■

Eventually, Jessica took me by the shoulders and held me at arm's length. 'All right, *darling* Timothy. I really cannot take much more.'

'Much?' I lifted her arms and leant forward for another passionate kiss.

'Any, then.' She side-stepped and, smiling sweetly, caught my wrist, twisting my arm behind me and forcing it up my back towards my shoulder-blade.

I yelped. 'All right! Jess, I yield.'

'You'll have to, Prince Charming,' she chided me. 'I couldn't take any more without a rest for oxygen. Wasn't that enough, for you? You've only been off the island for twenty-four hours. And you have more important things to think about just now.'

'Like Uncle Wilfred, you mean? More serious, maybe, not important,' I grumbled. 'Hey, Jess? You're not supposed to put an arm-lock on me yet. Arm-locks are for after the wedding. And then you won't need one; not when I've promised to love and to polish...'

'And I have not promised to obey?' She frowned. 'I'm still thinking about that one.'

'I'm not,' I assured her. 'This is the modern world. Why should you promise to obey me? I'm not asking you to.'

'I know. If you did, I wouldn't. Yet you haven't. And I think I therefore might.'

'Eh?' I appealed for male support. 'Hey, Keith! Do you think women are incomprehensible?'

Keith glanced over his shoulder. 'Yes,' agreed my boss. 'That's why I've tried to lose the habit. Successfully, for the moment.'

I gave Jess a supercilious smile. 'There you are. You are incomprehensible. Or at least, you will have to remain so until you explain yourself to me later.'

Keith and Simon both turned round, grinning.

'Good,' said Keith. I'm glad that's settled. And now we can say hello properly to Jessica. You look great, Jessica.'

She smiled and leant forward to give Keith a polite kiss on the cheek. 'Thank you. Now – Tim, should we be running to catch the harbour bus? It's about to leave.'

Keith shook his head. 'You can all have a lift in the Land Rover. Didn't I make the offer earlier, Tim? I meant to. And, Simon? We didn't know you would be on board, but you're welcome also; we owe you more favours than one lift, in any case.'

Jessica and I leapt into the back of Keith's official Lifandoy Reserve vehicle on the pier, leaving Simon to take the front seat. Shortly, Keith eased the Land Rover along the bumpy old wooden pier. As we drove onto the quay and around the harbour, we could see little knots of people standing outside the port shops and business premises, reading from phones or listening to portable radios or just talking with worried faces. 'You've heard the latest about the Earl's plane?' asked Jess.

'Yes. And I can see the news has broken with a vengeance,' I replied.

'We're all devastated up at the Estate Office. Especially about Lady Lifandoy – she was such a lovely person. She knew every secretary in the Estate Office by name.'

'I know. But the death of the Earl will have a bigger impact on us all. The livelihood of the whole island is at stake. We have been worrying about who might inherit the estate...'

'With the heir dead as well?'

'Yes. And the Earl's son had no heir himself, of course.'

'He may not have made a will.'

Keith pursed his lips. 'If Vivian died *with* his father, then it could be his father's will that counts in any case.'

'I can check our office files,' offered Simon. 'I'm sure we have a thick file on the Earl himself.'

I frowned. 'Perhaps the Factor might know about the Earl's will, or someone else at the Estate Office?'

Jessica shrugged. 'Perhaps. But I've never heard the will mentioned while I've been a secretary there. Someone in the legal department might know. But I don't.'

'Perhaps nobody outside the family knows. It could be complicated – the estate could pass to any of a whole set of nephews or nieces. Or even to all of them.'

Jessica was silent for a few moments. 'I wonder. It runs in my mind that there might be someone else.'

'Eh? Who?'

'You should ask your Uncle Wilfred. But does the name *Dominic* mean anything to you?'

'Dominic? As a first or second name?'

'First. The second name is Lifandoy.'

Simon looked around. 'As in the Earl? The Earl's full title is Lifandoy of Lifandoy, isn't it? So Lifandoy is his surname as well as his family seat.'

'Yes. I mean someone in his family,' said Jessica.

'But he has no brother,' I interjected, 'and we know the names of all his nephews; none of them is a Dominic.'

'The name means nothing to me,' offered Keith.

'Nor me,' added Simon.

I thought hard. 'It's coming back to me now. I have a vague idea – yes, wasn't there a *second* son?'

'Really?' Simon and Keith both glanced backward in surprise.

'It was a long time ago. I think I remember Uncle Wilfred mentioned him once. He was born with a severe lung problem and mental handicap and was flown abroad for treatment. To Canada, if my memory can be trusted. Uncle Wilfred thought that it failed and the child died, long ago. Yes, I think he was called Dominic.'

Simon was still gazing over his shoulder at us. 'If he died then it means nothing,' he said. But there was a gleam in his eyes as he looked Jessica. 'I take it you have no evidence to the contrary?'

She hesitated. 'Well...'

'Jessica's work at the Estate Office is confidential,' I pointed out. 'She can't tell you anything, Simon. She could lose her job.'

Jess shook her head. 'It's not anything I learnt at the Office,' she said. 'I would never have mentioned it, if that were so. Actually, it was something I saw on a letter that the postman once delivered wrongly.'

'To you?'

'To my Auntie Jenny, actually. She lives in the end cottage on Top Street, looking over the Estate Office. Hers is the first house the postman delivers to on his round after he goes up to Lifandoy House. Two or three times he has delivered letters for the House to her in error.'

'When was this?'

'About a year ago. I was visiting her and she asked me to pass an envelope on. It was addressed to the Earl; it looked like a small birthday card, which would fit, as the Earl's birthday was that week.'

There was a stillness in the Land Rover. 'And?' said Simon.

'It was from Canada. The address was badly handwritten, in rather faint ink. I remember thinking that the writer was probably a small child or old, if they were sending a paper card. On the back, the name of the sender was given as Dominic Lifandoy.'

'What was the address? Can you remember?'

'Yes. It stuck in my mind because it was unusual.' Jessica wrinkled her clear brow. 'The full address was something like Fourjohns Hospital, Niagara Falls, Ontario, Canada.'

'Fourjohns Hospital? Built by four chaps named John, I imagine,' said Keith.

I nodded. 'Unless it's at a place called Fourjohns. Niagara. I remember, now. Dominic *did* have a lung problem. That was why he was sent to Niagara for treatment – the Earl would have sent him anywhere in Europe or America for treatment, no matter how much it cost, and Niagara was the most humid civilised place anyone could think of.'

'The Earl visits Canada occasionally,' added Jessica. 'Probably he visits him.'

'But Dominic never came back,' I finished.

'Well, if he's alive, he might now,' murmured Keith thoughtfully.

22

3 – Wilfred's Hole

On the lawn of West Doy chapel, the entire Lifandoy island police force was by now indeed looking into Wilfred's hole. Both of them were there, in the burly forms of Sergeant Farquhar and his carrot-haired young constable, William Williams. Along with them, a number of other people were also peering into the hole, for it was quite a wide one, which dramatically terminated the smooth stripe of the lawnmower's path. It looked easily capable of swallowing up one short but not insubstantial uncle, as well as the chapel's even more substantial antique lawnmower. The bystanders looked up as we arrived.

'Hello, Timothy. Hello, Jessica.' A white-haired, apple-cheeked lady with an expression of gentle exasperation on her face greeted us warmly.

'Hello, Martha. Is your worse half still down there?'

'He is.' Martha sighed. 'And he wants me to go down there to join him, of all things. I've told Wilfred that retired schoolteachers with respectable reputations do not take up pot-holing. Anyway, now that's you're here I shall leave you with the job of persuading him to come up out of there. I have some soup and sandwiches to make up, for I'm sure Wilfred will want his tea soon even if he stays down there, to say nothing of all these good people who need refreshments while they work here on his behalf.'

Martha smiled at us and walked away, while we turned to the remaining crowd. As we did so, several smaller figures near the hole edge caught my attention. I approached them. In the middle was a small girl of about eleven, standing on a low wooden box. One of her fists was clenched tight around some small objects. She was accompanied by a slightly taller and thinner analogue of herself. Both girls had features closely resembling Jessica's. The taller girl was holding a clipboard, on which she was writing busily. The smaller girl appeared to be inciting the other children to speak out in some way; as I came near, I could hear her words of exhortation.

'Seven to four, six-thirty. Two to one, seven o'clock. Five to two, seven-fifteen. Or what about two to one on, five-thirty? Come on, speak up! Quickly now, before I put the odds up.'

I interrupted. 'Alice? What are you and Rosalind doing there?'

Alice declined to look in my direction. 'Rosalind,' she addressed the slightly taller girl, 'cancel the seven to four. And don't forget to charge Carmen the full rate. She can afford it.' Briefly, Alice loosened her fist just enough to jingle a few coins held tightly in it.

One of the other children, a spectacled small boy called Oliver, replied to my question. 'She's running a book on what time they will get Mr. Corn out of the big hole. Do you want to place a bet? Seven o'clock still seems to have quite reasonable odds.'

'You're joking!' I was about to address Alice angrily. But another voice spoke first, in the coolly magisterial tone of an eldest sister's.

'Alice?' The smallest girl went white in a moment. 'Rosalind? I'm *sure* that neither of you would ever, under any circumstance, gamble upon church property, would you?'

Alice flushed. 'Er, no, Jessica. I'm only responding to customer demand. But the odds aren't worthwhile, anyway.'

Jessica smiled sweetly. 'That's a relief. But it was good of you and your friends to make a collection, to provide free drinks for the Sergeant and Constable William. I'll take that money now.' Jessica held out her hand; Alice, with a look of consternation, opened her fingers weakly and let several small coins tumble out. 'But – Jessica, it's not all mine!'

Jessica beamed at the other children. 'I'm sure Alice will repay from her pocket money any money she has borrowed from you all.'

The children cheered faintly, looking puzzled. Jessica bent forward and whispered a few words in Alice's ear, then did the same to Rosalind. Both girls paled further; Alice's face was now chalk-white. Alice stepped quickly off her box and, without a backwards glance, stumbled away.

At the hole edge, William Williams greeted me cheerily as an old friend. 'We'll soon have your Uncle Wilfred out, Tim. In fact, he can come out any time he wants. The lawnmower might be more of a problem. But we have a ladder down into the hole now. Sarge was wondering if you could just ask Mr. Corn, for us, to make use of it?'

'*Ask* him to?' I stared at him, and then bent forward over the ragged crater in the turf. Beneath was not quite complete darkness; it seemed to me that a surprisingly large cavity opened out in the gloom.

I called down into it, somewhat self-consciously. 'Wilfred? *Wilfred?* Are you down there? What on earth are you playing at?'

'Or what under it?' chuckled one of the crowd.

There was silence for several seconds. Then a weird, scraping sound could be heard. Further back in the gloom, something came dimly into view. The thing – whatever it was – paused. Then it moved a step further. It paused again. All that could be seen was what appeared to be two unequal eyes: a large, dull, pink-and-brown one marked with evil-looking black veins, and a small, feebly glowing orange one. Unnerved, I tensed myself, ready to spring back if necessary.

Then the two eyes moved forward once more. As they came beneath the hole, they were illuminated by pale daylight. The orange one was the light of a fading torch, its batteries almost extinguished. The larger pink one was the bald head of what had once been an ordinary-looking uncle, but was now an uncle whose face and pate were besmeared from bushy sideboard to bushy sideboard with dark strands of ancient cobwebs and a rich layer of good Lifandoy soil.

'Timothy? Excellent.' A broad grin could just be discerned under the slime. 'Come on down. I'll hold the ladder. Have you a good torch?'

'What? Wilfred, we're trying to *rescue* you.'

'Oh, there will be time to do that, as well, before tea-time. Bring a good torch and come down the ladder. Carefully, now.'

Constable Williams handed me a large, shiny torch. 'You'd better borrow our rescue torch, Tim.'

Bewildered, I turned to Jessica for reassurance. 'It's dark down there,' I bleated.

She eyed me lovingly. 'Would you like me to go down there instead of you, darling?'

A couple of sniggers came from the bystanders. Keith enquired whether I would prefer a push or a shove. Simon carefully positioned himself with his camera.

I set my jaw. 'Give me the torch,' I snarled. 'I'm going down. But make sure Wilfred keeps that grin off his face, and his hands off that ladder.'

■ ■ ■ ■

Even with my eyes shut I would have known that the hole led into somewhere seriously old. A smell of dry mustiness surrounded me as I descended into a dimly lit, long space. In addition to the debris of the collapse, much dust had obviously been raised by the fall-in. A little of it puffed up under my feet as I stepped off the ladder's foot onto a heap of loose soil and turf.

The lawnmower still lay, half buried, in the heap; both it and Uncle Wilfred had evidently had quite a soft landing. They could easily have had otherwise, however, judging by the weight of earth they had brought down. 'Are you all right? You would have a headache by now if that lot had flattened you,' I remarked.

'Oh, I could have been much flatter than that by now,' my uncle replied, glancing upward.

I followed his gaze. As I did so I noticed that the walls of the hole were made of small close-fitting stones and sloped upwards, as though we were standing under a long upturned boat. Above us the stones nearly met; and the resultant gap was bridged by large stone slabs. But one of the slabs had evidently slid to one side at some time in the past. It now hung partly unsupported above us, while the remaining part of the roof was only soil, through the hole in which Wilfred and the mower had fallen and through which the ladder now protruded.

I stared up at the stone slab. 'For crying out loud! Is that really secured?'

Wilfred sniffed. 'If it hasn't fallen down in over a thousand years, it's unlikely to drop during the five minutes you're standing under it.'

'Hah! Alternatively, it could have been hanging on all that time in order to turn us into sandwich filling! Is it – hey, is this place

26

old, then?' I noticed for the first time that more large stones formed one end of the chamber. A black square in the gloom was clearly an entrance, low in the wall.

My uncle sighed. 'Even in these days of falling educational standards, I would have thought...'

'That's enough about falling,' I snarled. 'So this is why you're interested in this hole? As part of your historical hobby?'

My uncle gazed at me pityingly. 'I suppose you would have dismissed Tutankhamun's tomb as just a hobby collection?'

'Certainly not. But that was full of gold. This has...' I looked around and waved my hand 'This has stones and nothing else. Unless...' I stared at the dark square hole. 'Unless there's gold in *there?*'

'Sadly, no. Or at least, no treasure that *you* would value. The hole leads to a Neolithic burial crypt, which is far older even than this chamber where we stand.'

'What's this one, then?'

'We are standing in the main space of what is called a *souterrain* – a secret underground storehouse, dating from the Iron Age. Usually they had passages leading to them, but this one was obviously accessed through the older prehistoric chamber for convenience and security. It would have been built of stone then covered over, and its builders would have hidden here in times of danger. It is exceptionally rare to find one that is still standing. It's also unusually high and long – normally they are only up to head height.'

'But there is treasure of some sort next door?' I peered hopefully at the gloomy square hole in the stone wall. 'What's in there?'

'In the tomb? Come and look in there first, now you are down here.'

Taking the new torch I had brought down, Wilfred bent and clambered into the square opening. I was glad when he shone the torch behind him to guide me. I squeezed into the metre-square opening, banging my elbow as I did so.

'Ouch! It's an inconvenient way to keep safe. Hey – *aah!*' The floor of the tube-like opening vanished, and I slid clumsily forward, banging my other elbow as I landed on a very hard floor. I rose painfully and cautiously, feeling above my head with one hand for any obstacle.

Wilfred shone the torch around. We appeared to be standing in a solid stone box. At the other end of the box was a second square opening like the one by which we had entered; but this one was blocked by large, jagged boulders. It was extremely cold; I shivered. 'How have you survived down here for so long? You must be frozen.'

'Adrenaline is keeping me warm.' Wilfred bounded around like a young sheepdog. 'There's so much of interest.'

I surveyed my surroundings with a jaundiced eye. 'So much? I can't see anything of *anything*. It's entirely empty.'

'Of course it is,' my uncle agreed, pointing. 'Except for *these*.'

I peered at the focus of his interest. On two or three of the stones were a number of long lines of deep, crude scratchings. 'I presume this is prehistoric writing?'

Uncle Wilfred eyed me pityingly. 'No. Prehistoric times are called that because writing and written history had yet to be invented. This was written less than a thousand years ago, after the other chamber was built.'

'Eh? So someone broke into an empty grave to scratch on its walls?'

Wilfred's look of compassion intensified. 'They did not know it was empty until they entered it.'

'So who were they?'

'A whole series of raiders seem to have been in here down the centuries. I can show you traces left by Saxons, Irish Picts and Vikings.'

'But no gold? Huh.'

'No.' Wilfred smiled. 'Only the graffiti the various raiders and other visitors left behind, which is of great value to me, though not the greatest treasure I shall show you. I can translate some of these runic inscriptions. Here – this one says "These runes were carved with the axe Kali brought from Snaeland." Snaeland was a Viking name for Iceland. The one below it even has a name we can date: "Crusaders broke in here. Thorny carved these runes for Earl

Rognvald". He was a Viking on his way to the Second Crusade in about 1150 AD.'

'How did they get in here?'

'Most of the visitors must have entered by that second entrance, the one which is now blocked with boulders.'

I gazed around and pointed to an inscription near the entrance. 'Here – what does this inscription say?'

Uncle Wilfred glanced across. A slightly pained expression appeared on his face, and he chose instead to focus on a small legend near to the large one I had noticed. 'This small one here is interesting. At least, it would be if I could read it. But...'

'No, I meant this one.' I redirected his gaze. He looked up and pursed his lips primly. 'Er – yes, I have translated that one.' He paused. 'It probably dates from the Viking period. It reads: "Ingigerd was bedded here. Olaf says so."'

'What?' I guffawed. 'Wilfred, your hobby of ancient archaeology suddenly comes alive for me. I had no idea there was such interest to be found in it!' I gestured at the chamber around us. 'Who knows what history might have been made in this very spot!'

Uncle Wilfred sniffed. 'This grave is of far less interest to me than the first chamber you were in. Now, go on back through the tunnel. Let me show you some *real* treasure...'

4 – Secrecy

We clambered back into the large chamber with the lawnmower and the ladder. To our surprise, we were not alone there. Wilfred was pleased.

'Hello, Jessica. Nice of you to drop in. Is that a better torch you have brought down? Excellent! Timothy and I have just been looking at the grave.'

Jessica shivered. 'Grave?'

'There's a prehistoric morgue next door,' I informed her. 'The Saxons, Picts and Vikings have already raided it, though. It's empty.'

'That's a relief.' Nevertheless, she wound a warm arm tightly around me. I was pleased, and not only because she made my hormones flow; despite her shivering, Jessica's skin temperature was now several degrees above mine. She gazed around. 'So what was *this* place used for, then?'

I grinned. 'Yes, did a bit of nooky go on in here as well, Wilfred?'

'A bit of nooky? Under the chapel lawn?' Jessica gave me a scandalized look.

Wilfred answered. 'Not here, I think. This was just a store-chamber – at *first*.'

'What did it become after that?' I looked around. On a stone slab near the square opening I noticed some more markings. 'I see there is more graffiti here.'

Wilfred's voice was quiet. '*That* is not graffiti. Look closer.'

I did. 'Oh – it's a *cross*.'

'It is.' Wilfred shone his torch onto it. 'A Celtic one. Carved into the stone. I've only ever seen one like that once before.'

Jessica spoke. Her voice was soft. 'Was this once a place of worship?'

Wilfred turned to look at her. 'I think it was. The first church on Lifandoy.'

She gazed around. 'A real underground church.'

Uncle Wilfred smiled. 'I suppose it is. Yes, this chamber was a place of secrecy, but not a place of retreat of the amorous

30

kind. Or at least, those who were lovers here were not in the business of devoting their affection to their fellow worshippers.'

'You mean this really was a religious place? Like for monks or nuns?' I shivered in turn. 'Well, last winter you were complaining that the chapel central heating system was feeble. But this cave is definitely a place for God's frozen people! It's a wonder they're not still praying their last prayer!'

'Oh, that would never have been possible for them.' Uncle Wilfred was strangely firm. 'Of all people, *they* would never have *stayed* here.'

'Who? Why not?' My interest was piqued. I turned to Jessica with a puzzled frown. But she was nodding her head.

'Of course not,' she said. '*They* would have moved on – although they would not have known where they were going. None of them did. They were as mysterious as the wind... Let's get Wilfred out of here and he will tell you about them.'

■　■　■　■

Uncle Wilfred's lecture on the wanderings of the ancient Celtic Christians was, I had to admit, fascinating. 'They rarely built lasting places of worship,' he said. 'They had neither the time nor the resources to do so. They lived on the edge. They wandered for the love of God – *peregrinatio pro Deo amore.*'

'How did they get home?'

'Home? The idea probably never entered their heads. They did not expect to be long in this world at all – especially if some Viking raiders passed by. As Jessica said, they were like the wind, moving as they were led by God's Spirit.'

I leaned back, enjoying the comfortable armchair. We were sitting talking, with Jessica listening quietly, in the warmth of Uncle Wilfred's sitting room. There we were being fussed over by Aunt Martha, at whose stern command Wilfred had finally consented to be rescued from his subterranean prison. 'So what will happen to our Celtic cave now?'

Wilfred put down his soup and rubbed his nose thoughtfully. 'That's a good question. I've already contacted the British Museum, which is sending someone over immediately. They are very excited;

31

the archaeologist I talked to said the site might be taken out of our hands by the Government.'

'What? The chapel would be confiscated?'

'Nothing like that. It would be designated a national heritage site, owned by the nation. We would still look after it. But compensation would have to be paid to the Earl of Lifandoy as former owner. There are two other sites on the island to which that has already happened.'

A sudden silence fell. I broke it after a few moments. 'Er – former owner...? You haven't heard, then?'

'Eh?' Uncle Wilfred blinked at me. 'Heard what?'

■　■　■　■

My uncle was devastated by the news of Lord Lifandoy's disappearance. 'It *can't* be true. The consequences could be terrible.'

Aunt Martha appeared from the kitchen. With Wilfred safely rescued, Martha's sandwiches and soup had become redundant, so she had invited us back to Big Cottage to consume them. Keith had departed but Simon had been persuaded to join us with the promise of food.

Martha confirmed our news. 'I'm sorry, Wilfred. They've just said on island radio that all three of them were definitely on the Earl's plane.'

'Vivian too? *He's* definitely gone, as well?' Uncle Wilfred had a weary, faraway look. 'I remember him when he was little. He was one of the cleverest children I ever knew. And strong and healthy with it, quite unlike his brother Dominic.'

I nodded. 'We were talking about *him*. Most people had forgotten that the Earl had a second son, but I thought I remembered his name was Dominic. Jessica has seen an old letter that gave his address as a hospital in Canada. I suppose he's dead now.'

'Oh, no!' Wilfred interrupted. 'Dominic is still living. Or at least, he was living less than a year ago. I know that to be true, because it was the Earl himself who told me.'

'Really?' Jessica and I both sat up. 'Then Dominic is the new owner of Lifandoy island!'

Wilfred looked worried. 'That may be so. But perhaps there may be some other outcome.'

'What? Surely it's better for the island to stay in the family? And if Dominic is an invalid, he would surely leave the Estate Office to run the island for him as it does now...'

'Unless he wanted to work through another party.' Uncle Wilfred wore a darker expression than I had seen on him for a long time.

'Like who?'

'I'm not sure.' He hesitated. 'I'm probably adding one and one to make three.'

He now had the attention of all of us. Reluctantly, he spilled what beans he possessed. 'When I spoke with the Earl about Dominic – it was at the last Estate Office Christmas party – he gave me the impression that Dominic had got into something that seriously worried the Earl and his wife. He didn't spell it out in detail. But I gathered that the private hospital where Dominic lives had come under the control of a rather strange charitable trust. The trust in question was being monitored by the Canadian police.'

'Why?'

'The trust was rumoured to have a link with the leader of a secretive religious community – a doomsday-type cult. And apparently Dominic had gained an interest in the beliefs of the cult. In fact, the Earl suspected that Dominic was in some way being brainwashed by the cult. He raised the subject with me because he wanted to know if I had ever heard of the organization, or could give him any advice on dealing with such groups.'

'And had you?'

'No. The cult is called the Cult of White. Its members also use the name "The People of White", which makes them sound harmless, but I'm sure they're not. They seem to be fanatical about secrecy.'

We agreed. 'They obviously have something to hide from the Canadian authorities, for a start.'

Wilfred went on. 'I'd never heard of their leader, either. I think I would have remembered his name if I had heard it: he is called Johnson Shining.'

'Johnson Shining? Not really?' Jessica giggled. 'He sounds more like a window-cleaning firm than a false prophet.'

Simon had a thoughtful expression. 'I think I might have heard of him once. But not in a happy association.'

'Anyway,' finished Wilfred, 'I told the Earl that Martha and I would pray for Dominic, and I put him in touch with a Christian group that specializes in helping families with cult problems. And I hoped we would hear no more bad news – which was the case until now...'

At that point Martha came in and a discussion started on how cults chose their names. Wilfred was just saying something about white being a symbol of purity when the telephone rang.

'Wilfred, it's for you.' Martha handed her spouse the handset. 'It's the Factor himself, from the Estate Office.'

Wilfred was surprised. 'What is Tom Fothergill doing in his office at this time of a Saturday evening?' He started to listen. 'Wilfred here.'

Relaxing, we half listened to half the conversation. 'Yes, I heard a little while ago,' said my uncle. 'And I do want to say how shocked I was...' He paused. 'I'm sure that will be the case, although obviously...'

Rather abruptly, he stopped and continued to listen. Sensing a change in his manner, we glanced at him. A serious expression had occupied Uncle Wilfred's face. His eyebrows rose and contracted a little. Plainly events were taking a turn he had not expected.

'I'll do that,' he said, rather tersely. 'And I will be with you by seven.' He put the phone down and frowned at Martha. 'I can finish my soup, dear. But the rest of my meal will have to become supper rather than tea.'

Martha was not pleased. 'Mr. Fothergill has called you to the Estate Office? Whatever for?'

'A meeting.'

'A meeting? What sort of meeting? He has no interest in your sheep farming, has he?'

Uncle Wilfred pursed his lips. 'I'm afraid I'm not allowed to say.'

■　■　■　■

And that was that. When my uncle wants to keep a secret, he clams up as tightly as if he has a million dollar pearl in his mouth. He finished his soup rapidly, sat for a minute or two looking thoughtful, oblivious to the surrounding conversation, then made his excuses, grabbed a battered straw Panama hat, and left.

As soon as the door closed, we all looked at Martha. "What's up, dear aunt? Come on, you must be able to guess something?'

She wrinkled her brow. 'I'm not sure I...'

'We are, though. You should tell us.'

She shook her head. 'I was not going to say that I should *not* tell. I simply can't; I don't know anything. Although I was just thinking that there could only be one reason for Mr. Fothergill to want to speak to Wilfred in these circumstances.'

'Which is? Tell us the secret.'

'Oh, it's no secret. I would keep it if it were. But Wilfred is one of the Estate Seigneurs. You know that yourself.'

Simon looked interested. 'Estate Seigneurs?'

'They're a room full of old buffers who do ceremonial things to look after the island,' I said.

'I thought Lifandoy island was managed by the Estate Office and a board of appointed professional trustees?'

'It is,' said Jessica. 'But in theory they are appointed by the Seigneurie, a body of senior island citizens...'

'Mostly doddering old grey-heads,' I interjected. 'Who have a dinner once a year on Trinity Sunday to see how many of them are still alive.' Jessica and Martha both scowled at me.

'And Wilfred is one?' asked Simon.

'He became one three years ago, when his father died,' explained Martha. 'Seigneur is a hereditary position. But what significance it has just now I cannot imagine. Perhaps it's something to do with arranging a replacement for the Earl on the Estate's management board. But why that should be so urgent is beyond me.'

■   ■   ■   ■

There seemed little further appetite for conversation. We made a manful attempt to demolish Martha's mound of sandwiches, then offered our thanks and headed back down the path through the colourful garden of Big Cottage to the street.

Simon glanced at us hopefully. 'Would anyone object if I reported in the *Manx Chronicle* that the Estate Seigneurs had held a meeting to discuss the plane crash? Can we assume that's what it was about?'

'I see no problem,' I said. 'But there is going to be no revolution on the island.' I reached Wilfred's gate. I rested my palm on the gatepost for a moment. '*Yeaagh!*'

The others looked at me. I lifted my hand, to reveal the vomit-coloured blob of chewing gum now stuck to it.

'Oh dear,' said Jessica. 'Whose could that be?'

'I'll give you one guess,' I snarled. 'But you can ask her yourself. Here she comes.'

Alice and Rosalind, at the head of a group of worried-looking young people, were trotting down the street. 'Hey, *you!*'

Jessica's sisters slowed and turned to me without altering their worried expressions, which was unusual. I held up my hand to expose the regurgitated blob.

'Haven't you left something behind?

Alice inspected it minutely. 'No. That's banana flavour. I detest banana flavour.'

'Gum should be banned on the island!'

She gave me a strange stare. 'Yes. That's what we are afraid of.'

'Eh?'

Rosalind also scowled. 'We've heard a rumour that the island is going to be taken over by people who are ideologically opposed to the chewing of gum.'

I snorted with laughter. 'The island taken over? What film have you been watching?'

Jessica eyed her younger sisters penetratingly. 'Tell.'

They shrugged. 'There isn't anything to tell,' said Alice. 'We heard that from a source who must remain unidentified, even from our big sister. We've done nothing wrong, after all. You can't expect us to expose our informant to danger just to satisfy your curiosity.'

'I suppose not.' Jess frowned. 'But one of you can take your banana-flavoured gum with you, wherever you are going.'

'Oliver!' Rosalind spoke, as if to a dog. The urchin Oliver sidled up, scraped the gum off my hand with the end of a small ruler, and retreated. I looked around for something to wipe my hand on, considered Alice, then chose a bit of hedge instead.

Simon cleared his throat. 'Er – may I ask–?'

Alice gave a doubtful look. 'It's against the policy of our Cabal to speak to the Press.'

'*Quite.* Mind you, unidentified sources in high places sometimes find it convenient to leak news to trusted correspondents. The Press can be useful if you want to put pressure on someone. If your group – er, Cabal – had some information that you wanted made known anonymously...'

Rosalind turned away but Alice nodded thoughtfully. 'Just say that a reliable source has reported that dastardly political manoeuvring on Lifandoy has created a threat to the healthy dietary needs of the island's future population.'

I spluttered. 'Dietary needs? Banana flavoured chewing gum? And *what* politics?'

'Actually,' said a soft voice behind my ear, 'It's not politics. But it might be religion.'

5 – Arrivals

We turned. The speaker was a slightly stooped, thin, olive-skinned man wearing a dog-collar. From under a thatch of stiff grey hair he smiled a small smile with his mouth but one that lit up his eyes with surprising warmth, as though he were gazing at us through a shadowed window with a gleam of sunshine just catching his face. He was carrying a rather worn-looking pair of binoculars.

'Hello.' He stuck out a hand. 'I was looking for one of the nature reserve wardens. I heard that a rare seabird had been reported.'

I took his hand. 'Who told you?'

'For one, I was talking to the helmsman on the ferry. Angus Donald? He's an old acquaintance. When we were much younger, we served once together as deck hands on a cargo freighter.'

I nodded. 'Angus did a spell in proper ships when he was young. And he has been seeing dark-rumped petrels from the ferry. We've seen one for ourselves now. But you won't see them from the shore.'

Alice and her group had lost interest at the mention of birds. They wandered off down the street. Jessica and Simon were still listening.

Simon frowned. 'Tim, you never explained about these birds. What is so special about a Storm Petrel with a black bottom?'

I shook my head. 'Rump, not bottom. That's the lower part of the back, above the tail. What's special, is that in the early 1980s a new sort of petrel was found in the Atlantic, one that had only ever been found in the Pacific Ocean before.'

'Had it moved?'

'It may have, or it may have been here all along, in very tiny numbers. It's called Swinhoe's Storm Petrel. Our normal British petrels – the ones that breed around the British Isles – are the ordinary Storm Petrel and the Leach's Petrel, which we used to call the "Fork-tailed Petrel". We have Stormies on Lifandoy.'

'What do you mean by "here"? Not in the UK?"'

'No. Swinhoe's is now thought to nest on some tiny islands between Madeira and the Canary Islands. Nowhere else in the Atlantic.'

The olive-skinned minister agreed. 'They are called the Selvagens Islands.'

I eyed him with interest. 'You know something about them?'

He laughed. 'I was on a tanker that nearly hit them once.'

'I'd like to hear about them. Did you see any black-rumped petrels at the time?'

He chuckled again. 'No. It was at night.'

Jessica had been listening. 'Do they fly by night?'

'Well, when they are breeding they fly ashore by night,' I said.

'How mysterious.' She was delighted. 'So they are *night* birds?'

'If you like. Especially since they are black all over.'

Simon winced. 'I think I heard that phrase earlier.'

I looked at the minister. 'I'm Tim Corn, assistant warden of the Lifandoy Reserve. You want to know what other birds we have here?'

'I'd love to. He stuck out a hand. 'John Khourei.'

Simon had a gleam in his eye. 'John, you said that religion might be a problem. Surely not for chewing gum? Do you know something about the island?'

John shook his hand. 'You have a reason for asking?'

I shook a finger. 'Look out, John. Simon is the Press; and he will quote you. Although from my point of view, he is the good Press.'

John frowned. 'In that case, I had better be careful to say only what I know. But have you not heard the news on your local radio? The driver was playing it on the little bus that I caught up here.'

'About Lord Lifandoy's plane?'

'And about the fact that the island has changed hands.'

■　■　■　■

'What?' There was a stunned silence.

Simon was astonished. 'How did my office not tell me this?' He pulled out his mobile phone. '*Aaagh*! No signal. I should have stayed on the ferry! I'd forgotten that you live in the dark ages, Tim. It's more difficult to contact people on this island than on the Moon! They're probably sending up rockets to try and find me. Folks, I have to get back to work. I have to file the story of your Uncle Wilfred's descent with his lawnmower into the Underworld; and then it sounds like all hell has escaped from there, too. But I'll stay just long enough to hear what John has to say.'

We turned back to our visitor. 'The island has changed hands? That's not possible!'

'I didn't grasp the details. But apparently you have some archaic laws on your island. Are you one of these funny little places that is not covered by proper laws? I visited Sark in the Channel Islands last year...'

Jessica nodded. 'We are rather like Sark. I know that from my work at the Estate Office. Like Sark, ordinary British law doesn't apply here. Or any other outside law.'

Simon stared. 'And the radio news said that that applies to *inheritance* law, too?'

'Exactly. No waiting for long legal processes. The island is under the personal and immediate control of whoever is your Earl of Lifandoy.'

'And that means Dominic, the younger son? There's no long legal process? He owns everything *now?*' We all reeled at the thought.

Simon was staring at John with a grim expression. 'But you as a vicar know more?'

'I'm just a Reverend. I'm actually retired now; I was running a children's home in the Holy Land, which is the land of my birth, until last year; this is a long retirement holiday, the first I've had in years.

'But yes, I do know a little. Before I went back to the Holy Land, I was seconded for a few years to the Anglican Church in Canada. I have met the people who now own your island, the Cult of White. I know them rather well. And yes, they will ban chewing gum. And they will not stop with that. I think you aren't going to like them one little bit.'

■　■　■　■

Wilfred nodded. 'I hear it's public knowledge now. That was fast.'

Jessica and I were back in the kitchen of Big Cottage. Simon had headed off to get connected to the modern world again, and our birdwatching minister had gone off to birdwatch. 'It's all true, then?' I scowled. 'That radio broadcast of the change of island ownership is correct?'

'Entirely. Though it is not clear to me why someone put it about over the airwaves to the whole island. People will be unnecessarily worried.'

'Unnecessarily? Not from what our visiting reverend says.'

Wilfred looked up. 'Your what?'

I explained about our meeting with John Khourei. Wilfred was intrigued. 'What an interesting person. I look forward to meeting him. But he actually knew something about the island's new owners?'

'Apparently they are a strange but supposedly harmless group who claim to be Christians but don't pay a lot of attention to normal Christian beliefs. They are called the Cult of White because they spend all their time studying just those verses in the Bible that talk about anything *white*. They don't seem to think the rest of it matters very much.'

'What, you mean like white clothing and so on?'

'John listed several things – he has apparently been involved in heated debates with them at times. There were white clothes of all sorts, white wool and linen, white stones and white horses, white teeth...'

Jessica took up the list. 'White snow, white hair, white clay, white milk, fields white for harvest, even the white of an egg...'

'They seem to have a fanatical attraction to all of those.'

Uncle Wilfred snorted. 'I don't suppose they mentioned white patches of skin disease, or white tombs?'

'No.' We laughed. 'It sounds a harmless set of obsessions.'

'Far from it,' warned Wilfred. 'It's a distortion of the Truth, and that is far more hazardous than an outright lie. Well...' he sniffed unhappily 'Canada is a long way away. It will probably be a long time, if ever, before anything like that disturbs the peace of Lifandoy.'

We thought so too; and there followed a peaceful island Sunday, during which Jessica and I found reason to forget things black, white and any other hue. It was a rather exquisitely relaxing lull before the storm. But what might Monday bring?

■　■　■　■

Like a joyful lark, I was up early and already waiting at my garden gate with a last cup of coffee, when Jessica walked past on her way to work at the Estate Office. Jessica normally only worked part time, but all the Estate Office staff had been called into work to deal with the complications of the Earl's loss. My reward was a long kiss.

'That's enough, Timothy. You should be off to work, too. You can't lounge around Little Cottage all day!'

Sadly, I shut my front door – no-one in Little Doy village locks their door – and headed up the street towards Keith's office. Coming the other way was a mean-looking posse of teenage girls, with Alice at the head.

'Ooh, look at the lipstick on his cheek!'

'No, I think that's a heat flush, or a love bite. Unless it's strawberry jam.'

I grimaced. 'Just keep your chewing gum away from me, that's all. Which reminds me: who is this secret source that has been feeding you information?'

They grimaced back. 'As we said, that's none of your business.' They stalked off. Beyond them, further down the street, a skinny, pimply lad was lounging by himself. As they approached him, Rosalind walked ahead of the group and approached him with a flounce. He gave her a toothy smile and wound an arm around her waist as he walked on beside her.

A voice spoke behind me. 'Do I see young love in action?'

I turned. Uncle Wilfred was standing at his garden gate, following my gaze. I sighed. 'I suppose even my young sisters-in-law-to-be have human feelings. I wonder who that Lothario is? Rosalind has clearly started entwining him in her charms.'

'And vice versa.' Wilfred gave a beaming smile. 'They'll make a lovely couple. He'll be a fine catch for Rosalind.'

I was surprised. 'Do you know him, Wilfred?'

'The lad is the Factor's younger son. I think his name is Julius. Julius Fothergill.'

'Ah.' I was thinking. 'Perhaps that is how Rosalind and Alice's crowd got to hear about the island takeover.'

Uncle Wilfred's expression suddenly became unreadable. 'Yes. Well. I hope to hear nothing further about that.'

I glanced at him. 'But you're worried about it?'

'I can't say. Although…'

'Come on, uncle. Spill it. I am flesh and blood.'

He sighed. 'I don't suppose it will be confidential for long. I suppose I can say that there is a rumour we might receive a visitor – or possibly even visitors – later today.'

'A visitor?' I frowned. 'Who? A lawyer?'

'I don't know. Possibly.'

'Not Dominic – not the Earl's son?'

'Oh, no. I understand he is very frail. He's certainly far too ill to fly over from Canada himself.'

■   ■   ■   ■

I left Wilfred to ponder mysterious likely arrivals and walked on to the Lifandoy Nature Reserve office, my place of employment. Outside it, the various attractive noticeboards and displays had already attracted three or four visiting tourists and naturalists. Keith was already giving couple of them directions for their bird-watching day on the Reserve. Also standing there, by himself, was John Khourei, who gave me a smile of recognition.

'Are you able to tell me where on the Lifandoy Reserve I might see some interesting seabirds?'

'Certainly.'

'But not Storm Petrels, of course?'

'I'm afraid not.' I set out to discourage him from an impossible task. 'A few may nest on the Reserve, but it would be a major expedition by night even to locate them. Even then you would probably only hear them. And I would strongly recommend against trying. The Raw Head cliffs are dangerous enough even by day.'

'Oh, the daytime birds will be fine.' He laughed. 'I never expected anything else. So you don't monitor any petrel nests yourselves?'

'Not on the Reserve. It would be like looking for a black needle singing softly somewhere inside in a black haystack on a cliff face. Even if we wanted to look, we would not do so on Raw Head, which is where you will be going to today.'

'But there *is* somewhere on the island where you do monitor Storm Petrel nests?' he persisted. 'I am well used to these things: I have stayed on several Scottish islands and I have seen Storm Petrels being ringed on Fair Isle, for instance.'

Keith had emerged from his office to talk to the visitors. He joined us, listening. I glanced at him. 'Well… we know of a colony outside the Reserve which can be reached fairly safely,' I admitted.

Keith eyed John carefully. 'Keith Potts. You're…'

'John. John Khourei. Reverend.'

'And you know the Fair Isle colony? Well, there are Storm Petrels nesting in the boulder slopes south of Sound Point.'

'Sound Point? That's the Isle of Lifandoy's north-east tip?'

'Yes. On the slopes that face toward the Isle of Man, the ones that look across what is called the Sound of Doy.'

'Do you census them?'

'Yes, we attempt a census each year, of all the birds we can hear churring – calling – in their nests. We do it in late July – around now, in fact.' Keith paused. 'How long are you on the island for? It's somewhat hazardous, and it would be entirely at your own risk. But if you were interested, I might be glad of another pair of sharp ears…'

John was delighted. 'I'm here for at least a week. I'd be very pleased to help. I have boots and have done a lot of hill-walking and scrambling through rocks. When would it be?'

Keith thought for a moment. 'I'll have to check the weather forecast. It needs to be a dead calm night. Look, give me a number I

44

can contact you on in an evening and I will let you know if it happens.'

John provided his details and set off for his day on the Reserve. I looked at Keith. 'That's one job lined up for the week, then. What else? Shall I go on repairing the marsh path, or have you any other extras for me?'

'You can spend the morning rebuilding the muddy section of path beyond the big bend,' he said. 'And I'll join you when I've finished my paperwork. But at lunchtime you can come along to the Estate Office with me. I want to convince the Factor that the Estate Office should make a contribution towards buying a quad bike for the Reserve.'

'How do you propose to do that? The Reserve is not Estate Office property.'

'No, but a lot of the Estate's tenants benefit from the Reserve. And quite a few of them damaged bits of it earlier in the month, when they all went digging holes looking for buried gold.'

I laughed. 'You're blaming the Factor for the Lifandoy Gold Rush?' I was referring to the last hilarious event that had recently made our little island famous.

'Well, it's worth a try.'

'I wouldn't miss your attempt to mug the Factor for the world.'

Keith gave me a stern look. 'Tim Corn? You don't care a fig about the Factor. Just get it into your head that if your best beloved Jessica is not in sight when we walk into the Estate Office, you will *not* try to find her while you are on time that I am paying you for.'

'I know,' I sighed. 'She wouldn't pause to give me even a venial kiss while she was editing spreadsheets and presentations, in any case. But I might just glimpse her braided tresses for a moment or two.'

6 – New Owners

Tragically, Jessica was not in sight when Keith led me into the smart, low building in which all the important business of Lifandoy is done. I wept hot tears of denied love inwardly, but Keith looked around with interest.

The Estate Office is carefully designed to avoid being a blot on the landscape. It stands behind a tiny ridge so that from a distance it appears, misleadingly, to have only a single storey. The entrance is thus grander than most visitors expect.

It was also newly decorated. Keith was impressed. 'This has taken serious money,' he commented.

'Haven't you seen it before? They did it last month.'

'I don't have the same cause to come here as often as you,' he said. 'I'm not marrying any of the Office's employees.'

'I'm sure we could find you a secretary,' I offered. 'Or a senior manager. Jessica tells me the next Factor is likely to be a woman.'

Keith scowled. 'God made man. Then he added woe, and made woman.'

'Don't say that sort of thing here,' I warned him. 'You're surrounded by Amazons. And I'm on their side. And so is God, too.'

'Is God female, then?' he snorted. 'That puts me off Her even more.'

'If you're talking about the God of the Bible, then maleness as far as God is concerned is not about gender. Think of it this way. If two people were approaching a narrow doorway, one of them has to go first. That's simply a matter of mathematical order. Should it be the man or the woman?'

'What? Well, I like to think I'm a gentleman. And men are generally stronger. If there is something *nasty* beyond the doorway, the strongest should go first.'

'Yes. But if there is something *nice* there, he should step back and let the woman lead. Exactly. Either way, the stronger – presumably the man – took the decision; because *someone* had to.'

'So God has the initiative?'

'Well, that's a bit different; but certainly, *He* made *Creation* and not the other way round. But Creation itself contains both male and female, in any case.'

'I still think your idea of God is sexist.'

'If there is a maker and a made, one can't be the other. Or can you suggest any other alternative?'

'No,' he grumbled. 'But then, I don't believe in a Creator.'

The receptionist, a cheerful young man who I knew from many nights out, eyed us with what seemed a sort of relief. 'Mr. Potts. One-thirty, that's right. Please take a seat. I'm afraid Mr. Fothergill is running behind with his appointments.' He was obviously having a complicated day already.

We sat down in plush, too-soft chairs. A couple of other visitors – both off-island, by the look of them – were already waiting. The foyer was busy with a constant traffic of staff travelling between offices and meeting rooms.

One of the passers-by caught my eye. It was Graham Fytts, the estate farm manager, my least favourite fellow Lifandoyer. He hesitated, and then scowled at me without a word, turned to nod to Keith, and marched past into a meeting room, the door of which he slammed behind him.

I glared back. 'Fytts is being as pleasant as usual, I see.'

'Maybe he has something on his mind.'

The receptionist, whose name was Tony, heard Keith's comment. 'I think everyone has a lot on their mind this morning.'

'Is that why the Factor is running late?' asked Keith. 'The Earl's loss must have thrown the whole Office into disarray.'

'No, actually,' said Tony. 'The Earl has nothing to do with the detailed running of the office and the island council. The implications of his death will be a matter for high-up legal people, not us. And we don't expect them to start talking to the Factor and the managers for a couple of days, until the paperwork has been looked at. We don't anticipate any immediate impact, at our level, from…'

Tony's voice tailed away. He was gazing at the entrance doors, and our eyes followed his.

▪ ▪ ▪ ▪

Walking in through the double doors were three figures that were well worth a stare. That was, firstly, because they were very difficult not to notice. Two men and a women, with one of the men in the lead, they were all dressed in pure white.

The men wore suits of the spotless sort one sees in religious films when one of the characters is playing God or an angel, and white shoes. The woman wore a long, floor-length white dress that made me wonder, for a moment, if she was a mistaken escapee from a queue of patients waiting for a hospital X-ray or an operation.

Secondly, they wore fixed smiles. Even if we had no idea where they were from, it would not have come as a shock when the leader addressed us with an accent clearly grown on the further side of the Atlantic.

'We have come to make you our *brothers*,' he said with a Canadian twang. 'Brothers-to-be, greetings. My name is Simeon Silver.'

He was clearly addressing not only Tony but also Keith, me and the couple of waiting business visitors. The latter both turned away abruptly, snatching their mobile phones and suddenly discovering they had a caller they needed to speak to.

Tony adopted a professional, if slightly stunned smile. Keith and I just let our jaws drop. As Mr. Silver advanced, we were forced to stand in order to shake his hand. Or so we thought; as we held ours out, he and the other man held their right hands on the wrong side of ours, and tapped the backs of their hands against the backs of ours. 'Er – Keith Potts,' mumbled Keith.

'Friedrich Frost,' offered the second man. 'Serena Snow,' added the woman.

Before I could offer my name, the two men swivelled as if joined at the hip. They greeted Tony with dazzling smiles. 'We are here. You have our assistance now.'

Tony had clearly been well trained in handling awkward visitors. He gave them a coolly professional half-smile. 'And you are here to see...?'

They glanced at each other. 'A Mr. Fothergill? We believe he has been called the Factor. Until now...'

■　■　■　■

48

Tony smiled coldly again in return, facing them with admirable aplomb. 'I'm afraid these two gentlemen have an appointment before yours.' He glanced at us. 'But there may be time after *they* have seen the Factor. If it is important?'

Keith and I looked at each other. 'Well...'

At that moment, the door of the Factor's office opened and Mr. Fothergill emerged. With him, to my surprise, was Uncle Wilfred. They shook hands and the Factor turned inquiringly to Tony. Tony paused.

Keith spoke up. 'Mr. Fothergill? It looks as though you have visitors from a distance. Would you prefer Tim and me to come back at another time? It was just about the grant for the quad bike...'

Mr. Fothergill was staring at the visitors with an expression approaching horror. Without looking at Keith, he answered him weakly. 'Er – yes, Mr. Potts. I'll approve your grant for the quad bike. Just give my assistant the details and I'll sign the paperwork.'

Keith beamed. 'In that case, I don't believe we need to take up your time any further.' He nodded to Tony. 'These gentlemen and lady may have our appointment.'

Mr. Fothergill turned toward his office without greeting the newcomers, and walked unsteadily through the door. They followed, walking with a polished smoothness that seemed almost a glide. The door closed behind them all with a soft thud, like a closing manhole.

I turned to Uncle Wilfred. 'And who on earth are *they*?'

■　■　■　■

'So what were you seeing Mr. Fothergill about, Wilfred?' In the absence of further information, we had abandoned speculation about the strange visitors for the time being. Keith and I were walking with Wilfred along the island road below the sloping lawns and neo-Gothic bulk of Lifandoy House. We had just crossed the East Burn and were being preceded and followed along the gravel roadside path by groups of tourists who were en route to view the House and its treasures for an exorbitant admission fee.

Wilfred brightened. 'I was telling him about the wonderful archaeological discovery we had made.'

'Do you mean the hole in the chapel lawn?'

He pursed his lips. 'I wish you would gain a better perspective on the history of the island, Timothy. This is the island history discovery of the decade. I was trying to persuade Tom Fothergill that we should take it over and make it a historic monument as soon as possible, to protect it. If we leave it to the British Museum they could take months or years to get proper protection in place.'

'Did he agree?'

'He said he would look into it. But I suspect his new visitors will put everything else out of his mind for the moment, unfortunately. If that proves to be the case then I may have to might get the lads from the farm to help me put a temporary roof over the hole.'

We reached a fork in the road. Uncle Wilfred continued on to his shepherds and sheep at Lifandoy House Farm while Keith and I walked down to West Doy village and back to the Reserve Office.

There Keith pulled out a large-scale map and we started to look at the landscape of the coast near Sound Point.

Keith put his finger on the map. 'This is the main Storm Petrel colony, of course, near the Point itself. We know the lie of the land there pretty well. And our average count of likely nest sites in use, for the last five years, is around a hundred and fifty. Compared with...'

'Compared with only half a dozen on Raw Head?'

'Yes, if that. But we will never know. No-one can survey those cliffs safely. But that wasn't what I was about to say. Look at the map. Do you know *this* cove?'

'That's by the next headland south of Sound Point? Is that the one with the two big caves – Two Cave Cove, as some people call it? I've walked there with Jessica; and before that long ago with other lads from the school when we were playing truant now and then.'

'Yes, well. I'll report you later. But after we finished our survey last year, I went up to the Point and did a long walk by torch along the cliffs. It was an absolutely calm and windless night. And above that cave, I heard more petrels. Or I think I did.'

'Think?'

'They seemed rather harsher sounding than the ones at Sound Point. But maybe the calls were just echoing around the cove.'

'But you want to survey that possible colony as well?'

'You never know what you might find.'

■　■　■　■

Jessica was the centre of attention when she returned home that evening. After tea, she came round to Little Cottage. Keith joined us, along with Jamie and Bob, the two graduate students doing ecology research projects with us on the Lifandoy Reserve. Even Uncle Wilfred and Aunt Martha came round for a chat, although Martha spent most of her time pointedly cleaning up the mess in my filthy kitchen, something to which I did not object.

'Mr. Fothergill seems to have been presented with a *fait accompli*,' reported Jessica. 'Simeon Silver and his friends from their Cult of White had already blitzed the paperwork, and arrived with all the legal documents and authority they needed to take over his office.'

'What? Have they sacked the Factor?' Wilfred was shocked.

'Oh, no. But they have made his post just a chairman's instead of an executive one. And he is no longer the Factor. They have changed his title. He is now called the Lifandoy First Pale Disciple.'

Keith exploded with laughter. 'What? You can*not* be serious.'

'I think they want him to convert to their cult so they can make him white.'

'Well, in that case, I shall remain firmly outside the pale.'

Martha looked across from my sink. 'Very witty. So who is administering the Estate Office now?' asked Martha. 'Is it this Silver person?'

'No, I think it's actually being run directly from Canada by Mr. Johnson Shining, the leader of the cult, himself. Simeon Silver is just the mouthpiece for him and his son.'

I looked at my uncle. 'Where does that leave the Estate Seigneurs, Wilfred? Obviously you can't tell us what the Seigneur

Council actually discusses. But presumably their legal status is no secret?'

Jessica thought the same. 'I think their positions cannot be touched. Not without an Act of Parliament or something.'

Wilfred confirmed her view. 'That's correct. But whether anything we say will be taken seriously now is anyone's guess.'

Bob, one of our students, spoke up. 'Surely these incomers are not going to try and make the islanders believe in their ridiculous cult?'

I shook my head. 'Most people would never go for that sort of thing. But we might have some rules and regulations imposed on us that we don't want.'

Keith looked at me. 'It's a good job the Lifandoy Reserve is not under their control. At least the environment is safe.'

Wilfred raised his bushy eyebrows. 'I hope we don't find ourselves having to move in with your rabbits and seabirds,' he said gloomily.

■   ■   ■   ■

The others departed in various directions. Jessica and I decided to take a romantic walk. But we were only a hundred yards up the street, en route for the coast path, when Rosalind and Alice came running up.

'What can we *do* about our chewing gum?'

Jessica frowned. 'What do you mean?'

I eyed them sourly. 'Yes. Spit it out.'

'We don't like it mint-flavoured.'

'Eh?'

'All the fruit flavours are going to be banned. They're not *white.*'

I scowled. 'Don't be silly. If it's in the shop you can buy it, whatever colour it is.'

'But it *won't* be. It won't be allowed onto the island at *all.*'

Jess and I looked at each other. 'Look, go back and play with your toys. Whatever else happens on the island, no-one will tell anyone what they can or cannot sell here.'

Alice gave us an angry stare. 'That's what you think. You've got a lot to learn! If you've any sense, you will stock up right now on anything edible that isn't white. While you still can.'

'Why?'

We're being taken over by people who want *everything* white. They will try to feed us as many white things as possible, until we join their evil cult.'

Jessica smiled. 'If you say so. In that case, I think I'll wear that nice white blouse to work tomorrow.'

Alice looked worried. 'I'm afraid they won't like that. *Wearing* white is for cult members only. They plan to confiscate all white clothing on the island.'

I chuckled. 'Oh, yeah? Does that include my string vests? And other things?'

Alice flinched. 'Well, maybe not. But they will stop any more being sold, or sent to Lifandoy.'

Jessica shrugged. 'I like coloured clothing. Don't you like me looking bright and summery, darling?'

I beamed at her. 'I like you in oodles of colour, joy of my heart.'

Rosalind grimaced. '*Yeeugh.* Come on, they aren't listening to us.'

'They never do,' said Alice.

7 – White Power

The girls headed off down the street. Jessica looked at me. 'What nonsense!'

'Well, they are your sisters. Anyway, where are we walking to?'

'Let's go up onto the ridge and walk down to Crystal Bay. I love the shell-sand there.'

We walked past Keith's deserted office and up onto the long West Ridge that stretches right down that side of the island, paralleling the shore.

The sun was in our eyes as we looked out over the long stretch of Machair Bay and the marshy pools and *machair* grassland behind it. Eastward, the whole of West Doy village lay below us, with Lifandoy House and its Farm across the valley. The green uplands of the island's centre were fairly featureless, but beyond them to the north-north-west we could see the round mass of Sound Hill. I pointed it out.

'That's where the next job will be for Keith and me. We will be counting the Storm Petrel nests on Sound Point. By night. You could come if you liked.'

Jessica giggled. 'I'm not sure Keith would trust you and me to disappear into the darkness together. No, I'll leave that scrambling around the rocks to you.'

We carried on to the triangulation pillar at the southern end of the ridge, then left the path and descended toward a small track running up from the hamlet of Borve. We crossed it and then, taking our shoes off, walked barefoot through the late summer *machair* flowers down to the edge of Crystal Bay.

'Crystal Bay is famous for good reason,' I commented. 'They say it has the purest white sand in the whole of Lifandoy.'

'I can believe it.' The shell-sand beach shone pure silver against the wine-dark sea.

I helped Jess to leap over a line of squelchy rotting seaweed above the high tide mark. Then we walked down to the edge of the waves and, standing with them lapping around our toes, occupied ourselves for a long time with pleasantries that form no part of this account.

Eventually, our lips were so worn out and our toes so cold that we walked hand in hand up the beach to where another track from Borve curled along its edge. There we had an unpleasant surprise.

■   ■   ■   ■

Where the track met the shore, a large, ugly noticeboard stood screwed onto a rough-hewn post freshly hammered into the turf at the edge of the sand. It was facing away from us. We walked round to its front and read what was on the plastic notice sheet stapled to it.

It read:

PRIVATE BEACH. OWNERS ONLY. NO WALKING ON THE WHITE SAND. TRESPASSERS WILL BE CONDEMNED.

I looked at Jess. 'Who's put this up? What is James Kelly doing banning people from the beach?'

'And who is he banning?' she asked. 'There's no-one else at Borve who could have put this sign up. Is he being hassled by tourists, or something? Even if so, "condemned" seems a bit strong.'

We walked on, a little annoyed. No-one was around to ask at the Borve croft, so we continued up over the hill and down toward the harbour.

'The river path?'

Jessica shook her head. 'Not yet. I fancy a drink in the Harbour Inn.'

'A very good idea.'

■   ■   ■   ■

The *Harbour Inn* was Monday evening quiet. At first. We were nicely settled down behind a pint of real ale and a port and lemon, in a snug corner, when more customers started to arrive.

The first was Jack Dooley, owner of the Harbour Garage, which was a misnomer for the biggest heap of junk machinery on the island. He nodded. 'Evening, Jessica. Timothy. Do they still sell beer here?'

'Why shouldn't they, Jack?'

'Someone told me it was all going to be lemonade, white wine and vodka from now on. Or at least, once stocks run out.'

'That'll be the day, Jack. Don't believe everything you read in the tabloid press.'

He gave a relieved smile and took a drink off to another corner.

Shortly, the grizzled figure of Tom Soss shambled in. He nodded to us and took a pint of ale across to Jack.

'I wonder why Tom is here? His normal hostelry is the *Doy Arms*.'

'Oh, he'll be down here to see Jack for some reason. They are cronies.'

The following peace lasted only seconds. With a bang, the door flew open. 'Oh, *no!* It's the Darren Stocks crowd.' We sighed.

A loud, clumsy, noisy crowd filtered into the bar. Its leader caught sight of us. 'Ah! The gorgeous Jessica and her fiancé.'

We scowled. 'What are you rowdy lot doing here?'

Darren spread his arms wide, pleadingly. 'We're desperate. The *Doy Arms* has run out of real ale.'

I snorted. 'You couldn't tell real ale if I poured a bucket of it over you. You lot aren't connoisseurs.'

'Well, we can't survive on white wine.'

'What are you talking about? Tom Soss said something about that. Has the *Arms* forgotten its order or something?'

■   ■   ■   ■

Darren started to reply, and then paused as the door opened again. Into the bar entered four smiling young strangers, all dressed in white. They all had the same haircut, an odd crew-cut with a ridge down the middle. They walked up to the bar, excusing themselves politely as the crowd at the bar fell aside in astonishment, and called over the nearest bartender, a cheerful brunette called Daisy.

Her face fell as she saw them. 'C-can I help you?' she asked nervously.

The foremost cult member replied in a Canadian accent. 'The owner or manager, please.' He gave her a dazzling smile.

'Michael?' She called over the landlord of the *Harbour Inn*, a hot-looking bald-headed, plump figure well-known to us all.

He winced as he saw the newcomers. The leader addressed him, in a voice with perfect diction that was audible in every cranny of the room. 'Mr. Michael O'Mourne? We are *delighted* to meet you. We are under instruction from the Estate Office. My name is Paul Pristine. I think you will have received a phone call warning you of our arrival.'

The landlord scowled. He was evidently minded to bluff it out as long as possible. 'I get a lot of nuisance phone calls, to be sure. I'm not sure if I...'

Paul Pristine gave him a hard look, and unfolded a legal-looking document on the bar, turning it for the landlord to read. 'You are still the landlord? For now?'

Michael blanched. 'I'm employed by the Estate Office, of course.'

'Then you will be familiar with the Lifandoy First Pale Disciple's signature?'

Behind the group leader, Darren Stocks suddenly exploded in laughter. He gave a near shriek of hilarity, and slapped Mr. Pristine on the back with a force that thumped the slender Canadian painfully against the bar. 'You boys in white really mean all this stuff, don't you? Hey lads, let's buy them all a pint of real brown ale. Mikey? Serve them up! This one is on me!'

Paul Pristine froze, and then straightened himself. He glanced at one of his colleagues, who immediately pulled out a very slim and expensive-looking mobile phone and started speaking into it.

I nudged Jessica. 'All very hi-tech. Darren is going to get the third degree, I think. But *not* by the Cult of White making use of the awful mobile phone reception of the *Harbour Inn*.' My prediction was fulfilled as the cult member with the phone stopped, stared in astonishment at his instrument and then at his fellows.

Darren's mates, who could see that their leader's beverage offer had not gone down well, cautiously pushed him to one side. As he was sidelined by the group, he came within earshot of us.

I hissed at him. 'Darren!'

He turned, his silly grin fading slowly.

'These White Power types have no sense of humour. If I were you, I would make a quiet escape while they're not looking.'

Unfortunately, Paul Pristine turned in our direction in time to hear my words. He focused on me with a thunderous look. 'Did you say, "White Power", sir?' he demanded.

One of his colleagues had stepped rapidly out through the door onto the street. He reappeared immediately, followed by a well-known island figure who had clearly been standing outside waiting for orders.

In full uniform, it was police constable William Williams. He looked extremely unhappy. Paul Pristine pointed to Darren and me. 'Officer, I wish these two men to be arrested. The first assaulted me in the presence of all these witnesses. The second has just carried out a culpable act of religious discrimination.'

William's face gained nearly the same hue as his carrot-coloured hair. 'Er – there were witnesses to these assaults?'

'Three of us,' announced the second cult member. 'It was a violent blow of resistance against a clear, correct and authorized act carried out on the instructions of the Lifandoy Estate Office.'

Darren's mates could have protested, but to the surprise of no-one they deserted their fallen friend. They shuffled back, leaving him staring at them in wordless wonder.

William slowly pulled out a handcuff and fastened it to Darren's nerveless wrist. 'I think I had better take Darren away for his own safety. If there is evidence that a proper assault has been carried out then you will need to present formal statements at the police station.'

'We may well do that.' Then the cult members turned to look, with far more piercing and malevolent expressions, at me. 'Now please arrest the perpetrator of this savage act of religious hostility and incitement to hatred.'

At my side, Jessica tensed. I realized she was about to stand up, so I started hurriedly to anticipate her. But I was myself beaten.

With force, the bar door opened again, startling us all. Into the bar strode two grim figures, both bearing such angry looks that even Paul Pristine stepped back in alarm.

The first was William's boss, Sergeant Farquhar, the island's other and principal representative of the police. The second, to our wonder, was Uncle Wilfred. He turned to me, and quietly whispered. 'I could see there would be trouble here, and I knew you had come this way. I persuaded the sergeant to come down to Port Doy with me in case there was trouble. We were listening outside. Leave it to us, now.'

Sergeant Farquhar waved a hand. 'Back, Constable. I'll handle this one. Leave Mr. Stocks to me.'

William, clearly with great relief, stepped back with alacrity.

Farquhar gave the cult members a cool stare, and then turned to the landlord. 'Mr. O'Mourne? Did you witness a violent assault here this evening? In the last few minutes?'

The landlord glanced uneasily at the cult members. 'Well...'

Uncle Wilfred interrupted him. 'Don't be alarmed, Michael. There were many witnesses. The truth will not be hard to discover.'

The landlord nodded. 'There was no assault. In my view, Mr. Stocks was simply taken by a fit of great enthusiasm, for which I am sure he is now sorry. No doubt, no offence was intended. But it's up to this gentleman to realize that, of course.' He looked at Paul Pristine.

Encouraged by the arrival of the cavalry, Darren's mates had all recovered their spirits. They were now crowding around in a slightly intimidating manner; the bar had suddenly gained a very full feeling indeed.

Paul Pristine suddenly switched on a smile so dazzling that it almost seemed to outshine the bar lighting. 'It is not a part of our mission to conceal the truth,' he beamed. 'I accept that this misguided young man was merely careless. Provided that he is prepared to join one of our Education Classes, I see no reason why we should not pardon his weak ways as we set out to build true spiritual strength in him.'

After a moment's pause, Darren's jaw dropped. 'Huh?'

Paul gave him a look of such benevolence that it might have penetrated an iceberg. 'Thank you for your co-operation. We will see you in the hall of the Lifandoy Island School at seven tomorrow evening.'

Sergeant Farquhar rapidly unlocked the handcuffs and pocketed them. Darren started to protest. 'But I play darts on Tuesdays...' But his mates surrounded him and silenced him, carefully pushing him behind them.

Paul gave a piercing look at the landlord. 'You will, of course, understand our requirements as to the drinks you serve from now on? For health and safety reasons, no coloured drinks are to be offered for sale on the island any more. But to show all these gentlemen that we only have their best interests at heart, please give all of them one small vodka each, and send the bill to the Estate Office.'

There was a confused small cheer, and Darren and his mates surged forward as Michael reached for the liquor. Then Paul Pristine turned to stare hard at me.

8 – A Breather

'That does not, of course, apply to *this* primitive person.' Paul Pristine gave me a look that I did not like at all. He was clearly out for blood. 'He must be…'

'*My fiancé.*' Jessica pre-empted Uncle Wilfred, who had opened his mouth. 'His name is Mr. Timothy Corn. *Not* "he". And *you*, sir, are not the representative of a faith organisation with *any* understanding of being a good witness to your fellow creatures on God's earth if you describe another human being as primitive on your first meeting with him.'

I had never seen Jess so angry. In fact, I had rarely seen her in such a forceful mood of any kind. Paul stared at her. She stormed on. 'And if you, sir, claim to be a member of a group that respects all things white, perhaps you can tell me why your hair and that of your companions is *brown*?'

The four looked at each other; their crew-cuts were all certainly far from pale. Like an angry lioness, Jessica shook her blonde hair out as if she was unfolding wings to pounce on Paul.

Unsurprisingly, he recoiled in shock. 'Well – but – we hadn't thought about our hair. Yours is certainly… But "White Power" is a deadly insult to us.'

Uncle Wilfred stepped in smoothly. 'I understand that you are Canadian, Mr. Pristine? You are aware, of course, that different cultures use similar words in different ways? I am sure that your generous, lasting and thoughtful care of the present Earl of Lifandoy must have shown you that English and Canadian ways are not identical? Even as a child, Dominic must have shown you that. And Lifandoy is a remarkable community, which will take you time to understand it.'

Sergeant Farquhar added his bit. 'I am not familiar, sir, with Canadian laws on religious discrimination. But I do not have the legal right to enforce them on Lifandoy. You can, of course, quote the passages from the relevant Act of Parliament under which you wish me to take action here?'

The leader of the cult team scowled at me. But he set his jaw grimly; there was no gleaming smile this time.

'We will expect you to accompany Mr. Darren Stocks to the Education Class tomorrow evening, Mr. Corn,' he muttered.

'I'll be there too,' said Jessica, giving him a sweet smile. 'I'll make sure Timothy comes to no harm.'

Wilfred looked uneasy. 'And I'd like to know more about these Classes, too.'

As the door closed behind the four strangers, everyone else in the *Doy Arms* gazed at each other in silent concern.

■   ■   ■   ■

The Education Class did not happen on Tuesday evening. Evidently, the members of the Cult of White had over-reached themselves for the moment. Uncle Wilfred came round at breakfast-time on Tuesday to Little Cottage to tell me the good news.

'It seems that Simeon Silver has decided not to start imposing any more silly regulations or events on the islanders for the moment. We have a breather for now.'

'But it will come?'

'Yes. I've heard that all of the cult members, except for Johnson Shining himself and the ones running the hospital where Dominic lives, are planning to relocate to Lifandoy. In a week the island will be crawling with them, I'm afraid. And your Education Class appointment will not be forgotten then. But we have a breather before that happens.'

I sniffed. 'I don't much care. They've shown their true colours already. Five or ten times the number will not endear any of them to me.'

Wilfred frowned. 'I think we will all have reason to take a lot of notice of them before long.'

'Well, I shall be spending time thinking about other things until then.'

He nodded. 'Like preparing for marriage? You and Jessica have some marriage classes to attend instead, I believe?'

'Er – yes.'

■   ■   ■   ■

At the Reserve Office, Keith was amazed by my news of the *Harbour Inn* confrontation. 'This sounds like the beginning of a military coup,' he commented from the chair in his office, as we drank our pre-work coffee.

I shrugged, put down my mug and stood up. 'Right. I'm ready to go. So, what bit of the Lifandoy Reserve needs my loving attention this morning, then? What are your orders for today, O Senior Reserve Warden and boss?'

Keith made no attempt to rise. He gestured me down. 'Not just yet, Tim. Sit down again for the moment.'

Surprised, I did so. 'Ah. It's time for a business meeting, is it? It is a little while since our last paperwork session.'

Keith grimaced. 'A little time? Not half. Reserve paperwork and being glued to a screen are the bane of my life. I avoid them for the longest periods I can get away with. But I wasn't talking about routine business. Tidying up the books can wait for another week yet. But there are a couple of more fundamental management matters we need to discuss.'

I regarded Keith with suspicion. 'That's the look,' I said, 'which you give me each year just before my annual performance review. But you're not due to haul me over the coals for another five months yet. Have I done something awful?'

He grinned, and relaxed. 'No. Not yet. But your personal circumstances are shortly going to change. I want to discuss how single-minded your approach to the job will be thereafter.'

'Single-minded?' I laughed. 'When I get married? Not at all.'

'Good.' Keith grinned broadly. 'I'm certain your marriage to Jess will be brilliant news for the Lifandoy Reserve, as well as for you personally.'

'For the Reserve? I'm sure that having an attractive PA coming to live in Little Cottage will not hinder my warden's work...'

'Except when you describe her in those terms!' Keith rolled his eyes. 'If the future Mrs. Jessica Corn hears you describing her like that, she will make sure that it's you who becomes her personal assistant! No...' He put down his papers and leaned back comfortably. 'I'd just like to congratulate you on behalf of the Nature Reserves Society.'

'Thanks.'

'And to do more than that.' He paused. 'The Society will do more than just recognize the fact.'

'Really? How? A pay rise?'

'*No*. I'm talking about security of tenure.'

'Tenure?'

'As you know, Little Cottage is leased for the assistant warden from the Lifandoy Estate. The lease is in your name. But assistant warden is an optional appointment, so if you left the job the lease would end. Or if something happened to you.'

'But when I am married…'

'The Society will add Jessica's name to yours on the lease. So that if I ran you over with my tractor, Jessica would still have a roof over her head.'

'Ah. Yes, I hadn't thought of that. That's really useful.'

'And I think we can do more than that. I shall attempt to touch Head Office for the funds to give you a decent wedding present as well. And if they prove mean, I shall personally wipe out the Reserve's petty cash fund to make sure you get something.'

I chuckled. 'I really appreciate those thoughts, Keith, even though I know that the petty cash tin has about enough in it to buy a pair of teaspoons. But I'll certainly tell Jessica what you've arranged. And you'll get an invitation to the wedding, of course – as best man!'

He recoiled. 'Oops! I should have seen *that* one coming.'

We laughed, and chatted for several minutes, discussing my forthcoming nuptials. 'And you are really planning to have your Uncle Wilfred lead the service?' Keith was amazed. 'You really think he won't wreck it with some sort of mishap? You've asked him already…'

'For better or worse? I'm afraid so,' I acknowledged. 'I know he is the most disaster-prone person on the island. But I think he's reasonably safe in church services.'

Keith paused and regarded me curiously. 'You've changed, Tim Corn. You've really changed. If someone had told me a year ago that you would be having a church wedding, I should have laughed in their face. This religion thing has become important to you, hasn't it?'

'Religion?' I shook my head. 'Religion means rules. That's the difference between me and the Cult of White. I haven't become a Pharisee. I'm a Christian now, yes. But all I do is pray and read my Bible.'

'What, all of it?'

'All of it. In fact, I first seriously found God in the depths of the Old Testament.'

Keith sat back. 'I think that story must wait for another day.'

I grinned. 'One day you may want to hear it all.'

'Perhaps.' It was his turn to shrug. 'Perhaps not.'

∎ ∎ ∎ ∎

Just then, our student researchers Bob and Jamie bounced into the Reserve Office. 'Keith? Do you want our help to count the Storm Petrel colony this week? When are you doing it?

Keith glanced at me. 'I have Tim and one other volunteer so far. But I'd like to cover more of the cliffs than we did last year. So, yes, you would be helpful.'

'Great. We like stormies.'

I looked out of the window. 'It's blowing a bit this morning. When are you thinking of doing it?'

Keith thought for a moment. Not tonight or tomorrow night. And the weather forecast is bad for Thursday. Perhaps Friday.'

'Friday?' I protested. 'That's pub night. I need my fix of real ale.'

'I thought it was white wine now?'

I winced. 'Not when the ghostly brigade aren't there – at least until the taps run dry.'

Keith stood up. 'Come on. You have a path to mend. I'm clearing that overgrown ditch. And Bob and Jamie have to finish their projects before their grants run out.'

∎ ∎ ∎ ∎

We piled out of Keith's office. I collected a wheelbarrow and spade, and wheeled it down onto the start of the Reserve track. We had just set foot on it when some activity near the chapel opposite caught our attention. I walked up to the low chapel wall.

Uncle Wilfred was directing four of the Lifandoy House Farm staff as they lifted several heavy planks out of a trailer. We attracted his attention.

'Wilfred? Are you building a log cabin?'

He walked across the lawn. 'No. I've given up on Tom Fothergill. I'm not waiting for him to sort out the protection of our archaeological treasure. I talked to Graham Fytts for an hour or two about how magnificent a discovery it was; so he gave me permission to borrow a team.'

'Yes, that was probably less painful for him than listening further.'

'What? Yes, so I'm putting a temporary lid on the Iron Age chamber myself.'

'Won't that mean you can't get into it?'

He gave me a pitying look. 'There will be a trapdoor in our roof, and a ladder.'

'Won't it look rather unsightly? All those dirty planks in the middle of the chapel lawn?'

He rubbed his chin. 'I see what you mean. Yes, I think we had better cover them. A covering of thick turf will retain the humidity of the ancient chamber and preserve everything down there. After all, the chapel is a feature for tourists. Yes, when we have done that, they won't know anything is under there for now. I'll get my chaps to do that before they finish.'

■　■　■　■

We plodded on up the Reserve track to our various duties. I was left to repair my muddy section of track. Before long a shower wet me, then another, then another. It was evidently one of those days. I worked on for hours, getting muddier and muddier. From time to time, birdwatchers or tourists walked past through the Reserve, gratefully stepping on the new path I had created and eying me cautiously as if I were a warthog in a wallow, which was not far from the mark. When the sun came out for a few moments, I stopped to eat some butties, and then went on.

Near the end of the day, a particularly heavy shower was enough to make me throw my spade ringingly into the barrow and set off home. As I passed the chapel, I glanced incuriously over the wall. Uncle Wilfred had done a good job repairing the lawn; there was no obvious evidence he and his lawnmower had ever plunged through it.

I dumped the barrow at Keith's office and set off for a hot shower at Little Cottage. I was nearly there when a splutter of giggles and laughter made me raise my head.

'Watch *out*, girls! *Mud* Man is about!' Alice and Rosalind, at the head of a raiding party of some sort, were warning of my approach.

I growled at them. 'I've done a lot harder work than you have. Leave me alone.'

They were not in a good mood. 'We've had to work hard, too!'

'How so?' Remembering that they were my sisters-in-law to be, I searched the depths of my soul and found a forgotten crumb of interested sympathy.

The bespectacled small figure of Oliver at the tail of the gang burst into tears. 'I had to draw *lines* all morning.'

'I think you mean *write* lines. You must have done something naughty.'

'No, he's right,' said Alice wearily. 'The rotten Culties have confiscated all the school exercise books with lines in. We had to use ones with blank pages and draw the lines in for ourselves before we could write our essays.'

'Did you use white ink?'

Hostile stares met my humour. Realizing that I was outnumbered by far, I avoided passing too close to the girls and plodded on. The hiss of a peashooter followed me; but I was so covered in wet earth that the pea simply embedded itself somewhere near my left shoulder and presumably started to germinate.

Once I had scraped myself clean under the hot dribble that was all I allowed myself for financial reasons, I felt mostly human again. I microwaved a large potato, opened it up and filled it with baked beans. By the time it was inside me, I was feeling friendly toward the world again. Which was why it seemed most unfair, when the world arrived on my doorstep in a thoroughly unfriendly way.

9 – Nothing!

The knock was imperious. I shambled to the door and opened it curiously. Standing on the doorstep was Paul Pristine with three new white figures, not the ones that he had led two nights previously.

He walked in uninvited and looked around. 'Thank you for your co-operation.'

'Were you requesting some?'

He smiled with his eyes only. Evidently, I was still on a blacklist. 'You are privileged, you know. You have been chosen to be among the first. You will thank us when you understand.'

'But not yet?'

His smile dimmed further. He held out a sheet of paper. 'I think you will recognize the signature.'

'Thomas Fothergill. Yes.' I scanned the sheet. 'What? This is effectively a *search* warrant! "All properties owned by the Estate Office and occupied by its tenants…"' I carried on reading the rest of the sheet.

A noise from my bedroom made me look up. Paul's three companions had walked on into it without me noticing them. I stomped to the door. 'Hey! What goes on?'

They were clearly well trained. They had already searched right through my chest of drawers and my wardrobe. They turned, with expressions of amazement on their faces. One of them, who was holding one of my string vests with two fingers, put it down on the bed delicately and stepped away from it.

Oddly, Paul Pristine seemed as surprised as I was. 'Haven't you collected *anything?*' he asked his associates.

One of the three shrugged and held out his hands. 'No. He doesn't have *any*. Nothing at all.'

Without another word they turned and walked out in line. I was enraged. Standing on my doorstep, I called after them.

'You do realize that I am not an Estate Office tenant? This is a leased cottage! Your search warrant doesn't apply here.'

Paul turned in obvious surprise. He appeared genuinely disconcerted. '*Really?* In that case, I apologize, sincerely.' He looked upset; he sounded almost sorry for me. 'We were incorrect. We should not have invaded your privacy.' There was a regretful quirk on his lips. Startled, I realized that he really was apologizing. Beneath the stern rigidity of the Cult of White's fixed smile, he seemed to be peeping like a little boy caught out.

The flash of humanity departed and he turned and walked away. As he did so, a series of shrieks rent the air. Alice and her crowd of plug-uglies rose into view from behind my front garden hedge.

'"Nothing at all!" We all heard it! Nothing at *all.*'

Alice marched up the path toward me. 'How much is it worth?'

'What?' I furrowed my brow. 'What are you talking about?'

'You know very well. Ten quid will do for now.'

'Eh?' I was bewildered. 'Are you seriously suggesting that *I* should give *you* money?'

'Well, it's better for you than the alternative.'

Rosalind joined her. 'She'll be here before long,' she said in a warning tone.

'Who will? What alternative?'

'Jessica, of course. Just wait until she finds out! Your life won't be worth living.'

I fixed them with a grim stare. 'You're obviously trying to blackmail me. But it won't work. How could it? My conscience is clear. I haven't done anything.'

Alice snorted. 'That's the point. You just haven't done it at all recently, have you?'

'I haven't done *what?*'

She turned and gazed in helpless wonder at the others before replying. The Globe Theatre could have expected little more melodrama. 'You haven't kept up with your laundry, brother-in-law-to-be. You don't do proper *washing!*'

'You offensive little...' I frowned. 'But what do you mean? How could you know?'

They giggled. 'If you don't pay us off, it will be all around Little Doy village in twenty minutes time. And Jessica will be the first to hear.'

'What?'

70

'The fact that the People of White came to your house to confiscate every piece of white clothing they could find. And they didn't find any. Because absolutely everything you own is *grey*.'

■　■　■　■

Jessica was in a bright mood when she arrived. 'What about walking down to Doy and seeing that new film?' she suggested.

I scowled. 'I'm a bit short of loose change at the moment.'

'You wastrel.' Her expression clouded. 'How much do you spend on real ale? I thought you only went to the pub on Fridays.'

'I do.'

'Well then, you must have enough money to buy me some flowers tomorrow, then.' She gave me a sweet smile. 'I'll expect them with pleasure. Never mind, I'll pay for the cinema.'

We walked slowly down the street. Rosalind and the others were smirking at the first corner, but Alice was nowhere to be seen. 'Where is she?' I hissed to Rosalind.

'Alice? She's networking.'

'*Networking?* She should be captured in a net and released into a cage. She would make a good cage fighter.'

Rosalind gave me a supercilious smile. 'You're not used to diplomacy, are you? It must be all that mud.'

I was about to reply bluntly when Jessica yanked my arm half out of my socket. 'Come on, darling, we'll be late.'

The film was about a family that travelled constantly from one comic disaster to the next. One of the characters was the same age as Alice and one or two of the disasters she inspired seemed uncomfortably familiar. I started sulking and hunkered down in my seat, which was at the end of the row next to the wall. A familiar sound caught my attention; I leaned with my ear almost against the wall and realized that through a freak of the acoustics I could hear a conversation taking place two rows in front of me. The speaker was Alice.

'I realize that you got me into the film for free because your big sister is an usher, Yvonne. But you owed me three favours already. Now I'm calling them all in. It's your Dad's help that I really need.'

The reply was inaudible.

'He goes on the ferry every week to the Isle of Man with a van full of toffee from your toffee factory, for the mainland. He could bring us back a *crate* full of chewing gum. And you would get some of it, too.'

There was another faint reply. 'But surely you want a change from toffee? We've already eaten three boxes of the caramels your sister is selling.'

Disgusted, I drew back my head and sat back next to Jessica. Then I put my arm around her. Then she snuggled up to me.

What happened next in the film was anyone's guess. We weren't watching.

■　　■　　■　　■

After saying a sweet goodbye, I walked Jessica to her home. I would have walked her past it, into a sexy clinch in a dry bank of the long grass overlooking the Reserve, but she protested that she had a meeting first thing next morning.

I was returning down the street, passing Big Cottage, when I met Keith, who was coming home the other way from a visit to a pub in Doytown. Big Cottage was in darkness; Wilfred and Martha were evidently already in bed.

Keith eyed me curiously. 'You seem glum.'

'Jessica has just sent me away, for a start. And worse, I have to buy her some flowers in the morning,'

'So?'

I scowled. 'It's a cash-flow situation.'

He snorted. 'You're a wastrel, Tim Corn.'

'Not you, too! She tells me that. It's an unjust accusation.'

'Well, I pay you enough. Is someone extorting money from you?'

'Yes. Alice.'

Keith nearly fell into Uncle Wilfred's hedge from laughter. 'You're helpless, then.'

'But I need flowers,' I whined.

'There are plenty of daisies on the Reserve.'

I ignored him and walked on to my gate and up to my front door. I marched in angrily without turning the light on, and then paused. The room was full of scent; I sneezed hard two or three times, partly from surprise. For a moment, I wondered if Jessica had sneaked back to me for a romantic encounter. But when I switched the light on I saw only a large vase full of colourful flowers on the table. Around it, the room looked as though it had been steam-cleaned.

'Martha, you're a wonder,' I grinned. 'And those flowers! From Wilfred's herbaceous border, no doubt.' I paused. 'Now why do *flowers* ring a bell?'

■　■　■　■

On Wednesday, I continued repairing the Reserve footpath, and returned home as muddy as the day before. But after a shower, I found some nice paper and gathered Martha's flowers up into what looked to me like an attractive bouquet. I was sure it would be indistinguishable from one from the flower shop in Doytown.

I strolled into my front garden carrying it. Jessica had not appeared; and at first no-one else was in sight. Then to my surprise a white van rolled slowly up the street.

It slowed to a halt at my gate. As it did so, I started to sneeze again. Paul Pristine looked out. 'Those coloured flowers are not good for you, you know.' He seemed much less hostile than before.

I was bent half over with my eyes streaming. Before I could protest, he reached over the hedge and took the bouquet from me. 'Would you like some better ones?'

'Where could I get them?' I spluttered in astonishment.

He smiled and stepped back into the van. 'Wait here. We'll be back in twenty minutes.' Before I could respond, the white van spun round and purred down the street.

I waited impatiently, looking around to make sure that neither Martha nor Wilfred had been in sight. The street remained empty; only ten minutes later the van hummed back up the road. Paul opened the door and stepped out with an enormous bouquet of pure white lilies, done up in a huge cone of silver wrapping. 'With the compliments of the People of White,' he grinned. 'Better than what you had. Those other flowers would have been lovely if they were white, but in any case someone had wrapped them up in rubbish paper.'

He beamed as I accepted the lilies with delight. In moments the van had turned and departed again. It was only a couple of minutes out of sight when Jessica came walking tiredly up the road.

I hid the bouquet behind the hedge until she reached me. 'I think you were hoping for some flowers?'

Jessica was astounded. My sweet, delightful, sexy fiancée's jaw dropped in a manner that made me feel very nice indeed. 'Oh, *Timothy!*' She took them from me gingerly. 'They're so *lovely* that I hardly dare touch them!'

'They're nowhere near as lovely as you, my oodles-of-sweetness love,' I oozed.

'Oh, I *love* you!' She bounced through the gate and forced such a lengthy a kiss on me that I was left gasping. 'I *must* show them to Mummy and get them into water. But I'll be back!'

She departed up the street, all tiredness gone, walking as proudly as if she were carrying an Olympic torch. As she disappeared, the door of Big Cottage next door opened and Uncle Wilfred pottered down his path to the street.

He smiled. 'Did you like the flowers Martha left you? I put some of my really strong-smelling evening stocks in with Martha's other flowers last night.'

I gulped. 'Ah – they were *very* strong. So strong, in fact, that they started my hay-fever. I'm afraid I had to give them away.'

'Oh, what a pity. I can understand, though. My stocks this year seem to be dripping with scent. Did you give them to someone who really wanted them?'

'Oh, yes. Very much so.'

■   ■   ■   ■

I retreated inside and watched the street nervously through my open door, wondering if I had got away with my deception. Shortly Jessica's sisters came skipping down the street. They paused at my gate, and then marched up to my door.

Rosalind was full of admiration. 'For the first time, I am beginning to think that I might be getting a brother-in-law who shows Jessica the respect she deserves, and treats her properly,' she declared.

Alice fixed me with a hard, cold eye. 'That's one interpretation. Another is that Timothy has money to burn. He's won the lottery, or something.' She sidled up to me and hissed. 'Pay me another bribe and I won't raise Jessica's suspicions.'

I gazed down at her condescendingly. 'Do you seriously think that you have any way of putting me into Jessica's bad books for the rest of this week?'

Alice drew back a trifle, a frustrated expression on her face. 'No, I suppose not.'

'And hadn't you better get on with arranging your smuggling? That crate of chewing gum you are arranging to have shipped in under the radar?'

She was astonished. 'Perhaps you are a future brother-in-law nearly worthy of the name! What sort of espionage provided *you* with *that* knowledge?' She leapt forward and grabbed me by the throat. 'And it is secret information. Remember that! But how did you *know?*'

I gave an airy smile. 'Obviously I can't reveal my sources.' I paused. 'But I might let you work with me one day, if you become good enough.'

She gave me a sour look. Then she hesitated. 'No bribe?' she said sadly. 'What about a goodwill partnership bonus?'

'No.'

Behind her, Uncle Wilfred appeared at my gate. He called to the girls. 'Alice? Rosalind? Are you coming to choir practice at the chapel this evening? Remember that you need to keep your attendances up if you are to be allowed on the choir outing next week.'

The girls turned. 'We'll be there, Mr. Corn.'

'And, of course, we have a special event to prepare for, in two weeks' time.'

The girls walked to my gate and I followed them. 'Oh,' I said with mild interest. 'What's that, Wilfred?'

Both the girls turned to me and stared with open mouths. Wilfred grinned broadly. 'It's your wedding, Timothy. It's your wedding.'

'What? *Already?*' I stepped back in astonishment, fell over a brick at the side of my path and landed rear first in a bush.

They all stared at me without a shred of compassion. 'Does Jessica know you do things like that?'

Alice turned her back dismissively. 'She will soon.'

10 - Invasion

I decided that I had better meet the challenge like a man. Uncle Wilfred and the girls headed off up the street to the chapel and I followed. Jessica appeared, dressed in a rather nice dress. I forgot all my fears as I gazed lovingly at her.

'Hello, gorgeous.' I leered. 'Is that a dress that we must not get dirty?'

'Oh, I'm not that innocent.' She leered back. 'I was wondering if you fancied examining the nice soft grass beyond the chapel wall again.'

We walked slowly to the reserve track. It was slow going because we paused for a kiss every few yards.

All was quiet; inside the chapel we could faintly hear Aunt Martha starting up on the piano. We walked past and turned right, looking for a spot that was catching the evening sun. We found one and started doing the sorts of things that a couple about to take part in chaste Christian marriage has always done. It was ten minutes before we lay back pleasantly, soaking up the evening rays.

Behind us, we could hear the choir at full belt. I was a little surprised when another sound intruded itself on the quiet evening. It sounded rather like the white van of Paul Pristine. Whatever the vehicle was, it purred up to the chapel gate on the far side of the chapel lawn and stopped there.

It was now behind the building from where we lay, and we were out of sight of the chapel itself in any case, unless anyone were to walk to the chapel yard wall and climb up on it to see us.

All at once the piano and choir stopped, in the middle of a chorus. We lay, listening incuriously. There was a series of confused noises, and what sounded like a door banging. Shortly we heard the van start up and drive away again.

A loud noise of children's voices arose. 'That was a short practice,' I said.

'Some people don't need much practice,' murmured Jessica. 'Personally, I think I need a lot.'

'So do I.' We forgot the rest of the world and shut out all their noises. It was a beautiful sunset.

■ ■ ■ ■

I was in a good mood on Thursday morning when I turned out of my gate and met Wilfred just starting off for the farm. He looked tired and pale, not unlike the weather which was grey and threatening.

'Are you all right?'

'No, I'm not,' he snapped.

I was so startled at such an uncharacteristic reply from my uncle that I stopped dead. 'Good grief, Wilfred! What's happened?'

He set his jaw grimly. 'The Cult of White has taken over.'

'I know that.'

'But now they have gone far too far.'

'How?'

He stared at me. 'Didn't you hear the hubbub in the village last night? They drove up to the chapel while we were at choir practice, and walked right in…'

'We heard some noise. Maybe they were just visiting…'

'And they picked up every pew Bible in the chapel, and took them all away.'

'What?' I was astounded. 'Didn't you try to stop them?'

'We didn't want to distress the children at the choir practice. We tried not to let them know that it was an invasion.'

'But the Cult of White stole the lot? Every Bible?'

'Well, they tried to replace them. With a distorted translation of their own. We threw those out, of course.'

'How do you know they were distorted?'

'All the colours had been written out of them. For instance, do you know the Bible verse from Isaiah that says *"Though your sins are like scarlet, they shall be white as snow"*?'

'I've heard it. How did they change it?'

'They made it "Though your sins are like scar tissue…" Scar tissue? I ask you!'

'It certainly wrecks the symbolism.'

'And it is a lie. The Bible simply doesn't say that!' Wilfred had as dark an expression as I had seen on him for a long time.

'Oh, well I'm sure you know how to stick to the truth.' I smiled and turned away. But I found myself facing another pale-

78

faced figure, someone who had walked up behind me without my noticing them.

The newcomer gave a thin-lipped smile of his own. He was not dressed in white. So he was presumably not a Cult member. But nor did he look like an amateur naturalist, for his costume was a blue windproof over a jacket and tie, and he carried a laptop briefcase with a clipboard and the unmistakable air of someone on official business.

'Can we help you?' Uncle Wilfred was still behind me, as curious as I was.

'Is either of you two gentlemen Mr. Wilfred Corn?'

'I am.' Uncle Wilfred stepped forward.

'Dr. Edwin Winchester. From the British Museum, Antiquities Section. I trust you were expecting me?'

'Of *course*. Welcome to the Isle of Lifandoy.' They shook hands. Wilfred introduced me. 'This is my nephew Timothy. He was one of the first to see the chapel and burial chamber, after I found a way into them.' Uncle Wilfred gave me a sideways glance and a slight wink. I presumed that was a plea for silence on the subject of lawnmowers. I shook the archaeologist's hand and obediently left the talking to Wilfred.

My uncle was clearly relieved to have something to take his mind off the Cult of White's invasion. 'I understand you were already planning to come here on a general survey?'

'I may be here for a few days.'

'But you will want to see the chapel straight away, I expect. Timothy and I can walk you to it now – it's not far.'

I followed half a step behind, as the conversation immediately turned technical. When we reached the chapel, the antiquarian gazed around, puzzled. 'I thought the excavation was in the chapel lawn?'

Uncle Wilfred led us up to an anonymous-looking piece of grass. He lifted a flap of turf, revealing a metal ring, which he pulled. The turf square rose, and he bent and lifted it aside to reveal a square entrance and the top of a ladder.

Dr. Winchester was delighted. 'What a wonderful way of preserving the contents in the correct atmosphere!' He produced and donned a head torch, leapt for the ladder and began excitedly to descend. Uncle Wilfred produced two more head torches, handed me one and followed him.

To my surprise, the Iron Age store-chamber's floor was level and clean. The lawnmower had been removed, but the mound of fallen soil and turf I had landed on previously had also been moved to one side. The space was larger than I remembered.

Dr. Winchester was already climbing through the square hole into the Neolithic burial chamber. We followed and listened while he examined the inscriptions, enthused about the design and generally became rather intoxicated by his own excitement.

When he went off on a particularly obscure rhetorical lecture, I nudged Wilfred. 'Is he talking to us?'

'Oh, he's just overjoyed.' Even Wilfred seemed to be becoming a little weary of the expert's endless chatter. When Dr. Winchester produced a clipboard and started sketching the inscriptions, Wilfred coughed gently. 'Would you like a camera with a flash?'

The expert frowned. 'I have everything I need here, thank you.'

I nudged Wilfred again. 'I'm starting to freeze solid.'

Wilfred agreed. 'I think we would need thicker clothing to stay down here for a long time.' Dr. Winchester appeared impervious to any such trivial consideration. But Wilfred and I climbed back through the square entrance into the bigger chamber. 'It's a bit warmer here. It's not lined with rock,' he said. 'With proper clothing one could easily stay down here for an hour or two.'

I was puzzled. 'Why should anyone want to do that?'

Uncle Wilfred gave a faint grin. 'Oh, probably no reason,' he said. He gave me a practical task. 'Here, Timothy, while you are with us, can you help me clear this pile of fallen soil from the floor? If you could climb the ladder and go to the chapel shed, you should find a shovel, a bucket and a length of rope. If you could lower the bucket down to me I could shovel this soil into it and get the floor clear.'

'Clear? What for?'

'Oh, just for tidiness' sake.' The glint was still in his eyes. 'Do get on, dear boy, if you will. I'm sure you have other things to get back to of your own as well.

■　■　■　■

Back on the Reserve, I told Keith why I had been delayed. 'Oh well,' he grumbled, 'I suppose it was something important for the island. But have you finished rebuilding that path yet?'

I gave my boss a pitiful look. 'It's going to rain today. You said so yourself.'

'And how am I going to get all the paths mended when you get married and disappear for your honeymoon? Assuming I allow you one?'

I decided the soulful eyes look was the best tactic.

'Oh, never mind. Look – get yourself down to Port Doy and collect a package for me. Angus Donald should have delivered it personally on the *Bagpipe* yesterday evening, but I had no time to collect it yesterday. It should be in Brendan Todd's office, with a label on it.'

'In the harbour-master's office? Since when has The Buoy played the part of your postman?'

'And take your car. I don't want my parcel getting wet.'

'Really? It's that valuable?'

'No. You're that clumsy.'

■　■　■　■

I trundled in my battered Ford down through Doytown toward the harbour. As I arrived in Port Doy, I found the *Bagpipe* just fastening up at the quayside. I parked and walked across curiously. Angus Donald was first off the ship, so I accosted him.

'What's up, Angus? This isn't a ferry day! Have you come to the wrong island by mistake? What are you doing bringing the *Bagpipe* to Lifandoy on a Thursday? I've just arrived to pick up Wednesday's mail.'

He gave me a strange look. His voice was subdued. 'Someone has paid a lot of money to change the ferry schedule.'

'Who?'

Angus walked on without a word. I stared after him. Behind me, there was a thunder of feet on the gang-plank. I turned.

Descending it were a whole army of white-clad figures, all carrying white suitcases. They gazed around as they stepped onto island soil.

One of them, a grim-looking character wearing a platinum and diamond ring, stared at me. 'I am Shining-son,' he announced.

Feeling that I should show at least a minimum of island hospitality, I stuck out a hand. 'Timothy Corn. Welcome to Lifandoy.'

Without accepting it, he stared past me. 'You will be, I hope. Is that your *car?*'

'The Ford? Yes.'

He stared at it in manifest astonishment. 'What *colour* is it?'

I winced. 'Underneath the mud, you mean? Ah...'

Before I could finish, he walked past me. As if on parade, a file of followers matched his move. They lined up at the bus stop, evidently waiting for their transport to be unloaded from the ferry.

I headed over to the harbour-master's office. The Buoy looked very harassed. 'The parcel for Mr. Potts? Angus could have given it you directly, if he had known he was coming today.'

'Did he not?'

Brendan Todd eyed me coldly. 'No, he did *not*. And nor did I know that an unscheduled ferry was going to turn my harbour upside down.'

'Never mind, Todd.' A new voice spoke across the office. 'Visitors to the island mean money in its economy. And we need it, with so much of the island given over to useless nature conservation.'

I turned, my hackles already raised as I recognized the acid tones of my ideological enemy. 'Good morning, Graham.' It was Graham Fytts, the Lifandoy House Farm manager, Wilfred's boss and my nemesis.

'Ah, I *thought* that was the back of our junior nature reserve warden that I saw there.' For some reason, Fytts was in a jovial mood. 'How are your little birds today?'

'As an assistant warden I deal with big birds, not little ones,' I retorted.

'And you are marrying one, I hear. I suppose someone needs congratulating for that.'

I decided his response was genuine for once. 'Thanks.'

His face twisted as if I had taken his meaning better than he intended. 'What's in the special parcel?'

'I don't know. Not birds.'

He rumbled in amusement. 'Good. There may not be room for them before long.'

Before I could ask why, Graham walked out of the office and across the road. I was surprised to see him walk up to the stern figure of Shining-son, who turned and started talking with him.

Brendan Todd stood at my shoulder. 'Like friends already, they are,' he muttered in his soft Irish accent.

'They act as if they know each other.' I was curious.

'Oh, they do.' His voice held a dark note. 'All too rapidly and all too well.'

I looked at him. 'How? Who is this Shining-son? Is he, by any chance...?'

'The son of the cult leader, Johnson Shining? I believe so. He will be in charge here. He will plan it all.'

I frowned. 'Plan what?'

The Buoy turned to me. 'The new centre for their Cult. Haven't you heard? The Cult of White has decided to build a city on Lifandoy.'

'A city?'

'Well, a colony, then. A sort of university, I believe. A college, at any rate.'

I was aghast. 'What? Where?'

'That's why he's talking to Graham Fytts. It will be on the Lifandoy House Fields, just opposite where you live in West Doy. It might spread across the burn onto your nature reserve land: the Cult has some legend about a white bridge over a dark stream, apparently.'

'Over my and Keith's dead bodies, more like. And Fytts has agreed to them building on his best fields?' I could not believe it.

'Oh, he will be making a great deal of money out of the commission on it,' said the Buoy. 'Your favourite farm manager is going to be very rich.'

11 – Health, Safety and Flight

Back in Keith's office, I nearly dropped his parcel in fury before he could take it from me.

'Hey! Be careful with that.'

'Aren't you appalled too?'

He scowled at me. 'I don't believe it. The Buoy must have got the story mixed up.'

'Well, Fytts and this Shining-son were cosying right up to each other.' I stared angrily at the parcel, which Keith was unwrapping. 'So what is this golden delivery?'

He opened a box and lifted its contents out reverently. 'On loan from our Head Office: a pair of night vision binoculars. For watching Storm Petrels as they fly to their nests.'

Briefly, I forgot the invasion. 'Wow! Really? Can we try them out now?'

Keith rolled his eyes. 'Yes, if you can find some night to stare at in the middle of a Thursday morning.'

'Oh.' I returned to my news. 'Could they really build there? The whole village would be wrecked as a place to live! And could they build a bridge over the stream?'

'I doubt that. The Lifandoy Reserve land could possibly be used for another purpose; but it could never be built on.'

'So no work can be done on it at all? Definitely?'

'Oh, I wouldn't say that. *You* could do some work on it. The rain hasn't started after all. So you can go and work on the path repairs for a couple of hours. I'll see you at lunchtime.'

■　■　■　■

Infuriatingly, the rain came just as I finished my couple of hours of labour. By the time I was back at the office, I was drenched. Keith looked satisfied. 'I think you've done all you can for today. You look a muddy mess. You'd better get a shower. Then I want you to get some things for me from the hardware store in Doy. If I can clear this paperwork in time, I'll take you down myself. I fancy some fish and chips for a change.'

Half an hour later, Keith rolled up to the door of Little Cottage in the Reserve's Land Rover. I trotted out through the steady rain and jumped into the passenger seat. He peered through the windscreen. 'It would be unpleasant to be caught out in this lot.'

I did not deign to reply. We drove down the empty main street of West Doy village and were soon crossing the bridge into Doy itself. At first glance, Doytown appeared just as deserted. Then we noticed a colourful mass to our left.

'What are all those kids doing outside the parish church? And why do they look like a paint-shop gone mad?'

Keith glanced across past me. 'All the kids have to wear yellow jackets now when they go on school trips. And they all have red umbrellas. But what's the white?'

'But what's happening? It looks like a riot is starting.'

Keith parked the Land Rover outside the Doytown Co-op store. The rain had nearly ceased. Interested, we delayed our lunch and walked past the chippy next door, to see first what was going on. At the wrought-iron gate of the parish churchyard, a swirl of youngsters was surrounding three teachers. They were engaged in a stern argument with Paul Pristine and half-a-dozen of the Cult of White. Paul's voice was raised. '*White* jackets, not yellow, please.'

'I think I can guess what that argument is about,' I chuckled. 'Health and safety versus the Cult of White. The irresistible force meets the immovable object!'

Keith was equally amused. 'I'd like to hang around and see how this one turns out. But we'd better get our lunch.'

In the milling crowd, I spotted Rosalind. 'Rosalind? Are you taking odds on who will win this row?'

She looked thoughtful. 'It's an idea. Wait – I'll ask Alice.'

Keith was departing. 'Tim? Cod and chips? I'll order for you.'

'Haddock, if they have it, please.' I turned back. Alice had emerged. Her face indicated that her brain was engaged in calculations that should not be disturbed. Then she nodded.

'Good idea, future brother-in-law. Rosalind, make it three to one in favour of the teachers.'

I shook my head. 'Three to two, I would make it.'

'You don't know the power of modern health and safety.'

'If you say so. By the way, do I get a commission?'

She looked astonished. 'A *commission?*'

'My idea. Patent protected.'

She blew a raspberry at me. Unhappily for her, one of the teachers was just glancing our way. 'Alice Bull? That's half an hour detention for you. Insulting a member of the public is an insult to our school.'

Alice winced. 'A-*tchoo*! Please miss, it was a *sneeze*. It's all the pollen from the flowers in the churchyard.'

The teacher's face darkened. 'Pollen? After today's rainstorm? I don't think so. Make that an hour detention, for forgetting your science lessons.'

I turned away, not wanting to be blamed for further pain. Rosalind had also sidled away, sensing that her younger sister had become a lightning rod for punishment. She glanced at me. 'Who do you really think will win?'

I rubbed my chin. 'I don't know, and I'd like to find out. Hang on; let me collect my chips from Keith. Then I'll come back.'

I walked to the chip shop and acquired one of the two packets of fish and chips Keith had just bought. I strolled back, munching chips, and was surprised to find the crowd already breaking up. Alice was standing next to Rosalind, all smiles.

'No detention now,' she gloated.

'What? What did you do? Bribe your teacher with your life savings? No, that wouldn't even buy them chips.'

Rosalind explained. 'Alice was bending down to pick up a penny that someone had dropped, when she noticed that one of the Cult of White was wearing pale yellow socks. So she loudly asked the teacher what was meant by the word "hypocrite". When the teacher explained, she pointed to the socks and asked if it meant something like that. The People of White were so shocked that they forgot all about our yellow jackets and took their errant member away to discipline him. The teacher was so pleased she let Alice off her detention.'

I sniffed. 'A member of the public still wants to complain about a raspberry blown at him.'

'Raspberry? I hope not.' Another voice spoke behind us. 'Raspberries are red.' We turned. It was Paul Pristine, now alone. He gave me a quizzical stare. 'But you already know that we can replace colour with white if you let us. Were the ones we gave you acceptable?'

Alice and Rosalind were listening with interest. I suddenly realized my danger. If Paul had happened to mention the word 'flowers', I would have been dead meat. Urgently, I changed the subject.

'Oh – er – by the way, did you say something about classes that we needed to attend?' At my side, Alice's jaw dropped with an almost audible thud.

Paul was delighted. 'Do you know, I am *really* pleased that you have volunteered,' he said. 'Is that for both you and your fiancée?'

I had a sudden vision of myself leaping out of a frying pan into a fire. 'Ah – well, I can't speak for her.'

'She would be extremely welcome,' Paul said. 'We are indeed now ready to run our classes. Shall we say seven-thirty this evening, in the church hall just over there? We have already spoken to the vicar and he has said we can do anything we want.'

That fitted well with my concept of the Reverend Arthur Fetherstonhaugh, the vicar of Doy. A milk-and-water liberal of the sort beloved by television and radio producers everywhere, he had a reputation for changing his views to agree with nearly everyone he ever met. That did not include Uncle Wilfred, with whom he was reluctant to discuss all matters of religion, and who after a couple of debates he now avoided with a distaste verging on allergy. Once, recently, Wilfred had grinned at him and the vicar had retreated so fast that he had fallen into the West Burn. Even the members of his congregation were sometimes irritated by the vicar; one had once described him to me as the most sheepish sheep they had ever met.

Paul walked away. Realizing that Alice and Rosalind were about to demand an explanation, I stuffed half-a-dozen chips into my mouth, mumbled and pointed to the rest of my dinner. 'Keef needth me to fibish my food. Abd your teacher wabts you two.' I turned and stumbled hurriedly away.

■　■　■　■

Laden with fencing material and gravel, Keith's Land Rover groaned back into the village. He and I got wet again, unloading the materials, into the cavernous shed by his office which held all of the Reserve's hardware stores. He looked sadly at the filling puddles. 'I suppose you will have to go and do some paperwork yourself this afternoon. Have you completed reading that Head Office policy booklet on how to care for vulnerable children and adults yet?'

'No. Have *you?*'

He had the grace to admit that he had not read it either. Glumly, we separated to our fate. I plodded back through the rain to Little Cottage. I was just about to walk up my garden path when I realized someone else was just passing. Clad in an efficient set of walking waterproofs, it was the thin figure of John Khourei.

He gave a sad smile. 'I'd been cooped up all day. I thought the rain had stopped. Still, it's warm.'

I glanced at the sky. 'It will get worse before it gets better. Do you want a cup of tea while this really heavy downpour passes over?'

'Well, if you really don't mind.' He followed me inside. 'Tea or coffee?'

'I don't suppose you would run to Earl Grey tea?'

'Sorry, I'm a socialist. No Earls here.' I poured him a cup of the Co-op's best. 'Did you see some good seabirds yesterday?'

'Magnificent. That flat rock where you can stand and watch the birds flying right along the cliff edge is an amazing place. I spent two hours there taking photographs of birds in flight.'

'In flight?'

'A hobby of mine. Capturing birds in free flight is a challenge, requiring speed and good reactions, rather than just expensive equipment.'

'Free flight? Rather than just photographing the birds standing or sitting on their nests, which is hardly a challenge?'

'Or setting up a flash to capture a bird following a regular flight path that it keeps repeating? Yes. That's professional work, and boring. Exactly.' John passed me his digital camera.

I flicked back through some of his images. 'Hey, these are seriously good. Would you be prepared to let us have one or two for

88

the Reserve's use? I'm sure Keith would like that one of the razorbill in flight, for a start.'

'By all means. I'll put a few on a memory stick and you can transfer them and use them with my permission. As long as you don't sell them.'

'Will you bring your camera when we go counting Storm Petrels?'

'If that's OK?'

I nodded. I think we are looking at Friday – tomorrow evening, for that. As for this evening, I'm booked up. I have to go to this class the Cult of White is running in the church hall in Doytown.'

'Really?' John was surprised. 'Surely they can't force you to go?'

'It's complicated,' I sighed. 'I think I talked myself into it, to save myself from a greater embarrassment. But I'm hoping that my fiancée Jessica will go with me.'

John pursed his lips. 'Be careful. They are practiced brainwashers.'

'If they can brainwash Jessica, they will surprise me. And I have no brain to speak of compared with her.'

I paused as there was a knock at the door. Keith walked in. 'Oh, hello, John. The petrel census will be tomorrow evening, I think.'

'So Timothy said. I'll be ready.'

I held up John's camera. 'Keith? John has some really great flight photographs of seabirds along Raw Head. He has said we can use them for Reserve publicity if we like. Do you want to have a look?'

'I was thinking of creating a couple of new signboards. Can I have a look? But Tim, we forgot to pick up the two inch galvanized nails. We're stuck without some. Could you nip down in your car for them?'

I nodded. 'I'll leave you two to swap photos. Keith, there's a lightly used tea bag that I used for John's drink if you want one yourself.'

Keith grimaced. 'No, thanks. Oh, and one more thing. Tom Soss told me he had a couple of big green plastic sheets he had no use for. Could you drop in at the *Doy Arms*, which is where he will be by now, and ask him where to pick them up from, and bring them back with you? Tell him I'll buy half a dozen jars of his honey as recompense.'

'Will do.'

■　■　■　■

I drove through the rain back to the Doytown hardware store, and picked up the nails. Then I carried on down the valley road to the *Doy Arms*. I parked outside the pub and ambled in. It occurred to me, sadly, that I would not be able to down a quick pint as the *Doy Arms* had none left. I expected therefore that the pub would have few occupants, even on a wet afternoon. But I was wrong.

12 – Bootleggers?

As I entered the *Doy Arms*, I noticed a strange huddle in the corner furthest from the bar. Then my attention was drawn by a member of the Cult of White who was standing at the bar alone, with the erect pose of someone who is on station for a purpose. I wondered if he was policing the drinks being sold. But no-one was buying.

I frowned at him and walked up to the bar. I gazed unhappily at the wine, and then felt for coins in my pocket. 'A quarter of lemonade, please.'

The barmaid looked at me sympathetically. 'Did you say a *quarter*, luvvie? If things are that bad, you're even worse off even than we are.'

I took my meagre drink across to a table next to the huddle in the corner. I had noticed that Tom Soss was alone there on the table next to the muttering group.

'Tom? Keith told me you had a couple of green plastic sheets that you said he could have for the Reserve, in return for him buying some of your honey.' Tom was the island's beekeeper.

The old man lifted his grizzled head. 'I'll be glad of the sale. But I'm afraid the green sheets are no more. Those white vulture strangers saw them and confiscated them. They promised me white sheets in exchange, but they haven't delivered any yet.'

'I'll tell Keith.'

'You can have the white ones when I get them.'

'Thanks. I'm not sure we want the Reserve looking like a builder's yard, though.'

He nodded. 'Suit yourself.' He stared down mournfully at the glass in his hand. 'No coloured plastic is one thing. But white wine instead of beer is terrible.' He glanced over my shoulder at the group in the ill-lit corner behind us. '*They're* trying to do something about it. But I don't think they have found a way yet.'

I turned round. Six or seven heads were bent in close consultation. One of them lifted to look at me. It was Darren Stocks.

'Hey, Tim. Do you want to join our planning team?'

'Hah! *You* plan anything organized, Darren? You couldn't plan a boozy night out in a garden shed.'

'No-one will be planning boozy nights out unless we can beat the Prohibition Police.' He glanced cautiously at the white figure leaning against the bar.

'What are you scheming to do?'

Darren gave a toothy grin. 'Behold the Lifandoy Bootleg Brigade. We're ready to start smuggling as soon as we can work out how. There is a van-load of beer on the Isle of Man ready to be shipped here as soon as we have a ship.'

I raised my eyebrows. 'Presumably not the *Bagpipe*?'

'No.' His brow furrowed. 'They search her every sailing, before anyone is allowed off.'

I shrugged. 'Much as I would like you to succeed, I have no fast launches available to sneak across the Sound of Doy at night.'

'The Sound of Doy?' Darren gave me a startled look. 'Direct from the Isle of Man? We hadn't thought of that. That's a really good idea, that is. We were thinking out how we could sneak a cargo into Port Doy. But landing it in one of those quiet coves between Sound Point and Snaefell Bay would be perfect. Real smuggling!' He paused as whispered suggestions came from the bowed heads around him. 'It's the nearest point to the Isle of Man, so the boat would only have a short trip. And Johnny Davies at the Tystie Bay Hotel is not far away. He has a cellar which the Cult probably doesn't know about, where we could hide the booze. It's ideal!'

I snorted. 'You're mad!'

'Not at all. And we're desperate. Let's see, it's supposed to be a calm night Friday evening. I know someone who could hire a motorboat in Port Erin tomorrow. If you want to join us and get a share of your own, Tim, make sure you are up there, in that cove with the two caves down from Sound Point, at midnight tomorrow.'

My jaw dropped. 'Hey! We're doing our petrel survey along those coves tomorrow night.'

'Petrol?' Darren looked worried. 'I hadn't planned to start smuggling fuel, as well.'

'I'm talking about birds.'

He leered. 'Oh, I'm all for smuggling birds. Especially ones in very short dresses...' He paused. 'Why on earth are you bird-watching at night?'

'We're counting Storm Petrels churring – calling from their nest holes. They only call at the dead of night. Keith Potts is organising it.'

'But that's *perfect!*' Darren looked around at his conspirators. 'Lads, we've just become petrol watchers, too. If the Cult of White challenges us, we're part of your midnight survey team!'

'Darren? You and your lads would frighten every shy nesting bird away for the rest of the year. If you blithering well come within a *mile* of our bird survey, I will personally rip your tongue out so that you never taste another drop of beer again.'

He shrugged. 'Sound Point is open land. We can do what we like.' He saw me starting to rise from my chair, and backed down. 'All right, Corny boy. We'll look for another night. Tomorrow is probably too soon, anyway, and we do have canned beer at home for now. But your suggestion is still great. We'll be there in the darkness, listening to your charring petrols, one night soon.'

■　■　■　■

Since Darren outnumbered me eight to one, I left the *Doy Arms* before my temper led to me gaining a black eye.

Back at West Doy, the rain had nearly stopped and Keith and John had both gone. I sat down to spend the afternoon trying to read many pages of Lifandoy Reserve policies on health safety, vulnerable children, adults and birds. After eight-and-a-half minutes of Superman-speed scanning through the numbing pages of text, I decided I had done my professional duty and that building a path in the cold drizzle was less soul-destroying than reading such stuff in the warm and dry.

I was just walking past the Reserve Office toward the store for my wheelbarrow when Keith emerged. We eyed each other guiltily. Keith raised an eyebrow one millimetre. 'Done that reading? I've done mine. I won't stop you getting back to that path. You should be able to finish it this afternoon.'

Relieved, I plodded back to work. The drizzle faded away and a breeze sprang up. When the sun broke through the clouds, which were now scudding along from the north-west in puffy white masses, my hard labour suddenly became a delight. Larks started singing and redshank started calling like flutes from the marshy fields, while anxiously shepherding their almost invisible young through the long grass. By the time I put my path tools back in the wheelbarrow for the last time, I was in a sunny mood also. I trundled cheerfully back to the village. Walking back home, I met Uncle Wilfred coming the other way. We stopped to chat at his garden gate. There was a heavy scent arising from the flowers in his garden bed next to the gate.

'Had a busy day, Timothy?'

'I've been repairing the main Reserve path.'

'Using what?'

'The working man's shovel.'

'Oh.' He pursed his lips. 'That's a pity. I am borrowing the House Farm's small portable digger on Saturday, to create a new path at the chapel. I could have come along and dug holes for you if I'd known.'

Uncle Wilfred is the most dangerous person on the Isle of Lifandoy. The idea of him attacking the Reserve footpath with a hole-creating mechanical digger struck me as little less frightening than him trying to clean my cottage windows with it. 'Ah. I've missed that, then.' My tone was that of a driver who had just avoided hitting a tree. Uncle Wilfred failed to notice.

'That isn't,' he went on, 'the most difficult challenge I am facing, though. What about *Sunday*?'

I looked at him. 'Sunday? You aren't normally worried about Sundays. The joy of the Lord, and all that: isn't Sunday the height of your week?'

'It ought very much to be.' My uncle looked tired. 'But the Cult of White members have told me they intend to join all religious services on the island and if necessary to guide them in ways of religious purity.'

'Isn't that good? If they come to the chapel, they are more likely to be moved themselves by *you*, than to move others. Don't you believe God will speak through your preaching?'

'I have been warned that they might insist on preaching to the congregation themselves as well. And, even worse, on reading from their distorted version of the Bible. It's an outrage.'

'No-one will take them seriously.'

'There are those who might be misled by their fine show.'

'What do you propose to do, then?'

Wilfred's brow lowered. 'I am not having a blasphemous distortion of the Bible read out loud from.'

I thought for a moment. 'Well, just for the moment, what about finding Bible readings that just *happen* to be the same in their twisted version of the Bible and yours, so they can't object? And choosing hymns that don't mention anything white? And making the service so short that they have no time to add anything?'

He nodded. 'I'll have to do something like that. But how are we going to get on with the *real* business of meeting with the Lord Jesus Christ, of proper Bible teaching without their interference? I can't reduce the real work of the chapel to Sunday school level so as not to mention anything they would object to. We have to get down to business with Almighty God without heretics from this dictatorial sect interfering. How can we do it, when they will insist on being present at every public service? And they even want to know when and where our group Bible studies and prayer meetings will be. You and Jessica attend those – do you want to have the secret police sitting next to you? If I don't co-operate, they will find ways to close our chapel. They have all the levers of power on the island now. What can I do?' My uncle gazed sadly across the valley.

I sighed. 'I don't know, Wilfred. Maybe the real work of the chapel will have to go underground.'

Uncle Wilfred gave a start. Quivering, he turned slowly to face me. '*What* did you say?' Before I could reply, my uncle started to grin. Knowing that this was a warning sign, I watched uneasily as his grin spread right across his face to his white bewhiskered sideburns. I was starting to back away when he leapt forward, seized my hand and started to pump it up and down. 'Timothy, you have had a word from God.'

'Er – oh, have I?'

'Absolutely. *Underground*. Well, well, well.' Wilfred was almost bouncing.

I watched him with deep alarm. 'What are you thinking of?'

He was looking over my shoulder. 'I see one of the Cult approaching.' Instantly he was the very epitome of restrained old age. 'You didn't say *anything*, Timothy.'

'Ah – no. I rarely do say anything of significance.' I glanced at the approaching figure. It was Paul Pristine. I looked back at Wilfred. His face appeared placid, even mournful. Yet there was a twinkle in his eye that from long experience I knew meant that someone, somewhere, would deeply regret what it was he was planning.

■　■　■　■

Paul bore his usual rather plastic smile. Yet he greeted me with something like warmth. 'Good afternoon, Timothy. I have come to confirm that you are able to attend our evening class in the Doy church hall at seven-thirty.'

Uncle Wilfred was surprised. 'What's this?'

Paul gave him an official smile. 'We are beginning our de-education classes, Mr. Corn.'

'Did you say, re-education?'

The smile dimmed a little. 'The word I used was *de-*education. We have found that when dealing with groups of limited pure knowledge it is necessary to strip away various layers of tradition, misunderstanding and prejudice, before beginning our proper lessons. Nothing complicated; this first meeting is merely a little historical background, initially about why the People of White think white is an important colour.'

'Is it a colour?' Uncle Wilfred gave me a grim stare. 'Did Timothy volunteer to attend your meeting?'

Paul gave a broad smile. 'He did indeed.'

My uncle was amazed. 'I suppose he has his reasons. Although I would have wanted to know very much more about your classes. *Do* you intend to go, Timothy?'

The breeze had dropped temporarily and the heavy scent from Wilfred's flowers on the other side of the fence was filling our nostrils. I was considering saying no to Paul. But the flowers for some reason unnerved me. 'Well, I did say yes.'

Wilfred's grim expression darkened. 'And is anyone going with you?'

'Jessica is going with me.'

My uncle relaxed a little. 'Then I suppose you will be well advised, at least.'

Paul Pristine smiled sleekly. 'Everyone is well advised to learn more about the beliefs of our People. Everyone on the island will be invited in due course.'

'Are these meetings public?'

'Of course, and open to all. We detest the idea of anything being done in secret or in hiding.'

'Ahem. Yes, of course.' For some reason, Uncle Wilfred's cheeks were faintly pink. He nodded to me. 'Well, you'd better get on, Timothy. But don't forget, under any circumstances, to take Jessica with you.'

13 – De-education

Paul walked on and Wilfred and I went into our respective cottages. I got myself something to eat and made myself respectable. I wandered down to my gate with a cup of coffee and was waiting for Jess to walk down the street when two caricatures of her appeared.

Rosalind and Alice, to my wonder, were in coloured dresses. I had never seen Alice in a dress previously, except distantly in a choir stall at the chapel, and was astounded to realize that she had legs with skin. Until then I had always classed her as probably belonging to the same branch of the evolutionary tree that had produced the Daleks and R2D2.

'Where on earth are you two going?'

They scowled in unison, like two china monkeys in an antique shop window. 'To the same place as you.'

'To the talk in the church hall? What for? Or, rather, for what material gain? You two don't do *anything* for nothing.'

'That's an insult,' said Alice.

Rosalind rebuked her. 'Level with him, sis. He's nearly family, even if he will lower our standing in society.'

Alice eyed me for a moment, and then nodded. 'It turns out that mint is not the only flavour of white chewing gum. We've been told there will be a supply of milk-flavoured gum at the talk. We can live with that on a temporary basis, if there is enough of it. And it will be free.'

'But why the dresses? You look like...'

A gentle hand fell on my shoulder. 'My sisters look like *what*, darling Timothy?'

I felt like King Belshazzar, staring at the Writing on the Wall. Uncle Wilfred had been preaching about that Bible story last Sunday, and the words he had read out from the Writing's translation by the prophet Daniel began echoing in my ears. "*You have been weighed in the balance and found wanting...*"

Dizzily, I turned to my fiancée. 'Er – I was going to say that they look like small versions of *you*, my dearest oodles-of sweetness Jessica.'

My best beloved gave me a hard look of frank disbelief. She was in a dress, too. As I gazed at it in admiration, it seemed for one flickering moment as though there really was a family resemblance between her and her sisters. Then to my relief the hallucination evaporated. She made no objection as I twined my arm tightly around her side. Her sisters winced and walked on.

'We'd better go. I'll leave my coffee cup by the gate.'

■　■　■　■

Twenty-five people were seated in the church hall when we arrived, waiting for the Education – or De-education – Class to begin. Four were young friends of Alice and Rosalind, all of whom were looking longingly at a display of sugary white comestibles lying next to bottles of clear lemonade and white wine on a table at the side. Standing like a policeman behind the sweets was Paul Pristine and next to him, wearing a rather vacuous smile, was Reverend Fetherstonhaugh. The Vicar of Doy was busy explaining pedantically to Paul that he pronounced his name Fenshaw. Actually most of the island population called him Reverend Fency (or Fancy behind his back).

At the head of the hall was the meeting's obvious leader, in the tight-lipped form of Simeon Silver. The equally unfriendly-looking form of Serena Snow was hovering behind his left shoulder, whispering in his ear.

Alice and Rosalind joined their friends, who surrounded them conspiratorially, as their secretive Cabal went into immediate session. Rosalind had leapt into the seat next to pimply Julius Fothergill; the two of them immediately started twining themselves into a red-faced Gordian knot together. We looked around the rest of the seated crowd. Darren Stocks and two friends were there, showing the whites of their eyes and obviously desperate for alcoholic or any other form of escape. Amongst the others I noticed two grim-faced teachers from the school; a bewildered-looking Tom Soss; Mr. and Mrs. Ponsonby, whose daughter Lavinia was next to Alice, and also, to my surprise, Angus Donald.

I nudged Jess and we slid into the seats next to Angus, behind Alice's gang. On the other side of the *Bagpipe*'s helmsman was a competent-looking woman of about his own age, with short, raven-black hair, smart spectacles, a long green wool cardigan and an air of keen interest. After a few moments, I recognized her as Jane MacEachern, a locum doctor who was on Lifandoy temporarily to stand in for our senior GP, Dr. Livingstone, who was on holiday.

'Angus? Visiting your mother over here, I presume?'

'Yes, Tim. I was annoyed at having to crew the extra Thursday ferry, because I was supposed to be taking leave. So I refused to sail it back. My second did that and I'm with Mum here in Doy for a break. And also…' He glanced to his left. 'I was surprised to meet an old acquaintance. You'll have heard Mike Livingstone is away?'

'On safari in Africa, I believe? Yes. Perhaps we can presume he will meet Stanley?' The schoolchildren of the Isle of Lifandoy loved Dr. Livingstone; he was invariably addressed by them as 'Dr. L., I presume?'

Angus chuckled, making a sound like pebbles inside a barrel. 'Presumably. In the meantime, meet Jane.'

The raven-haired woman leaned across with a smile to shake hands. 'Pleased to meet you.' She had a Lowland Scots accent. As she sat back again, I whispered to Angus. 'An old flame of yours, by any chance?'

He had the grace to colour a little. 'Possibly. Meeting her was certainly a nice surprise.'

'It may be the only nice one for any of us this evening.'

We sat back as Simeon Silver stepped forward to a small lectern. On a screen behind him there appeared, surrounded by a misty glow, the face of a slightly rat-faced man with snow-white hair. In a voice that sounded as though it came from his stomach, Simeon Silver intoned a sort of chant. 'Johnson Shining is *pleased* that you are all here. He honours us all with his countenance.'

The second sentence was repeated under their breath by Serena Snow, Paul Pristine and six identical figures in white who had been standing unseen behind us. There was a pause as they all looked at us. 'Do they expect a response?' I whispered to Jess.

If they did, it was not the one they expected. A small boy in Alice and Rosalind's gang piped up hopefully. 'Can we have some milk-flavoured chewing gum now?'

Rosalind hissed at the urchin. 'Shut *up*, Nigel.' He burst into tears.

Simeon stared at her coldly. 'Blessings are earned. We cannot gain the favour of God and His Prophet without work.'

'Oh,' said Jessica brightly. 'Does it say that in your version of the Bible?' Rosalind turned round to look up at her big sister in admiration.

Simeon scowled for a moment then immediately replaced his expression with one of gentle weariness. 'We are here to reveal the truth about what the Bible really says. Many people have distorted its message for many years. But we have the true interpretation, thanks to our Shining Prophet. You have been brought here to study his revelation.'

I yawned. 'Haven't I heard things like that before?'

Serena Snow advanced and stared down at me like an avenging angel. 'You have heard nothing true before today.'

Jessica gave her a look sufficiently keen to make her step back. 'We will be the judge of that, I think.'

■ ■ ■ ■

At the end of the meeting, most of the adults tried the white wine. 'Not bad,' I admitted, after half a glassful. The dishes next to it were empty; within milliseconds of the meeting being dismissed, Alice's gang had cleaned out everything sugary on offer, and two of the bottles of lemonade had mysteriously vanished with them as well.

Paul Pristine was still standing there. 'What did you think?' he enquired with an oddly shy tone.

Darren Stocks was making a face at his own glass of wine. It was clearly not to his taste but he downed it rapidly. 'Boring. More in Tim and Jessica's line than mine.' He and his friends shambled off, obviously not wanting to discuss anything that required brain cells.

I shrugged. 'I thought we were about to get a religious inquisition. But instead of that it was largely a talk about the colour white...'

'Which isn't even a colour. It's a hue,' pointed out Angus.

Paul Pristine eyed us strangely. 'Look, this is not something I should really say,' he muttered. 'But you need to understand that influencing people is a sophisticated art, even when it's for their good.'

Jessica nodded at my side. 'If you think that talk was pointless, Tim, think again. Simeon was just softening up those who didn't understand what he was doing. For example, did you notice what he said about all colours really being white?'

'Aren't they, when they are all combined?'

'That wasn't how he put it. He was implying that all ways of looking at a thing become the same in the end, and *he* knew the only way that mattered.'

Angus nodded. 'He is trying to make his views seem so assured that you will soon cease to question him. When he has you following peacefully, he may spring surprises.'

Paul frowned. 'I believe those surprises will be ones you will welcome.' He turned away to pour out some more wine.

I glanced at Jess. 'Not a pointless talk, you say. Was it a harmless one?'

She shook her head. 'I'd like to talk to Wilfred. There was one thing in particular that he said that troubles me. Did you notice it?'

'I did.' The speaker was Jane MacEachern, who had been silent until now. 'You mean, about white being the source of only the *one* Light. He said that other lights should all fade; and he said that applied to other gods too. We should deny all other sources; only one beam shines from his so-called prophet onto us all.'

Jess looked at Jane with interest. 'Are you a Christian, Jane?'

'I think I'd rather describe myself as a stout-hearted member of the Church of Scotland. More stout-hearted than your vicar here, certainly.'

'That's not difficult,' I said.

Jess nodded. 'And you agree that Simeon sounded rather negative about...'

I wrinkled my brow. 'I think I see. You're suggesting he is trying to undermine the Christian idea of the *Trinity*? Only one beam of light...?'

'I suspect that is one thing which the People of White mean by "re-education".'

'It's a common way of steering off-course while navigating the Bible.' Angus nodded also. 'The Mormons, the Jehovah's Witnesses, the Christadelphians and what in the early Church were called the Arians. The People of White could be another of that clan. Their liking for appearing perfect is another typical feature. If Jesus isn't God and we don't need Him in the Christian sense – if He was just a Good Teacher, or alternatively if He were just God Himself and not human – then what we make ourselves, and how perfectly we can live, becomes the main story.'

Jessica was still thinking. 'I'd certainly like to talk to Uncle Wilfred about it all. We have to live with these people, so we might as well try to see behind their perfect masks.'

■ ■ ■ ■

Outside the church hall, we met an unpleasant hazard. '*Aaargh*!' I pulled the sole of my shoe with difficulty from the floor. 'Who left chewing gum on the *church* path?'

Jessica had a big sister's frown. 'I don't know but I'll find out.' She set off with a firm step. The culprits had not travelled far. 'Rosalind? That's not your gum that Timothy trod in, is it?'

Rosalind was old enough to see that sticking parishioners to their churchyard was more than just a small mistake. 'Nigel? I'll kill you. Get that up!'

'But it tastes horrible. Like milk.' The small boy scuttered to obey her, weeping as usual.

Alice appeared at my side. 'Brother-in-law to be? What do you think these Ghosts are *really* up to?'

'Ghosts?'

'That's one of our names for them,' said Rosalind. 'It was Lavinia's suggestion.'

'I don't know. But now that we've been to their class perhaps they will leave us alone. I understand they want to make the same presentation to everyone on the island. That will take them a while.'

'I wouldn't be too sure,' said Alice. 'There are a lot of Ghosts on the island now. But I could lay odds on how long...' She blanched as Jessica caught her eye. 'Oh well, maybe not.'

Then a glint came into Alice's eye. 'Hey! If we were the first to go to one of their classes, perhaps they might pay us for helping them to run others. And we could look after the chewing-gum displays.'

'That's your business,' I said. 'But I wouldn't recommend it. We may have to share the island with them now, but I intend to leave them strictly to themselves.'

'And so will you,' said Jess, addressing her sisters. 'Mummy will agree with me. That's an order.'

Alice looked dismayed. 'But there must be *something* we can do to make money out of them, or gain something from them? They are as naïve as...' Then she paused at a thought.

Whatever Alice had in mind was not about to be revealed. With a hiss and a nod, she and Rosalind vanished with the rest of their motley crew. At the church gate, Angus and Jane bid goodbye to us then turned and walked slowly, not holding hands but clearly in amiable company, into the town.

We strolled to the river bridge and leaned over its parapet on the upstream side, watching the water gliding toward us. The bridge spanned the Doy River with a single stone arch. At the end away from the town there was a second arch, through which water never flowed except in time of severe flood. For most of the time, the second arch was blocked with thick bushes on the downstream side. On the upper side it therefore formed a cave, beloved of small boys but sometimes muddy and occasionally smelly.

We walked across the bridge. The area was deserted, with just a single Land Rover parked near it with no sign of the driver. On the upstream side of the bridge, outside the entrance to the second arch's cave, a seat was positioned where it was just, at that moment, catching the last of the evening light. We descended three grassy steps and occupied it gladly, gazing over the West Burn valley towards the twilight glow and the stars already shining faintly above.

I looked at Jessica. 'It's a fine evening,' I murmured. 'What do we do now?'

She gazed at me in disgust, her dress fluttering below our seat in the breeze that had recently arisen. She murmured back. 'If you don't know, Timothy, you're a waste of space as a fiancé.'

I reached out to hold her tightly and leaned forward greedily for a kiss. But my lips never reached hers.

14 - Illumination

My lips were just millimetres from ecstasy when we both jolted upright in shock. From the second arch's 'cave' behind us, a light of paralyzing intensity suddenly fell on us. It appeared we had been caught in the beam of a searchlight. For a moment, I froze, with visions of a balaclava-clad team of armed SAS soldiers leaping out to pin us down, or worse. Or did the Cult of White possess shock troops of its own?

A voice sounded with what might have been a sharp command or exclamation. The light instantly went out. Then there was a horrible grinding sound from behind us, approaching at speed. When a pair of hands fell on our shoulders, I leapt forward with galvanic fear.

Then I heard Jessica giggling helplessly behind me. I turned.

Something was standing there in the gloom, with what appeared to be large white teeth as its only identifiable feature. Then, as my night sight slowly returned, I realized that the Creature from the Arch was not a stranger to me.

Uncle Wilfred was bearing one of his larger grins. 'Oh, I *am* sorry, Jessica. And Timothy.'

'Wh-wh-what was *that*?' I gaped at my uncle. 'What was that blinding light, Wilfred? And what are you doing emerging from the bridge like a monster from its lair?'

He beamed. 'It's powerful, isn't it? Better than I expected.'

'But what are you illuminating the underside of an empty stone arch at twilight for? Have you a contract from the tourist board to light the bridge up, or something? If so, why do it down *there*?'

Wilfred looked suitably apologetic. 'I was just testing the light,' he said. 'Jack Dooley down at Ferry Garage has welded a frame and stand for me, to hold a car battery and a powerful light. He makes a few for the roads department; they use them for mending holes and leaks at night in emergencies, in places where they cannot connect to an electric supply.'

'But why under the bridge?'

He laughed. 'Oh, I have no interest in the bridge. I was just driving back up to West Doy with the new light, when it occurred to me the dry arch would make a good place to test it. I wanted to see if it was strong enough to illuminate a large cavity.'

'Cavity? What do you *want* with such a light? Oh...'

He nodded. 'Exactly. We want to illuminate the underground chamber. But I wanted to test Jack's light before I went to the trouble of lowering it down into the souterrain. It weighs a lot and it's not a short drop down there. Here, since you're on hand, perhaps you could help me carry it back to the Land Rover.'

I obliged while Jessica finished wiping the tears of laughter from her eyes. Wilfred slammed the door of his Land Rover shut and turned to us. 'Do you want a lift? I have an idea there might be rain on the way.'

We accepted. I climbed in beside my uncle. 'Are you taking the light to the chapel now?'

'Yes.' He glanced at me and grinned slightly. 'Are you busy? I don't suppose you could give me a hand lowering it down now, could you?'

I frowned. 'What? *Now?* In the dark?'

He took a hand from the steering wheel and stroked his chin. 'I'd very much like to do all this when there is little chance of any of the People of White coming along to see what's going on.'

I sighed. 'All right. Jessica is in a dress, so she can be lookout, if it matters that much.'

'Excellent.' My uncle beamed again. 'It'll all be in place ready for the weekend.' I looked at him, but he did not elaborate on why that mattered. But I have never found it useful to try and follow all of Uncle Wilfred's arcane thought processes, so I left it at that.

■　■　■　■

Lowering the heavy light and battery by rope, down through Wilfred's trapdoor in the lawn, proved to be hot work, despite the cool evening air. When it was over and the chapel lawn looked like just a lawn again, he turned to us. 'Would you like a coffee?'

'*Yes.*'

Aunt Martha already had the kettle hot by the time we reached Big Cottage. 'I saw you all go up to the chapel in the Land

Rover half an hour ago, so I guessed that you were helping Wilfred and might soon be here.'

'You're a sharp-eyed darling.' Jessica gave her a kiss. 'But the men are the working thirsty ones.'

'They are always thirsty, if not always working.'

We settled down. Uncle Wilfred looked at us curiously. 'Had you been to that meeting in the church hall?'

'Yes.'

He looked at Jessica. 'What did you think of it, my dear?'

She responded with her own question. 'Wilfred? What do you know about the theology of the People of White?'

He pursed his lips. 'I would not describe them as at all Christian,' he said bluntly. 'Certainly not, that is, in my or the Bible's definition of the term, though Reverend Fenshaw evidently regards them as creditable.'

'That proves nothing,' I said. 'If a human-sacrificing Inca priest walked into Doytown church, Rev Fancy would greet him like a long-lost brother.'

'So what *do* they believe?'

Wilfred nodded. 'What did you make of the talk? I should explain that I have had a preview of it; they gave a shortened version of it to us in the Seigneurie meeting with them. I know that they go to great lengths to conceal the truths they are really trying to impose, underneath a lot of attractive and scientific-sounding material about light and the properties of everything white.'

'We realized that,' said Jessica. 'They were evidently steering us very gently towards a conclusion: that we should look towards only *one* light. My assumption was that they were starting to undermine the Christian doctrine of the Trinity.'

'I think so, too,' I added intelligently.

They ignored me. 'But,' Jess went on, 'in which direction? Do they blur Jesus into God, or blur Him into humanity?'

'What do you mean by that?' asked Aunt Martha.

'Take the beliefs of the Christadelphians and the Jehovah's Witnesses,' said Jess. 'Neither of those cults believes that Jesus existed before Mary conceived Him – which is, of course, exactly what the Jews that opposed Him believed in Jesus's own time. So to them Jesus is not *God* – not Someone to be *worshipped*. The

108

Christadelphians believe He was special, born from a virgin, but merely a picture of God's love. Jehovah's Witnesses believe he was perfectly obedient but ordinary until He became special – He became what they call Christ Jesus, three days after His crucifixion – but still not God. In both cases He is never and never becomes God Almighty, He is merely like an angel.'

I looked up. 'What about the Mormons?'

'The Mormons don't lift Jesus up to God; they bring God down to Jesus. To them, even God the Father started out as a human being.'

Wilfred spoke. 'You should also consider the Unitarians. They make a more subtle mistake. They accept the *divinity* of Jesus, but not His *deity*.'

'Eh?' I was puzzled. 'Aren't they the same thing? Don't both words mean God?'

'The Unitarians do not believe there are the three Persons of the Trinity. They believe only the Father is God. But they believe Jesus rose up to be *like* God, to be as admirable as He is. They like to think of Jesus as the ultimate in God-like examples. And they try to be like Him in that way. So they do not think that Jesus is and contains all of God, merely that Jesus is their perfect hero.'

'That sounds a rather easy belief.'

'Exactly. It is not unreasonable to describe Unitarians as people who decline to believe *anything* that is challenging. They like an easy, intellectually proud and confident answer to everything. But in fact they are what they are because of what they deny, not of what they believe.'

Martha was interested. 'Yet they seem closer to the line than the others. Are there Christian denominations that are close to the line on the *other* side?'

'Yes. The Coptic Church, for example.'

I wrinkled my brow. 'I don't understand this. *What* line?'

Jess explained. 'The line between Christian and non-Christian matters because it defines what Jesus could *do* for us, and has *done* for us.'

'Do you mean, in dying that we might be forgiven?'

'Yes. The point is that for us to be forgiven requires something from both *God's* side and from the *human* side.'

'From the human side, we need Someone perfect who can represent *us* and plead for us…'

'Yes. While from God's side, we need Someone who has all the *authority* of God to forgive us.'

Aunt Martha nodded. 'If Jesus is not fully man, He cannot act for humanity. If He is not fully God, He cannot act for God.'

I looked at Wilfred. 'So what does the Cult of White believe? Can you illuminate us on that too?'

Wilfred scratched his chin. 'Their views are quite subtle. I haven't yet worked out entirely where they stand. But they aren't Christian. And other signs of that are their enchantment with everything white; and their following what they obviously consider to be their infallible Prophet.'

'Johnson Shining, the furniture polish man?'

Wilfred chuckled. 'Don't let any of them hear you say that. Nevertheless, I'd very much like to hear from someone who knows more about their exact beliefs. What about that visitor you mentioned to me? Has he explained any of their beliefs to you?'

'John Khourei? No, but I'm sure he'd be delighted to.'

'Would you care to invite him around here for a chat? Tomorrow evening?'

'I'm afraid we're counting Storm Petrels tomorrow evening. And John has volunteered to help us. I'll ask him about Saturday or Sunday evening if you like.'

∎ ∎ ∎ ∎

Friday dawned fair, the more so since I had no more paths to repair. At the Office, Keith quizzed me about my paperwork but could not prove that there was bureaucracy I had neglected significantly more than he had.

'In that case, I have a different job for you. I've been talking for some time to Thomas Pandy, the shepherd up at Liffen Farm. He and I are concerned that the bridge over the West Burn there may become unstable if the bank of the burn continues to erode.'

'So it needs reinforcing? What do I do? Shovel gravel in?'

110

'No, this is not something we can do ourselves. I've contacted John Ponsonby at Marson's.' Marson's was well known to every Lifandoy islander as the island's only builder's merchant.

'Will he supply us with something we can build it up with?'

'No. As I said, this requires heavy materials. Rocks. John has ordered a trailer-load of small boulders from Sound Hill quarry. They will be delivered there this morning. And he will rent us the equipment to put them in place and arrange a driver for us to instruct. He might even drive the JCB himself.'

'Is the Lifandoy Reserve paying for all this?'

'Thankfully, no. The bridge is Lifandoy Estate property. The Factor – oh, I'm sorry, the First Pale *Disciple* – is footing the bill. But the work is on our side of the Burn so we have to supervise it.'

■　■　■　■

Thomas Pandy was pleased to see me. 'Good morning, Mr. Corn.' His Welsh accent was straight out of the Rhondda. He paused and looked worriedly over my shoulder. 'You have not brought your Uncle Wilfred with you, I see.'

'No, he is far away.' I carefully refrained from grinning at him, knowing the effect that a grin even related to that of my uncle might have on a simple islander like Thomas.

He relaxed. 'The rocks have already arrived; they are in a pile just across the bridge. Mr. Ponsonby is driving his little JCB up here now.'

We strolled down to the bridge, followed by Thomas's two suspicious sheepdogs. A rumbling noise prefaced the arrival of the JCB down the lane behind us.

The job was easier than we had expected and was completed in a couple of hours. Afterwards John drove up to Liffen Farm and I followed him to partake of Mrs. Pandy's hospitality.

We were gratefully making inroads into some flapjack she had made when I turned to John. 'I saw you at the meeting last night. Were you asked to go?'

'Not by these new island owners,' he said. 'For some reason young Lavinia desperately wanted to go, so Sarah and I decided to go with her.'

'What did you think?'

He raised his eyebrows. 'It all sounded quite nice. This thing about white is a bit odd, but I like the idea of everything clean and pure. Mr. Silver didn't seem to be saying anything I could disagree with.'

'Don't you think that they have any sort of hidden agenda? That he might have been trying to steer us toward something deeper? Like, say, revering their leader?'

It was plain that Mr. Ponsonby had no interest in looking for hidden motives. 'What's wrong with that? There have been many inspiring figures throughout history. I don't mind going along with someone who says things that seem reasonable.'

Thomas Pandy joined in. 'I've not heard anything from these Canadians myself. But if they help Lifandoy why should we complain? They've already persuaded the ferry company to put on an extra ferry when we need one. And I've heard that they are helping out in lessons at the infant school because the teachers are so stretched with this new curriculum.'

'I heard they offered,' said Mr. Ponsonby, 'and the silly teachers turned them down. But it's nice to have so many young adults around the island. And if the rumours about building a college on the island are true, it will be excellent news for Marson's for a long time to come.'

Thomas was equally positive. 'There will be a big demand for my mutton and lamb too, I hope. I think it's wonderful. We will never forget the day they came to Lifandoy.'

15 – Night Birds

Jessica was as concerned as I was, when I recounted the conversation to her at lunchtime at a café in Doytown. 'The People of White are going to persuade a lot of people with the money and business they can offer to islanders, she said.'

'And they are going to infiltrate a lot of island life,' I agreed. 'How are the First Pale Disciple and his estate office getting on with them?'

'I don't think Mr. Fothergill is keen on them,' she said. 'But there's not a lot he can do except obey their orders. The person who I think really does like them is Graham Fytts.'

I retracted my lips and snarled at the name. 'Is that because he's going to earn a fat commission from them when they build their new college?'

'You've heard that, then. I think it's more than that. He sees them as absolute paragons of virtue, as his ideal sort of people. He and Shining-son have meetings every day.'

'Shining-son? Is that what they call him? The Prophet's son?'

'I've never heard any other name. And he seems to regard Fytts as the person he wants to do things with on the island. We are worried that Mr. Fothergill might be sidelined in favour of Graham, or even sacked and replaced by him.'

'Or retired. How old is the Factor?'

'He's sixty-three. They could offer him early retirement if they wanted to get him out without a fuss.'

'But he has a young son. Julius is a long way from finishing his education yet. I don't think Tom would go willingly.'

'That depends how much money they have.'

I looked at her. 'Are they really that rich?'

'I have heard that Johnson Shining made a lot of money in Canada in mining. Nickel mining, I think. And they now have the rental income from most of the properties on Lifandoy. The Earl always ploughed the income back into the island. They might do it a different way.'

'There are certainly lots of old people who have been grateful for grants from the Estate Office over the years. Angus's mother, for a start; the Office paid for her house to be reroofed.'

Jessica pursed her lips. 'I suspect that kindly acts like that will be overtaken by a much harder business attitude now. The People of White don't plan to stop their spread with Lifandoy. They are already talking about setting up an office or a mission on the Isle of Man. Speaking of which, have you heard any more about Darren's idea of smuggling beer across the Sound from there?'

'No. Why?'

'Professional concern.' Along with her secretarial job, Jessica was on the crew list of the Lifandoy lifeboat. Her father had been its coxswain. 'I mentioned it to Barney during the lifeboat training session. He was quite alarmed. The Sound has a strong current at times. At night it's positively treacherous in places. Quite apart from whether Darren's plan was legal.'

'Would it be illegal? Darren would not be breaking any customs regulations. Anyone can bring beer from Man to Lifandoy, as long as they don't sell it. And I'd love to see you hoisting a dripping Darren Stocks aboard.'

'I would only touch him at the far end of a disinfected pole. Anyhow, I have to get back to work for the afternoon. Goodbye, darling.'

■ ■ ■ ■

There was a jovial mood at the Reserve Office as we prepared for our Storm Petrel survey. Storm Petrels are the maritime equivalent of swallows or, more precisely, house martins, with their white rumps. There are few birds more fairy-like or entrancing. Or secretive.

John Khourei arrived exactly on time. I was waiting for him while Keith, Bob and Jamie prepared their equipment. 'John?' I greeted him. 'Welcome. You look well-equipped.' He was clad with good boots, outdoor gear, two walking poles and a powerful head torch.

'I'm looking forward to it. It's a chance to get away from *everything*.'

114

I glanced at him. 'You look a little harassed. Have you been having an encounter with people who irritated you? People in white, by any chance?'

'Indeed. I was doing a favour for the lady who runs the guest house where I am staying. She had a letter to deliver to the Estate Office and she has a bad leg. I offered to put it through the Office letterbox as I passed the building on my way up here. Then I met Shining-son himself in the Estate Office car park.'

'Do you know him?'

'Indeed I do, from my time working in Canada. Let's say we crossed swords once in the past, when one of my flock in my church in Canada came under the influence of his people. In short, he was most put out to meet me on Lifandoy. The conversation was not pleasant. He even implied that he might arrange for my landlady to be told I was now *persona non grata* at her guest-house.'

Keith had overheard the conversation. 'If you get thrown out, John, we'll put you up.'

He was touched. 'That's really kind. I'm only here for a week or two, so I hope it won't happen. But thank you very much for that.'

■　■　■　■

Sound Point is the north-easternmost extremity of the Isle of Lifandoy. Made of rocks of Cambrian slate, it marks the northern end of a coast of slowly sloping cliffs with occasional hazardous gullies leading to deep clefts which occasionally descend to hidden coves or caves. By day it is dramatic and beautiful; by night it can be terrifying.

We approached the cliffs using the hard-beaten track that leads to the Sound Hill quarry. This conveniently runs near the cliffs until it climbs the hill, with several open areas where a Land Rover can easily park. Keith stopped in one of them and the four of us spilled out eagerly into the darkness.

It was nearly midnight and the night was cloudy. We could see absolutely nothing without our torches, apart from the lights of houses on the Isle of Man on the other side of the strait, which gave a useful bearing. Keith was stern. 'Stick together and use your torches at all times. Those steep gulleys are deadly.'

John Khourei was next to me. 'Can you hear that?' I pointed into the night sky. 'That musical sort of creaking call? That's two of the birds in a courtship chase.'

'I can hear one purring,' he said excitedly. 'That means a nest, doesn't it? On which parts of the cliffs do they nest?'

'We call it churring. A few occupy excavated burrows in the peaty turf. But most are in the sloping boulder fields where the cliffs slowly increase in gradient. We can only survey the upper flatter parts. Most nests are in cracks or crevices of the rock, under boulders or among loose stones.'

'On Fair Isle they nest in old walls.'

'There are two or three stone shelters along the cliffs, probably built by shepherds, which are particularly beloved by them.'

Keith had already explained the survey technique to John, Jamie and Bob. Each of us had a mobile phone with a recording of petrels churring. Keith marked out a ten metre square area of the boulder field and we explored it for possible nest holes, smelling for the strong oily odour of them.

'Try this one.' Keith shone a torch briefly on a promising hole. I helped John to play the recording using his phone outside the hole, for about five seconds. He stopped; and from within the sitting bird started its churring call in reply.'

'He is saying, "Get away! This hole is mine,"' I said.

John was puzzled. 'How do you know it's a male bird?'

'The females don't reply to our recording. They don't respond to the call of a strange male.'

'How can we survey the females, then? One bird is away at sea, presumably? But you don't know if the one here is male or female, do you?'

'We can't survey the females. But because the pair takes turns to stay at the nest we can just double our count of males to calculate the whole population.'

Slowly and patiently, we covered the whole of Keith's marked area. 'I make that seventeen', he said. 'Now let's take a look.' He reached into one of the burrows and withdrew a tiny morsel of life. He handed it to John.

'How much does it weight?' he asked in astonishment, holding it delicately.

'Twenty-seven grams, on average.'

'Less than an ounce. Astounding!'

Keith took the bird back and replaced it very gently. 'Now let's try a more densely occupied area.'

We moved on. John was amazed. 'The little birds are whizzing around all over the sky. It's so *noisy*,' he said. 'And if I didn't know what the sound was, it would be positively spooky.'

I laughed. 'You should visit a Manx shearwater colony,' I said. 'The call of a Manx shearwater has been likened to an opera singer being strangled. The arriving birds call from the sky and the sitting birds reply to them from tunnels under your feet.'

'Then they find each other?'

'Well, provided nothing is in the way. They are almost as blind as you are, of course. They have an ancestral memory of the shape of the hillside. But it doesn't include *you*. A Manx shearwater flying into your ear can give you a good thump on the head. Speaking of which...' I had detected a soft thud. 'There, that's definitely an occupied hole. Yours, I think.'

After two hours we were exhausted and Keith was very satisfied. 'I will have to extrapolate from our survey plots across the whole colony area. But at first glance the figures look slightly higher than last year's. We could have more than a thousand breeding pairs on the whole of Sound Head cliffs this year. I'd like to do another survey in a week or so, but tonight's has given excellent coverage.'

'Well done, everyone,' I confirmed. 'Is that it for tonight, then, Keith?'

He paused. 'Would you mind half an hour more? I would rather like to walk down to above Two Cave Cove. That was where I heard something odd last year.'

He led the way. 'It was right at the end of our last survey last year,' he said. 'It was four in the morning and the stormies had all gone silent. I was walking back to the Land Rover and I heard something call that didn't sound quite right, just a couple of times.'

We reached the slope above the cove. The waves were noisy on the rocks below. I could hear nothing. But Keith suddenly swung round. 'What was that? I heard a flight call. A sort of chattering, not like a Storm Petrel. It was more like the start of a Leach's Petrel call.'

We listened intently. No further sound came from the sky. Then a sound began from beneath a boulder a few paces from the path.

'It's like a Storm Petrel, but unlike,' said John. 'Each purr ends with a rising sort of note, instead of a gasp – a sort of *aaah!* instead of an *ow!* And the purring is harsher.'

Our student Jamie was excited. 'It sounds very like a Leach's.'

John was surprised. 'That's a Leach's fork-tailed petrel? I didn't think they nested anywhere in the British Isles outside Scotland.'

Keith was already busy with his phone. 'I have to get a recording of this. Are there any others?'

We explored the new boulder-field slowly. 'No, that's the only one we can hear. No, wait…' I thought I had heard one more.

Keith made his recording and started playing at holes under other boulders nearby. 'Yes – there's just one more. One more male, that is.'

We gathered together and shone our head torches around. 'Where are we? We must mark this spot. OK – in line with those two white boulders. That's it – *now* we can go home back to bed.'

■　■　■　■

Despite our late nights Keith and I were at the Reserve Office after breakfast next morning. Keith was playing the recording over and over again, comparing it with ones he had obtained from the internet. Jessica walked in, looking for me, and saw his furrowed brow.

'You all look tired.'

'We've been up half the night. We heard a different petrel on Sound cliffs while we were censusing the stormies.'

Keith sat back tiredly. 'I'm ninety-per-cent certain we have discovered a couple of Leach's Petrels nesting up there. But, oh *why* did I never think to see if I could lift one of them out of its burrow?'

Jessica frowned. 'Would you have wanted to disturb the nest of a very rare bird?'

'That's why I didn't want to do it. But...'

'But what?' I asked.

'Listen!' He played a recording of a churring petrel. 'Now that's a Storm Petrel.'

'Obviously.'

'And this...' He played another.

'Leach's?'

'Correct. But this...'

I listened. I looked at Jessica and watched her face as she listened. Keith stopped the recording. 'Is that the *same*?'

'I'm not sure.' Jessica and I spoke together.

'And nor am I.' Keith had a determined look. 'But we have to find out. We have *some* sort of petrel nesting on Lifandoy that isn't a Storm Petrel and – whatever it is – should not nest anywhere south of the Hebrides or east of western Ireland. And I *can't* absolutely identify it.'

16 – Sound and White

We left Keith grimly searching the internet, trying to download recordings or sonograms of every small oceanic petrel species known to man, of which there were evidently a number. He was trying to translate a Japanese scientific paper as we walked out of the Lifandoy Reserve Office. 'I don't work on Saturdays,' I muttered.

'Nor do I, normally,' said Jess.

I scowled at her. 'They're *not* going to call you into the Estate Office today?'

She shrugged. 'I think you need to realize, darling, that a lot of things are changing on Lifandoy. It soon won't be the island we have all known and loved. Mind you, I wasn't just referring to that. There is a forecast of a fast deep depression bringing high winds this evening. It could catch a sailor or two out, and a lifeboat alert isn't out of the question.'

'That's different.' I paused as another tired-looking figure approached. 'Hello, John.'

'Any conclusion about our last birds, yet?' Reverend Khourei was clearly interested in the feathered sort of flock for the moment.

'No. Keith can't be certain from the recording he made that it is a Leach's. I think he will want to go up on the cliffs again.'

'Tonight?'

'No, and not for a few days. There's a gale due.'

'Then I'll make the most of a sunny day.' John walked on slowly.

We were nearly at Little Cottage when a less respectable figure appeared. It was Alice, for once alone.

To our surprise, she walked past without looking at us. Jessica stopped. 'Alice? Is something wrong?'

'No. Only Rosalind.'

''What's your sister done?' I asked.

Jessica smiled sweetly. 'No more than I have, darling Timothy. I think Alice is weary of sisters who are joined at the hip to pimply youths.'

120

'Hah. Do you mind? I have no pimples and have had none for five years.'

Alice grimaced. 'Being sister-in-law to a Corn is bad enough. Being one to a *Fothergill* would be...' She stalked off angrily.

'What's up with her?' I looked after her. 'What has the Factor's son done now?'

'Or the First Pale Disciple himself?' Jessica nodded slowly. 'I suspect that one of Alice's schemes has been frustrated, probably accidentally, by Mr. Fothergill. And I think I know which one it is.'

'The only one I know of,' I offered, 'was her plan to import non-white chewing-gum via Yvonne's father, in his van that takes the toffee factory products across to Douglas.'

'Exactly. But had you forgotten that *toffee* is not white?'

'Oh.'

'Apparently Mr. Fothergill has been persuaded by the Cult of White to issue an order banning the production of brown toffee on the island. The Cult has agreed to fund a new purification unit at the toffee factory so that all the toffee can be made white. But it will take weeks to change over Yvonne's father's equipment...'

'During which there will be no van journeys and therefore no smuggling of coloured chewing-gum. Ah, well...' I sighed. 'Even Alice cannot evade all of the controls all of the time.'

Jessica looked back after her departing sister. 'I wouldn't be too sure. The face Alice has on her is not one of crushed despair; it's one of Machiavellian manoeuvring.'

■　■　■　■

The rest of Saturday morning passed in a pleasant blur as Jessica and I worked out which were the softest and most comfortable bits of each other while she sat on my knee in my armchair. After lunch, we set out for a walk. We were passing the chapel when Uncle Wilfred popped his head up above the wall.

'Hello, Jessica, hello, Timothy.'

Beside Wilfred's head appeared the bespectacled one of Dr. Winchester. He nodded to me. 'Your uncle knows a great deal about antiquities on Lifandoy.'

I smiled back. 'We live on a lovely island. Do you mean the antiquities under the chapel lawn?'

Wilfred replied. 'There is far, far more, Timothy. I would be delighted to show you some of it.' He grinned enthusiastically.

I stepped back a pace. 'Er – some other time, maybe.'

'Well, at any rate, Dr. Winchester and I are about to set out on a tour of the island. I thought I'd take him over to look at Fort Snowdon. Then there is a tumulus at the north end of Snaefell Bay that I would like his opinion on. Do you want a lift anywhere?'

Jessica looked at me. 'Afternoon tea at the Fort Snowdon tea-room would be a nice outing.'

We slid into the back of Wilfred's smart House Farm SUV. He and Dr. Winchester were so engrossed in their discussion that neither noticed us all the way to Fort Snowdon, which was probably a good thing.

We enjoyed the afternoon tea, and then found that Wilfred and the museum man were ready to leave at the same time as we were. 'You can come with us have an hour walking beyond Snaefell Bay, and then a lift back again,' offered my uncle. 'It will take us that long to examine the tumulus. Otherwise you have a long walk home.'

We agreed. As we disembarked overlooking Snaefell Bay, I looked up towards the cliffs. 'Hey – in an hour we could walk up to the rocks where Keith recorded that strange petrel last night, and back.'

'I'd love the cliffs,' agreed Jessica.

We walked round a small pebble-fringed bay that was a junior brother of the stony expanse of Snaefell Bay to the south. The cliff path was steeper than I expected. At the top, by daylight it was surprisingly hard to identify the two white boulders we had used as marks. When I worked out where the first nest hole was, I found it smelly but otherwise unremarkable. 'There's nothing to be seen by daylight. I knew that would be so. Still, I know better where the hole is now.'

We stood up and looked across the Sound of Doy. I glanced at Jessica. 'Would Darren Stocks struggle to bring a launch full of booze across from the Isle of Man one dark night, as he seems to be planning to do?'

'I certainly wouldn't recommend it, except at slack tide. If it was just at slack tide Darren might be able to do it. Or at least, a competent launch or dinghy sailor should be able to.'

'I *think* Darren knows one end of an oar from the other.' I sighed. 'Well, you of the lifeboat fraternity have been warned. Now we had better get back to the tumulus before we miss our lift.'

■ ■ ■ ■

When we reached the tree-topped mound, we found Dr. Winchester still busy with a measuring tape. But Uncle Wilfred was also standing looking across the water. His mouth was slightly open and his teeth were showing a little. The newborn grin hardened a little as we watched. 'It's not far, is it?'

'What isn't, Wilfred?'

He glanced at us. 'Oh nothing.' He paused. 'We have no Bibles now at the chapel. Except our own personal copies. The People of White will not let us order any except for ones in their own ridiculously distorted version. They are now controlling everything that comes onto the island through Port Doy on the *Bagpipe*.'

I shrugged. 'You'll have to find a way of bringing more Bibles onto the island, then.'

My uncle looked at me in an odd way. 'Yes I will, won't I?'

■ ■ ■ ■

Uncle Wilfred's antiquarian had decided he needed to get back to the mainland. So Wilfred drove Dr. Winchester straight to Port Doy for the late afternoon ferry sailing. We stayed in the rear seats until Port Doy.

Then we disembarked. 'We'll get home ourselves from here, Wilfred. Thanks for the tour.'

The harbour was busy as always. The island lifeboat was beside the inner quay. We strolled along past it. On the deck, the assistant coxswain Barney was busy with a mop and bucket. He grinned up at us. 'Nice to see someone is relaxing.'

Jess was surprised. 'You're working hard on a Saturday, Barney.'

He grimaced. 'We've been told we have to keep the decks as white as possible.'

'Are you going to paint the lifeboat white instead of orange?'

He scowled. 'I'd sink her first.'

We climbed down the steps to the deck. 'Barney? Do you know a lot about the currents in the Sound of Doy?'

He paused his mopping and rubbed his chin. 'Just after slack water there is a strong little current that sets in southward close to Sound cliffs. A sailboat was once caught in it and holed on that rock at the north end of Snaefell Bay, between it and the little bay.'

'Is that the reef below the spur the tumulus stands on?'

'Yes. But why do you ask?'

'Oh, we were talking to someone who was thinking of putting a boat out there.'

'Well, tell them to watch out just after slack water, then.'

■   ■   ■   ■

From the harbour, we looked up at the West Ridge. But the wind was already rising. 'The ridge would be too draughty a way home now. Let's walk up the river path.'

We reached Doytown bridge in half an hour. We walked up onto the bridge and glanced at the seat below. I could almost see a grin hovering in the air above it, like a Cheshire cat version of my uncle. 'Maybe *not*. Let's get a drink.'

Doytown was Saturday evening busy. We strolled into the town. 'What about the *Earl of Lifandoy*? I'm not going near the *Doy Arms*.'

'Suits me.'

To our surprise, several white-clad figures were visible among the crowd at the bar of the *Earl*. Only white wine, Martini, vodka and the like were on offer but the younger members of the People of White appeared to have no conscientious objection to Saturday evening alcohol.

With our drinks, we looked round for somewhere to sit. The only vacant place was at a table with two of the Cult already seated along with two others. We were already in the process of occupying the other two when I realized that one of the figures was Paul Pristine. He gave us a smile of recognition. His companion was a pretty girl with what looked like natural blonde hair. He looked across at Jessica. 'Nice to see another young lady with great taste in hair.' He introduced his companion. 'This is Anna Albion.'

'Hi, Anna.'

I was about to say something more when the couple next to Paul and Anna stood up and their places were immediately taken by a more familiar one. 'Hey, Angus. Jane. Good to see you. What can we get you?' I glanced down. 'And you two?'

Jessica murmured in my ear. 'Come into money, have we?'

'Keith paid me overtime for last night.'

Shortly I came back with a tray of various white drinks. 'Angus? Jane? This is Paul and – Anna.'

Angus chuckled. 'What colour are you people when off-duty?'

Paul smiled tolerantly. 'Still white.'

Jane nodded. 'A good clinical hue, at least.'

I chuckled. 'Doctors will have to wear a different colour now.'

Jane gave me a sour look. 'I've had to change to a pale yellow gown.'

Anna smiled sadly. 'That's not your own option.'

'The only one I would choose.' Jane's Scots accent became stronger when she was slightly nettled.

Angus poured oil. 'It's Saturday night. Shall we declare hues and colours off the menu for half an hour?'

Paul sighed. 'I must admit I think there are more important parts to our mission.'

I looked at him curiously. 'What *is* your mission? What comes first? Your Prophet, your beliefs or your lifestyle?'

Paul looked at Anna, and then glanced around. 'That might depend on whom you asked.'

'Is there a politically correct answer then? Would Simeon Silver or Shining-son give a different one to you?'

Jessica leaned over to me 'Well done,' she whispered. 'Divide and rule?'

Paul hesitated. 'They might.'

'Let me guess. They would put Johnson Shining on high.'

He was embarrassed. 'I couldn't possibly comment.' There was a quirk at the edge of his mouth that proved I had struck well. 'But how I live is important to me.'

Angus pounced also. 'You want to live well. Your beliefs follow on.'

Paul began to get angry. 'Are *your* beliefs not important to *you*?'

Angus sat back. 'I think Tim and Jessica have thought through their beliefs better than I have.'

Paul looked at us thoughtfully. 'Perhaps I should have a proper discussion with you. The thing is...' he looked uncomfortable. 'Our People are all strangers to your island.'

Jessica nodded. 'You're unhappy about imposing your beliefs on people that you hardly know yet.'

'I certainly know little of you. Look, I know we are alien to you. But on a simple human level, I'd like to think that we could share at least understanding. Perhaps eventually ... friendship?'

Jessica spoke. 'We respect you saying that, Paul. Yes, we would like to be friendly, as far as we can.'

Anna spoke. 'Why don't you tell us something about yourselves? We are all on this island together for now. What sort of things do you do, and what you are planning to do next?'

Angus chuckled. 'The second question is easy for *them*,' he said, looking at Jessica and me. 'They're about to get married.'

'Really?' Paul was genuinely pleased. 'When?'

'Two weeks.'

'Wow. Is everything ready?'

I looked helplessly at Jessica. 'I've no idea.'

'Most of it,' she said. 'My dress is still being made. It should be ready to bring over to Lifandoy in a week. It's being made by my auntie on the Isle of Man – she's a professional dressmaker.'

'How good is that?' Anna was excited. 'What colour is it?'

'White.'

17 – Persuasion?

There was a long silence. Anna looked sharply at Paul. He sat like a statue for several seconds. A gleam of sweat appeared on his forehead. Then in a low voice he spoke. 'I think I missed what you said, just then. *Don't* tell me it again.'

He was too late. Without warning, a tall figure had appeared behind him. Simeon Silver was staring down at Jessica, with a faintly contemptuous expression. He had obviously not heard Paul's quiet reply. 'I heard *that*. There will be no need to have a white wedding dress made. It would not be allowed on Lifandoy for *you* to wear.'

Anna was looking distressed. 'I'm terribly afraid you may have to go off Lifandoy to get married.' She was almost in tears.

Around us, the crowd had become aware of the tension. Among them appeared, to my surprise, the face of Darren. He had presumably crawled out of the *Doy Arms* and now clearly had had a vodka too many here. 'Hey, Silver!' Simeon Silver turned to face him in surprise. 'What do you mean by *you*? No-one talks to one of my *friends* like that.'

The idea of Jessica needing Darren as a friend startled me so much that I choked on my glass of wine. So I was not watching closely when Darren shoved Simeon Silver, and two of Simeon's companions promptly put Darren in a head-lock. A roar arose from the crowd standing around him

It was looking rather nasty when a large figure suddenly arose from the table behind Simeon. It was Sergeant Farquhar, out of uniform.

'Police!' The crowd stepped back instantly.

'Can you two gentlemen please release Darren Stocks? I want to take him down to the station to ask why he shoved Mr. Silver here, and to let him cool off.'

Simeon scowled, but with a gesture indicated Darren should be released. The sergeant, who was clearly not disposed to let Darren off this time, immediately clamped a strong hand onto his collar and led him away. Simeon and his two companions followed, evidently intending to ensure Darren went all the way to the police station.

That left our table of six sitting by ourselves, as the rest of the crowd grumbled indecisively. We all looked at each other. But mostly we looked at Jessica.

■ ■ ■ ■

I glanced around. 'I don't like this. There are too many of Darren's mates around here.' Several other white-clad figures were still present and staring sternly at the drinkers. Jessica had become a popular figure through her efforts in the lifeboat crew and the crowd had heard what had been said and was clearly in a truculent mood. A raw nerve had been touched.

Jessica, pale-faced, agreed. 'Perhaps we had better go somewhere else. I don't feel too much like socializing any longer.'

'Where should we go? Somewhere quieter.'

Angus looked round. 'My mother is out at an old-time concert for the evening. Would you all care for a coffee? She has a large living room.'

Paul was red. 'We wouldn't be welcome.'

Jessica disagreed. 'You and Anna are the human face of the People of White. Let's see whether we can get along with you, at least.'

Both Paul and Anna were clearly touched. 'It would be a privilege to be allowed into one of your homes.'

■ ■ ■ ■

The two Canadians looked around their first Old World home in surprise. 'It's beautiful. We ought to pay to come in here.'

Angus laughed. 'Mum has collected little antiques and china all her life. I've no idea what I'll do with it all when she departs this mortal coil.'

We settled down in a circle as Angus collected orders. He smiled at Paul and Anna. '*White* coffee, I take it?'

'Yes, please.' They laughed.

Paul looked at me hesitantly. 'Er – where *should* the wedding be? In the parish church?'

'Not likely,' I said. 'In West Doy chapel, where the real believers are.'

He laughed. '*You* have a low opinion of the vicar of Doy too?'

'Do you?'

'He agrees with absolutely everything we say. Then he agrees something quite different the next day.'

'That's Reverend Fancy for you. He fancies everything.'

'A good nickname,' he agreed. 'Is West Doy chapel part of the Anglican church too?'

'It's independent, though it is linked to other like-minded ones.'

'It's Christian, I take it?'

'Yes. And you're not?'

He winced. 'Why do you say that?'

Angus was interested. 'You don't seem to be denying it.'

'Johnson Shining would say that we are. I'm not sure that he means by it what I think *you* would.'

Anna looked worried. 'I hope this conversation will go no further?'

'Absolutely not,' Jessica assured her. 'Do you really want to take part in it? We don't want to persuade you to say something you'd rather not.'

'There's no fear of that.' It was clear that Anna was not a soft cookie.

Angus was interested. 'What aspects of Christian belief do you think that other Christians might suspect the People of White were out of order on? Or is that a secret that you don't want us to discover until it's too late?'

Paul grimaced. 'Do you see us as that insidious? I am *proud* to be a member of the People of White. We aim to live good lives, and I believe we do.'

Jessica nodded. 'From what I have seen of you at the Estate Office, I can find little fault. Almost *too* little fault.'

Anna laughed. 'We have been called the Teflon Tribe. But what's wrong with that?'

I thought for a moment. 'Nothing. But people aren't perfect. What happens when you make mistakes? What do you believe about forgiveness?'

For a moment, a hard look came into Paul's eyes. 'That's why I don't think we would really fit *your* definition of Christian. We fit your vicar's: he talks nearly all the time about good works and people who do them. I suspect you would talk a lot more about Jesus and faith.'

'That's true. But don't you?'

'Faith, certainly. But Jesus, and the Holy Spirit...'

I looked at Jessica. 'You and Wilfred were right. The doctrine of the Trinity is the sore spot. The Three in One God.'

Paul was not on the defensive. 'I don't think a lot of Christians – even your sort of Christians – interpret the Bible correctly. Frankly, most Christians that I have conversations with turn out, in the end, to believe effectively in *three* Gods.'

Jane came in. 'That's what is called tritheism, isn't it? It's a common accusation levelled against Christians by members of other religions.'

'It isn't true, Paul, even though you think it is, said Angus. 'But some Christians certainly do talk very confusedly. So much so that it's not *far* from the truth, for some careless Christians.'

Jessica countered. 'Whereas the People of White, I suspect, lean the other way. They *blur* the Trinity.'

'But in what way?' Jane was interested.

'In the Early Church,' said Jessica, 'there was a group called the Monarchians. They thought that within God, the Father *is* the Son *is* the Spirit. God was like one person with three roles – as, for instance, I am a daughter, a sister and a fiancée.'

We looked at Paul. He shook his head. 'No.'

'Alternatively,' said Jessica, 'a different sort of story is the one that Jesus is not *actually* God. Many groups have claimed that.'

'Is Jesus simply not God?' Again we looked at Paul. 'I don't believe that, either,' he said.

'A third option', said Jess, 'is a mistake called Adoptionism. That's the idea that Jesus was *rewarded* by becoming part of God. He was not one of the three Persons of God from before time began. He was more like an added *extra*.'

I turned to Paul. 'So which is it, Paul? Your picture of the "one white light" is obviously not inside the usual limits of what Christians believe. Do you believe Jesus is merely an added *piece* of the Almighty?'

■ ■ ■ ■

Uncle Wilfred was very interested in our discussion when I relayed it to him over our common garden fence on Sunday morning.

'So they *do* believe Jesus is God? They are not like the Mormons or the Jehovah's Witnesses or the Christadelphians or even the Unitarians?'

'Or the Jews or the Muslims? No, they're not. They are more subtle than that.'

He stroked his sideburns thoughtfully. 'But they think that Jesus simply got *added* to God? That He was no better than us but just improved until He became like God?'

'Yes. And, critically, they think they can follow the same course themselves if they are pure and white enough.'

He sighed. 'Then they need to learn that He came from eternity to be their *Friend* – one they *cannot* do without. Look, I think we should have a talk about this soon. In fact, I might even preach a sermon about it.'

'A sermon? But I thought the People of White were going to crowd into your morning service at the chapel, to make sure that you say nothing they disagree with?'

'They are.' My uncle sighed. 'But that is only the *morning* service.' Slowly, he began to grin.

■ ■ ■ ■

The morning service at West Doy chapel was indeed packed with members of the People of White. I expected Uncle Wilfred to rant and rave at them; but to my surprise the service was a tame affair, talking about generalities like love and kindness. Wilfred's sermon was, in fact, more like one I would have expected from Reverend Fenshaw.

Afterwards Jessica and I challenged him, as he shut the chapel door when everyone else had left. 'We didn't know you were a collaborator, Wilfred.'

He looked unhappy. 'It was a hard decision. But there is more than one way to skin a cat. The alternative was to speak so that the Cult closed the chapel and took it over lock, stock and barrel.'

'But what is the *point* of the chapel, if you are not preaching what the Bible says.'

'Oh, I will be. This evening.'

'I didn't know there was an evening service. You didn't announce one.'

He had a strange, soft light in his eyes. 'It won't be announced to anyone. Except by the Lord Himself.'

We turned as Paul Pristine came up. 'May I have your key, Mr. Corn?'

'What?' I stared as Uncle Wilfred handed the chapel door's big key to Paul. Paul locked the door and walked away. Wilfred nodded. 'Perhaps you begin to see now. Only services authorized by the People of White are now allowed in all church buildings on Lifandoy.'

'So *where* is the evening service going to be held?' I gazed at him. Then I watched as his eyes turned to gaze across the verdant chapel lawn. 'Don't tell me. No. You're *joking!*'

18 – Surveillance

We had Sunday afternoon to reflect on Uncle Wilfred's foolishness. 'He'll *never* get away with it. An underground church?'

'The service won't start until it is dark,' Jessica said. 'That will be at least ten o'clock this evening, I imagine.'

Since I possessed no deckchairs, we were lying on a blanket on the front lawn of Little Cottage. 'Well, I'll look forward to it. I hope no-one from the Cult finds out, for Wilfred's sake. But perhaps they will all be back at home by that time.'

We lay back. 'By the way,' I said. 'Where *are* the People of White all living? Are they staying in Lifandoy House?'

'No. That's the one place they are *not*,' said Jess. 'Simeon Silver and later Shining-son wanted to move in there. They told the Seigneurie that. But Wilfred and the other Seigneurs refused. They had conceded a lot by then, but the old dears rose up in fury. The Cult people were astonished. Your Uncle Wilfred was a hero. He stood up and said that if they moved into the Earl's home when the Earl's estate was not yet formally closed and his body had not been found, Wilfred would personally throw the suitcases of anyone else out of Lifandoy House. And all the old dodderers were on their feet shouting.'

'So?'

'Simeon Silver and his close acolytes are living at the House Farm, where Graham Fytts treats them like royalty.'

'Hah!' I spat in disgust.

'Don't spit, Timothy. It's unhygienic. Shining-son and his family are in the Doy Hotel. The other senior members are in a couple of guest-houses in the town, which they have taken over entirely. Also, two are in the *Harbour Inn*, one in the *Doy Arms*, and two are up at the Tystie Bay Hotel: I think Friedrich Frost is one of them. The rank and file are either scattered around bed-and-breakfasts in the town, or in caravans over at English Bay caravan site. Oh, and Paul and Anna are in separate rooms in the new bed-and-breakfast at the bottom of our village.'

'Shining-son has a family?'

'A wife and daughter. No-one has seen his wife. His daughter is called Minnie and is at Alice's school. In fact, I think she is in Alice's class. Apparently the schoolchildren were making fun of her white clothes – they called her Minnehaha at first – until she punched Alice's friend Oliver on the nose and knocked him right out. Now she has a group of friends who are now apparently the deadly enemies of Alice's little Cabal. They call themselves the Intrigue.'

We lay back in the sunshine behind the hedge. As we did so, we heard voices from the road. No heads were in sight, which was explained when we recognized Alice's among them.

'How can we get back at those Intriguers? And, more importantly, how can we get an angle on *all* the Culties? We have to have a plan of campaign.'

'I always thought your sister had a look of Napoleon Bonaparte about her,' I muttered. 'Small and with one hand always reaching for mischief.'

Jessica sat up. 'And do *I* look like Boney, too?'

A line of faces looked over the hedge. 'Hey! Come and watch. This looks like the first marital row. Who do you fancy?'

Alice's face joined them. 'Foregone conclusion,' she said. 'Not even worth laying odds.' She inspected us mournfully. 'But yet another problem to solve. We can't have them falling out two weeks before the wedding. Timothy must be lulled into a false sense of security now, until he's in chains. Jessica's day must not be spoilt. *Peace*, sis and brother-in-law.'

A line of youngsters walked into my garden, squashing my flowers and dropping litter on my grass. Alice perched ominously on a spade handle, like a hungry robin regarding me as the worm in the grass. 'What can we *do*?' Her mind had already reverted from our problems to her own.

We scowled. 'We might ask the same.'

She sighed. 'Minnie and her Intriguers are bad enough. But at least they understand the pain of having only two flavours of chewing gum. But our underground train has come off its rails. Yvonne's father can't smuggle for us. And we haven't got a plan B.'

'You'll have to bribe someone. Or blackmail them.'

134

She shrugged. 'I don't think the Culties are bribable.' Then her countenance brightened. 'But what did you say? *Blackmail?* That might have possibilities.'

I chuckled. 'To blackmail someone you must have compromising information.'

Alice brightened further. 'Information? Our Cabal are the information experts of Lifandoy. Little moves on this island without a report of it coming to me, if I need it. If there are things the Culties are doing that they shouldn't, I'll spot them. And threaten to report them, if it will help.'

'Help to turn the information into chewing gum?'

She was indignant. 'Not *just* chewing gum. If we can put on any pressure on about Jessica's wedding dress, we will do absolutely everything we can. Everyone I know is appalled by that.'

'I'm glad to hear it. The ants are on your side, Jess.'

'Alice did spot that pale yellow sock,' Jessica reminded me. 'And that created quite a fuss.'

Alice eyed me caustically. 'You don't believe I can collect good information? Did you have a pleasant evening with Paul Pristine and Anna and Angus and Jane, at Angus's Mum's house?'

I took hold of my sister-in-law-to-be by the jowls and started choking her slowly. Jessica reached across and pulled my hands away. Her basilisk gaze withered Alice's confidence. 'I had that from Ailsa, Sergeant Farquhar's daughter,' Alice admitted. 'When her dad arrived back to lock up Darren, she watched with her dad's binoculars from her back bedroom window at the police house, to see who else was on the street. She saw you all going in.'

'And then she set up a long-range surveillance microphone on an open window?'

'No, silly. We have our Cabal's reputation to consider. We don't monitor private conversations unless we suspect a crime.'

'You should suspect me more often,' I muttered. 'I'm sure I will commit one soon.'

Jessica was interested. 'What happened to Darren?'

'He was locked in a cell for twenty-four hours. Mr. Silver decided not to prosecute.'

'He was lucky. They have him marked down, now.'

I looked at Alice. 'So who will your spies be?'

She ticked them off on her fingers. 'Ailsa, of course. Spottie Mattie at Lifandoy House Farm – she's a bit suspect, because she's made friends with Minnie, but we can persuade her to watch Simeon Silver and his friends. Carmen at the Doy Hotel to watch Shiningson. Lavinia will watch for any secret use of Lifandoy House.'

'Can't you ask Minnie, if she will co-operate with you on this?'

'Tempting. But one should not be required to give evidence against one's closest relatives. Then there's Julius…?' Alice raised an eyebrow at her sister and Rosalind nodded.

'He'll be in,' she said with authority. 'If he wants any more snogging.'

'Then there's Cynthia. She lives next to one of the guesthouses the Cult has occupied; and with her electronic expertise she should be able to bug all the rooms next to her. At the *Harbour Inn*, Rosalind's friend Siobhan O'Mourne. At the *Doy Arms*, that's Karen Quilter. Helena Davies can spy on Friedrich Frost at the Tystie Bay Hotel. In the town, Patsy Junior will watch all the customers of Patsy's chip shop and tell Rosalind. At the caravan site, well, we'll have to investigate who could do that. None of our Cabal lives there. Perhaps one of the boys can persuade Mrs. Eccles at the campsite to give him a small job there.'

'That sounds a highly organized spy ring,' I said sarcastically. 'Has it a name?'

'Can you suggest one?'

'"Lucy" was a famous name for a wartime spy ring, wasn't it?'

Alice pursed her lips. 'Not a bad idea. *Lucy* says…' She nodded.

'And what about discipline? Do you need a political commissar?'

Alice glanced at a hard-faced girl next to her. 'Sally will exact punishment, if any is needed.' Sally nodded silently.

I sniffed. 'Well, what are you waiting for? Chewing gum heaven awaits you.'

Alice stared at me. 'There are times when I really don't think you take me seriously, bruv.'

■ ■ ■ ■

Jess and I ambled up to the Reserve for a short walk. As we were passing the Reserve Office, I noticed to my surprise that the door was open. We approached it. 'Keith? Working on a Sunday?'

My boss shook his head. 'Not really. I just thought I would have a look at these infra-red binoculars. I had forgotten all about them when we did our survey. I'd like them tried out.'

He handed them to me. I held them up and looked through them. 'It's all black and green.'

'The image is always green in night vision binoculars. That's because of the way they work.'

'Can I try them out sometime?'

'Anytime. If you'll look after them, you can take them with you to try.'

'Gosh, really? Don't you want to try them tonight?'

Keith shook his head. 'I don't want to stay up. Had you forgotten I'm off on the early morning plane to Manchester? I have four meetings and a training course at Head Office and I'm not back until Wednesday.'

'Of course.'

'But I'll break you into little pieces if there is a scratch on them when I return.'

'I'm sure you would. We're going for a walk, so I won't take them now. I'll pick them up and try them when it's going dark this evening.'

■ ■ ■ ■

As we returned from our walk the sun was low. We met Wilfred, standing by the chapel wall. He was squinting down West Doy's main street.

'Are you looking for someone, Wilfred?' asked Jessica.

'Hopefully not,' he answered.

'What do you mean?'

He glanced across the chapel lawn. 'I can't open up the chamber to let people down there for our underground service, if any of the People of White are around. Paul and Anna are staying in the bed and breakfast at the far end of the street. I don't think either of their bedroom windows faces in this direction but we can't take chances.'

I looked up at the chapel building. 'They could easily have seen lights in the chapel building, if there were any.'

'We could have blocked out the windows, with difficulty,' said Wilfred. 'But the chapel key has been taken from us in any case.'

'Do you think they have any reason to suspect you of doing something tonight?'

'No. But if they strolled up in the darkness, we might not see them.'

'Will you have a watchman?'

'Martha says she is too elderly to climb down into any Celtic cellar. She will sit in a chair on the lawn and listen from above. She will wave a rag down if anyone suspicious approaches. But her eyes are not very good in darkness.'

I walked across to the Reserve Office, unlocked the door, picked up Keith's night glasses and came back. 'Do you think Aunt Martha would be able to watch better for intruders, with the help of *these*?'

19 – Underground Worship

Everyone was dressed like Arctic explorers and had brought stools or boxes to sit on. And Wilfred's light, carefully placed so as not to shine through the hole above, produced a little heat of its own. So the atmosphere in the underground church was sufficiently warm in every sense. Jessica and I sat at the back, enjoying the need to huddle together in church.

Uncle Wilfred opened a hymnbook. 'We cannot sing down here, of course,' he said. 'The sound could carry too far. So we will do what persecuted Christian believers have always done, which is to whisper our hymns together.'

It was a thought-provoking experience. Then Wilfred led some prayers and took up a Bible. 'I'm sorry we cannot offer you Bibles, those of you without your own,' he said. 'They were all confiscated. We are working how to get new ones onto the island. But we haven't managed it yet. Now, if those of you who still have Bibles would turn with me to Hebrews chapter four... We shall read the passage entitled *Jesus the Great High Priest.*'

He read the passage. Then he flicked back a few pages in his Bible. 'At the beginning of the book of Hebrews we read these words, quoted from the Old Testament and addressed by God the Father to Jesus. *"You are my Son."* Now the book of Hebrews presents Jesus, as does in fact the whole Bible, as both God and Man.

'How can He be both? To help you understand this, I shall do something unusual, this evening. I shall tell you in detail how some people have got the Bible *wrong* – so that you may understand why the correct story is true. Those people include the Cult of White.

'In the Early Church there was much debate about how Jesus could be both God and Man. There were two major schools of thought, for a start, both of which were slightly off-course.

'Very roughly speaking, the one party, which was based in Alexandria, leaned toward the mistake that Jesus, though He was absolutely God and distinct from His Father, was *less* than His Father. He was a second-in-command, you might say. The other party, in Rome leaned a little towards the error of seeing Jesus as *blurred* into God rather than a distinct person. Jesus was less like an individual than, say, a musical part in a harmony of three. So Jesus was not everything that God was. In both of these mistakes, if you looked only at Jesus you would not see *all* of God.

'Our hero is Athanasius. He was an Alexandrian bishop who was persecuted and forced to move to Rome. His exile forced him to think about the beliefs of both schools. He steered a careful course, because he believed the deity – the full Godhood – of Jesus was central to Christian belief. The church as a whole came to agree that his view was the Bible's. Jesus is *all* that God is – and always was.'

Uncle Wilfred raised his eyes to the stony ceiling for a moment. 'There have always been those who have attacked ordinary Christian belief. And some of them have arrived on Lifandoy. But what *do* the People of White believe?'

He fixed us with a concerned stare. 'I believe that we are seeing *several* bad mistakes in the beliefs of the Cult of White, not just one. Or rather, we are seeing in them a *little* of each of several errors, which several different cults and erratic religious movements have made in the past.

'Thus, for instance, they are deeply focused on a shining, flawless lifestyle, which they see as of value just by itself. Like, for instance, the Mormons. Then, the Cult are very much of the view that they have to and can work their own way to heaven, like the Jehovah's Witnesses, and many other sects. Then, the People of White are quite close to Christianity, in that they see Jesus as God in *some* way. But for the Cult, Jesus is not *total* God from forever to forever, as Christians believe He is. These are subtle distinctions, but they matter a very great deal.

'This all sounds a bit heavy. But it raises two huge questions. First, why does it matter? It matters because of *forgiveness*. That is a word I have yet to hear on the lips of any of the People of White. Forgiveness happens *when someone who is able to offer it gives it to someone who is able to receive it*. But the Cult of White's Jesus is not all of God and so *cannot* offer it. What good is their sort of Jesus to them? That is a question we must ask them.

140

'Second, how do their mistakes arise? To answer that, we need to look a little more at the Early Church. This will be a little complex, so I'll take it slowly and I suggest you switch your brains onto high speed, just for a few minutes. I need to look at two *big* concepts: first, who Jesus is, and second, what the Trinity is.'

Wilfred paused and took a drink of water. Then he leaned across and lifted the cover sheet from a large flipchart. On it was drawn a diagram in the shape of a rough cross. The cross had coloured blobs at the centre and at the end of each arm.

'This sketch has nothing do to with the Cross of Calvary; it is just a diagram,' he explained. 'Now, during the first centuries after Christ, there appeared in the Early Church four great heresies – four basic mistakes – about who Jesus *is*.'

Wilfred took up a pointer. 'In the centre of my diagram is a solid green circle. That represents the Bible's perfectly balanced picture of who Jesus is. If God were coloured yellow; and humanity were coloured blue; then the green, made from the two together, is Jesus containing all of both God and man, in full. The green is not, in this case, intended to represent something which is *neither* yellow nor blue, but something that is wholly *both*.

'Then, each arm of this cross represents a fundamental *mistake*. If you look to the left...' We followed his finger. 'To the left I have drawn a single circle, full not of green but of blue and yellow dots. One error in the early Church was taught by an Egyptian called Eutyches. He said that Jesus was, in effect, a *hybrid* of God and man. Jesus was neither all blue, as it were, nor all yellow, but only partly each, and so neither fully God nor fully man. Jesus was only *some* of each. Another version of this came from a monk called Apollinarius. Apollinarianism said that Jesus had a human body holding a divine mind. I didn't try to illustrate that, but that could have been a circle with blue outside and yellow inside. Neither of *those* is the Bible's view.

'To the *right*...' We swung our eyes across like a tennis crowd. 'There I have drawn a blue and a yellow circle contained in – well – contained in a bag. This is what has been called the "pantomime horse" view of Jesus.'

I nudged Jessica. 'I like that. That's very descriptive. I understand that.' She nodded.

'This was the view of a Syrian called Nestorius. He thought that Jesus contained God the Word, and also contained Jesus the man, unconnected but in the same body. *This* is not the Bible's view.

'Now look *up*. Above is a large *yellow* and small *blue* circle.'

Jessica leaned toward me. 'I guess that means a Jesus who was mostly not human?'

Wilfred confirmed her guess. 'There was the Docetic heresy, which held that Jesus was a divine magician who did not suffer on the Cross at all. Another mistake, which I did not attempt to draw, was called the Monarchian heresy. That effectively held that Jesus *was* His Father – which would have meant God the *Father* was crucified. *Obviously*, neither of these is the Bible's view.'

'Finally, look *down*. At the bottom of my diagram are a large blue and a small yellow circle. I could write the names of many sects and even whole religions in here. I think the colour coding makes it obvious what the sects variously think: Jesus was more man than God, because He was originally *only* man. In the Early Church itself, the most famous version of this mistake was Arianism, the idea of a monk called Arius, which appears today in the beliefs of several cults.

'In every case, such groups claim that Jesus was *made,* not *born*; He was the Father's creation, not His eternal Son. He was an appearance of God in an ordinary man; that's like the Christadelphians. Or, He had a divine father – God the Father – but a human mother; that's like the Mormons. Or, He was the best of men and inspired by God, but only that or only a Son of God; that's like Unitarianism. Or, He was a man who became *a* god, but not *the* Creator God; that's like the Jehovah's Witnesses. Or Jesus was just a great Prophet or a good Teacher, which the other great religions claim. *None of these* are the Bible's view, either.

Wilfred paused for another drink. 'These are all mistakes relatively easy to describe. But also there is another, even more subtle idea, which lies behind *some* of those I have just mentioned. And from conversations I have had, I now know that this is the belief of the People of White. Imagine a theory of God which started at the bottom of my diagram and *moved*: one that claimed to move upward, toward the centre. This is perhaps the most tragic view of

God of all: the view that Jesus did – and by implication we also can – eventually become *like* God. We can lift ourselves up to Him – although in fact we are pulling Him down toward us.

'This is, of course, a very modern view, for it is related to New Age teaching, which sees all of us as potentially gods.

'But it still has one immense flaw; it presumes that Jesus died for *Himself*, and not for *us*. He is our example, *not* our rescuer. And so also, tragically, it does not require us to learn that He is our *Friend*.'

20 – Friendless

Uncle Wilfred paused and took a very long drink. Then he went on.

'On the subject of the Trinity, now. The Trinity is, of course, difficult to explain. I'm sure you will have heard various analogies, to try and describe how God could be Three in One. Incidentally, all the analogies that I have ever heard of – except for ones that originate from the Bible – have flaws.

'For example, one illustration that is sometimes used is the three sides of a triangle. But the members of the Trinity are not *identical*. Alternatively, St Patrick of Ireland is said to have picked a shamrock leaf to show that the leaf's three leaflets are all part of the same plant. But the members of the Trinity are not *parts* of a whole. Another picture is of three lights shining out through the three windows of a house that contains a single light source; but we can only focus on one window at a time and God does not show different modes or faces *in turn* to the world.

'Another is the shell, white and yolk of an egg; or the skin, flesh and seeds of an apple; but the parts of the egg or the apple are not the *whole* egg or apple, whereas each Person of the Trinity is wholly God. Another is the trio of ice, water and water vapour – but this is still inadequate, because the members of the Trinity do not appear as each other at different *times*, or change into each other.

'Unsurprisingly, the only good illustrations of the whole Trinity are those found in the Bible. I have no time to say more on that now, but *don't* start debates around individual verses of the Bible. The Bible is the whole Word of God; if *anything* in the Bible is true it will appear throughout its broad themes, not just in little quotes or statements here and there.

'Therefore, read in Genesis the stories of Abraham, Isaac and Jacob – grandfather, father and son. Those three men were biologically one, in the sense that all three were from the start, as it were, present in Abraham. Yet their three *lives*, the stories of which stretch through most of the first entire book of the Bible, represent in turn the *works* of the Father, the Son and the Holy Spirit. More about that another time.

'But the Cult of the White does not even get as far as the sort of childish mistakes about the Trinity that I have described. That is because they believe in a *progressive* Trinity: one that makes Jesus someone who *earns* His place in it. And so their severe mistake about the Trinity leads them to an even greater mistake about *Jesus*.'

■　■　■　■

Wilfred paused, rather breathless now. 'You will all be familiar with the most famous verse in the Bible, John chapter three verse sixteen, which says that God sent His Son into the world.

'In ancient Greece, many Greeks saw that the world around them was not perfect; but they believed perfection *must* exist. So they decided the universe must be in *two* parts. They believed that one was an active, perfect principle, which acted on the other, on the passive material universe. They called that principle or agent the *Logos*, which means Word, and they aimed to live in harmony with it.

'The Jewish philosopher Philo adopted that thinking; and he identified the Logos with the Jewish God. The Bible, in John's gospel, also extends the same idea from Greek or Jewish thought – or probably both – and presents *Jesus* as the Logos. *He* came as God. I do not see this Bible teaching as an extension from earlier thinking; quite the opposite, I believe all of history was *designed* to lead us, despite many misunderstandings along the way, to this truth – to *the* Truth.

'In the past, many of you will have heard this, and most Christians will have heard the first chapter of John's gospel read aloud in church at Christmas time, as a statement of this.

'But many people also stop their thinking about the Logos too soon! For, in the Bible's view, Jesus was not just sent to our world as a mere rescuer, like someone hanging on the end of a rope and calling to us.' Uncle Wilfred grinned. I could see he fancied the role.

'You see, the Jews came to understand something further about the Logos, something we often forget, or have never learnt. And the Bible's picture covers *this*, too. Philo and John's gospel both picture the Logos as being not in one place but in *both*. The Logos exists – that is, He lives – *both* separate from the world *and* entering into it.'

There was a stir of interest as people wrinkled their brows. Jessica looked at me. 'This is new to me.'

'Me too.'

My uncle went on. 'The Logos, Philo claimed, has two parts: an *unspoken* one as well as a spoken one. He called them "the spoken word" and "the word that stays within".

'And the Bible also presents this idea as explaining who *Jesus* is. The spoken Word is God come into, and active in, the world; but the unspoken Word is the Logos *still in God's mind*. It is the same as God's own active thinking and plan as He looks at the world. Jesus is God entering our world, all of the time. Yet He is still all of *God*.

'Jesus, even while walking the earth, was also *still* God's loving heart, the whole expression of our heavenly Father's love and purity and holiness. When we look at Jesus, we not only see what God always looks like – but we see His *thoughts*: we see all He is!'

Wilfred nodded slowly as he collected his thoughts for the summary. 'Because the Cult does not understand Jesus as *God*, they do not understand forgiveness. Because the Cult does not understand who Jesus *is*, they do not understand what He could mean to them. Because they do not understand where and how He came *from*, they do not see that He has come for *them*. They cannot climb up towards Him; He is already among them.

'This is the tragedy of Lifandoy today. *This* Jesus, the Jesus able to forgive us, the Jesus who is our Friend, the Jesus who is the eternal God come to us, is the Jesus whom the People of White *do not know...*'

■　■　■　■

There was a pause. A voice spoke up. It was John Khourei, whom I had not noticed earlier. 'Mr. Corn? Thanks for that explanation. I have some experience of the Cult in Canada, and I think your deductions about them are good.'

Uncle Wilfred beamed. 'Thank you. I meant to discuss this with you, so I'm glad you are here and agree. Now...' He turned to the rest of us. 'How can we best challenge these distortions?'

Several people made comments. Wilfred let them all offer their thoughts. Then there was a pause.

Suddenly, startling us all, the rag hanging down from the hole in the chamber ceiling leapt up and down. Wilfred leapt for the light switch and we were plunged into blackness. 'What is it, Martha?' he hissed upward.

We could see her face against the night sky, looking down at us. 'Oh, you can put the light back on, Wilfred. No-one is coming. I'm sorry if I startled you.' The cavern lit up again. 'No, *I* wanted to say something.'

Wilfred looked up. 'Yes, Martha?'

'You don't need to go further into theology and church history, Wilfred. All we need is to tell the People of White that we *forgive* them, with the forgiveness of Jesus. That's *our* Jesus who died for our forgiveness as all Man, and provided it for us as all God. *Forgive* them, Wilfred. That's all.'

■　■　■　■

I walked Jessica very slowly back home. That was necessary as it was only about thirty yards; she lived next to the chapel and we did not see why we should be denied a slow, hot lovers' walk because of geography.

'That's all.' Jess repeated Martha's words. 'That's all.'

I shook my head in the darkness. 'It's not that easy. I think there are already quite a few people on Lifandoy who will find forgiveness very hard. And the number will grow.'

'But some of those are not Christians.'

'Perhaps this is one of those tough moments when we Christians are called to do something that no other sane people would do.'

We leaned on Jessica's wall. The rest of the subterranean congregation had now dispersed, so conversation ceased while we engaged hotly in some things that Christians do that other people also do.

Finally, we both yawned. 'I'm sorry, darling.' Jess pushed me away. 'It's nearly midnight and we both have work to go to.'

I peered in surprise at Jessica's dark form. 'Work? Are you working on a Monday?'

'I'm afraid so. The Estate Office is all change now. And I won't be able to see you for a couple of days after that, because I'm catching tomorrow evening's ferry after work to the Isle of Man, to visit my auntie. She wants me to look at some of the trimming on my wedding dress.'

'I'll be there to see you on the ferry. But yes. What are we going to do about *the dress*?' I was suddenly in a grim mood.

'I talked to Wilfred. He says that we should set the wedding up and that I should simply appear with the white dress on. There will be such a crowd in the chapel that if the People of White try to stop the wedding there will be a full riot. He thinks he knows them well enough now to be confident that they would back down in the face of all that. It's not as if I would ever wear the dress again.'

'He may be right.' I frowned in the darkness. 'From the noises I have heard about what was said in the Earl of Lifandoy after we left the pub, your wedding dress has become a very hot topic of conversation on the island. A *cause célèbre*, in fact. But, that is once you have brought your wedding dress across to the island. They are searching everything that comes ashore from the *Bagpipe* or that arrives by plane.'

'I'll see if my auntie has any suggestions. Perhaps she could dye it with a temporary colour that I could wash out, or something.'

'Sounds unlikely.'

'I know.'

We kissed for a long time again. Then I leant back. 'I'd better go.' Sadly, I watched as she went to her door and disappeared.

I walked back past the chapel and down towards Little Cottage. I was just about to step in through my front door when I heard a strange sound. It occurred to me that Keith's night vision binoculars were hanging around my neck, after Martha had returned them to me following the service. Curious, I lifted them to my eyes and switched them on.

'What?'

21 - Evasion and Revolution?

At the side of Big Cottage next door, a small shape in the gloom was Wilfred and Martha's own car, a rarely used and venerable Mini. The noise had come from the car. There was no light in the windows of Big Cottage, so presumably Wilfred and Martha had gone to bed. It appeared that in pitch darkness someone was climbing in through one of the rear doors of their car. Through Keith's binoculars, I could see a boot waving in the air.

Car crime on Lifandoy scarcely existed. But the arrival of many strangers might have changed things. Feeling aggrieved at such disturbance of our island peace, I put the binoculars down safely in my porch and crept round on to the street. I felt my way through Wilfred's open gate, padded across the lawn and sneaked up the side of the car. I could just see the boot waving in the air. I grabbed it, and pulled.

'Come out of there!'

As the foot came towards me, a torch flicked on inside the car. It illuminated the unmistakable sideburns and face of my uncle. And his face bore a grin.

Unnerved, I let go and staggered backwards. I landed on a bucket of water beside my uncle's garden water barrel, which tipped over and soaked me. '*Aaah*!'

Uncle Wilfred backed out of the car and stood up. He reached forward and pulled me up, dripping like a sponge. 'Be quiet, Timothy. Do you want the whole street to wake up?'

'I'm *soaked*! Wilfred? What on earth are you doing?' In the light of his torch I could see that Wilfred had removed the back seat of the car and appeared to be excavating underneath it.

He sighed and turned the torch off. 'I was just trying to see how many Bibles I might be able to hide under the car seat.'

I restrained myself with difficulty. 'In the pitch dark?'

'Of course.' His face was no invisible but his surprise was obvious. 'What would be the point of showing everyone what I was about to do?'

I gritted my teeth. 'So how much contraband can you get in a Mini?'

He sighed again and looked at the car. 'Very little, I'm afraid.'

'Oh, well. You'll just have to try and bring your Bibles onto the island in full view. Perhaps they won't see them.'

My uncle turned slowly to me. Even in the blackness, I could see something that looked like a curved glow where his face should be. I could not remember from my last reading of Lewis Carroll whether the Cheshire cat was actually luminescent; but I had an unpleasant feeling about the expression that might be on Wilfred's face, all the same.

Wilfred reached forward and seized me by the hand. 'Timothy? I had forgotten that you are now a child of *faith*.' He was almost hopping up and down. 'After all these years, I can still be made ashamed by simple Christian trust.' He turned to me and grabbed me by the lapels. 'They would suspect me instantly. But *you* could do it, Timothy!'

'Do what?'

'You could evade the confiscators. You could bring a cargo of Bibles from the Isle of Man in full view, in our old car! We will pray that the Lord will protect you and blind their eyes. Timothy, when can you start our Bible smuggling?'

■　■　■　■

Wilfred was disappointed in the morning, when he came round, to find me sniffing and coughing. 'Sorry, Uncle. *Aatchoo!* I think it's a combination of days building paths in the rain, a night petrel hunt, an underground service, and a bucket. You'll have to find another driver.'

'I'm sure you will be fit when it is the right time, Timothy.' Whistling cheerfully, he went off to work.

The only entertainment open to me on my sickbed – or rather, sofa – was a further wad of health and safety literature that Keith had given me to read. With both Keith and Jessica away, I snuffled and coughed my way while reading it. Seven pages of it took me two full days to read.

On Wednesday I decided I was fit enough to get up. 'I'd better tidy up before Jessica arrives on the ferry. And I'd better get the new binoculars back to the Reserve Office before Keith gets back to find them missing.'

West Doy village street was nearly empty as I walked down to my gate with a coffee cup in hand. The only movement in sight was a gleaming vehicle pulling to a halt outside Wilfred's gate.

Its occupant got out and looked around. As our eyes met, we both scowled. 'If you're after Wilfred, you must have passed him on the way, Graham. He's gone to work.'

Graham Fytts did not appear at first to plan on any conversation with his ideological enemy. Then he changed his mind and looked at me sourly. 'If he comes back, tell him I want an urgent word.'

He started to get back into his car. 'What's so urgent on Lifandoy?' I probed.

Fytts paused and stood up again. His face was pink. 'Your damned uncle and his fellow old buffers in the Seigneurie have been obstructing progress on this island for far too long. *That's* what needs urgent attention!'

'Damned is the last word I would apply to Wilfred,' I responded. 'I can't say the same for you, though.'

His face went from pink to red. 'People like you aren't needed on Lifandoy at all, young Corn. We'll see whether the new regime will need the Lifandoy Reserve or whether it can be turned into useful farmland. In any case, I'm sure we can certainly bring pressure for the dismissal of its assistant warden. I can discover a few records concerning you that I believe both your employer and the People of White will take serious exception to. I'll go and start looking now.'

'Oh, if it is records you want to show to the new people, I have plenty.' A different voice spoke. Fytts's head swivelled to look. Aunt Martha was standing quietly in the porch of Big Cottage.

My aunt, smiling gently under her doll-like mass of white hair, went on. 'My nephew may not always have been a good boy, Graham. I'm sure there will be one or two embarrassing blots on his record. But I still have a couple of *your* old school exercise books from when you were in my class at school. And the language in those would shock any religious person to the core. Would you like me to send *those* to Mr. Silver or Mr. Shining-son?'

Fytts pursed his lips. 'Er – no.' His face had paled.

'No – *thank* you, Graeme,' prompted Aunt Martha. 'I did teach you manners once, you know.'

It was a wonder he could emit any audible words between lips that were so tightly compressed. 'No, thank you, Mrs. Corn.' It sounded like a snake breathing out.

Firing a look at me that if turned into solid form would have knocked a brontosaurus over, he got into his car and drove away. I turned and looked across toward the house next door. 'Thanks, Martha! I owe you one.'

'There was a twinkle in her eye. 'I can't have my nephew sacked just before his wedding.'

■ ■ ■ ■

Having spent two days doing nothing practical, I decided I should appear busy when Keith arrived back at the office. So I started to assemble a new noticeboard he had had delivered. By late afternoon I had just finished erecting it when I heard young voices coming up the street.

I turned. A large group of mostly girls was being led by Alice and a girl of similar age who was dressed all in white. I looked at them.

Alice nodded to the white girl. 'It's all right. This is Timothy. He's on our side. Or at least, he's harmless. Brother-in-law to be, meet Minnie.'

'Hello, Minnie.' I glanced at Alice. Are you two working together? Your Cabal and – what are they called – the Intriguers?'

'We have signed a Mutual Non-Aggression Pact, yes.'

'Like the one the Nazis signed with Mr. Molotov in 1939? Fair enough. Are you going to have a drink on it? A cocktail, perhaps?'

Alice's lip curled. 'We're on our way to campaign headquarters. That's my bedroom.'

'What? All of you?'

'Good point. Only our senior officers will attend the strategy meeting. We have given each other lists of our top officers –

Rosalind has their list and they have ours. The ordinary foot-soldiers will wait in the street.'

'Strategy for what?'

Minnie gave me a cold stare. 'I want to try strawberry flavour. I've *always* wanted to try strawberry-flavour chewing gum.'

Alice nodded. 'You will. I have a plan.'

▪   ▪   ▪   ▪

Keith failed to turn up by five o'clock. I decided that when he arrived the noticeboard would prove to him that I had not entirely wasted my time. I cleaned my face, shaved, washed behind my ears and walked down to Port Doy to see the ferry arrive.

Jessica was first off the ship. She noticed that I had shaved. 'Good boy, Timothy.' It was a long kiss.

'Am I allowed to ask about the dress?'

'It's wonderful. It will be finished by the weekend.'

'And then we just have to get it here. Any ideas?'

She looked downcast. 'I'm concerned it will get people into trouble. I've been wondering. Do you think we really should get married off the island?'

I put an arm round her. 'Let's have a drink before we think too much.'

We headed for the *Harbour Inn*. At the bar, we were served by the landlord Michael O'Mourne himself. He looked as mournful as we felt. 'I'm sorry, the drinks are still colourless.'

I eyed him sympathetically. 'You'll have to take up smuggling, Michael. Everyone else seems to be talking about it.'

'Is that a fact? Well, actually I know it is.'

Jessica smiled. 'There never has been much that you didn't know about Port Doy and the island, Michael.'

He laughed. 'I think my ancestors were smugglers themselves. It's in the blood. It's probably in the blood of half of Lifandoy. Evasion is native to us.'

'You could probably say that of anyone. But do you think *anyone* will find a way to escape the eagle eyes of the Cult?'

He shrugged. 'I couldn't possibly comment.'

I looked at Jessica. She nodded and spoke. 'If you do hear of any reliable means, Michael, we'd be interested to know.'

He grinned. 'It's like that, is it? Let me guess. Not chewing gum. Surely not beer? What then? Oh…' Abruptly, his expression darkened. 'Yes. The wedding dress. I've heard about that.'

'Have you? Who told you?'

The hoary landlord seemed almost near tears as he gazed at Jess. 'It's all round the island, how Simeon Silver humiliated you, Jessica. I'll tell you…' Suddenly he was fierce. 'There may be nothing else people will actually rebel about. The Cult is clever; they know just how far they can push folks; and a number of people actually quite like them, with their glossy lifestyles. They are busy trying to get me to buy expensive colourless beer now, and think they can bring me round with tricks like that. I think they will overcome most opposition by being smart, in the end.

'But if they really did confiscate your wedding dress, I think there would be an explosion. Revolution, even. Everyone in the Isle of Lifandoy remembers how your father and his crew were lost in the lifeboat – and how you have rescued folks yourself, since. So…' In Michael's eyes was a hard glint. 'If you want someone to help man the barricades … well, I'm not that far removed from my bloodthirsty forebears. Don't think that I have any intention of being a collaborator, or of being on their side if we all have to choose, one day…'

22 – Green Peas

Keith was astounded when we got back to the village. He was standing at the Reserve Office door as I walked with Jessica toward her home, so we went over to him for a word. 'Yes, I've heard the same thing. Revolution? The hotheads want to take over the asylum from the lunatics. Madness!'

'It certainly is,' we agreed.

'But did you know that the outside world is taking an interest?'

'Is Simon still reporting the story in the *Manx Chronicle*?'

'I'm sure he is. But I bought this at Manchester Airport.' He handed us a newspaper. To our wonder, it was a national daily. The story was at the bottom of page five; but the headline was bold. We read it and the first couple of lines:

BRITISH ISLAND TAKEN OVER BY CULT!

The little Isle of Lifandoy in the Irish Sea is being ruled by a Canadian cult which is hysterical about all things white. Only the cult members are allowed to wear white, while the islanders are only allowed white or colourless food and drink. A spokesman for the Government has said that they are monitoring the situation on the British island but that no health and safety rules have been breached...

'*British* island?' Jessica raised her fine eyebrows.

Keith laughed. 'They don't often call us that. The British Government's usual description of us is a pseudo-overseas tax haven which is a drain on their resources and a large net loss to the taxpayer.'

'Is it?' I asked. 'I thought all we paid our taxes?'

'The Estate Office staff and the Reserve staff both pay the standard UK rate of tax,' said Keith. 'But when it comes to the estate's own profits – that is, the Earl's own trust and empire of Graham Fytts – they do not have to be declared.'

Jess interrupted. 'The Earl actually puts back into the island more than he receives – or at least he did.'

'That's right.' Keith glowered. 'But Graham manages the Estate Farm's accounts separately. If he either pays tax in full to Westminster, or ploughs it all back into the Farm, then I'm a stuffed parrot. There is a huge black hole into which a lot of money in his hands has vanished over the years.'

Jess frowned. 'Are you suggesting Graham is crooked?'

'He doesn't act illegally. But there is a massive trust somewhere, and he draws expenses from it.'

I held up the newspaper. 'Do you think anything will come from this?'

'I have no idea.'

■　■　■　■

I took Jessica to her doorstep then left her to report to her mother at home. I turned to leave, down her garden path. 'Ow!' A dried pea stung me on the cheek, then another. '*Ow!*'

I looked up to the bedroom window to one side. Rosalind lowered the pea-shooter. 'We want you,' she said tersely. 'Chapel garden shed, five minutes.' Then she disappeared.

I considered going straight to the chapel shed and quickly digging a man-trap with poisoned spikes inside it. But when I reached it, it was already under armed guard. Two girls in ordinary school blazers and two in white ones lowered their pea-shooters reluctantly. 'Inside, you.'

'Charmed, I'm sure. I didn't know there had been a second wave of armed invasion of Lifandoy. And aren't dried peas green?'

One of the girls in white gave me a chill look. 'We use white pebbles. They leave a bigger bruise. We are grinding some down to sharp points, so think yourself lucky.'

Rosalind and Alice arrived with Minnie and their bodyguards. They seated themselves on sacks of lawn feed. I stood impatiently. 'Well, what is it?'

Rosalind glanced at the others then turned to me. '*Lucy* says…'

'Who's Lucy?'

Minnie stared at me as if I were a museum exhibit. 'Is he really that stupid? Or is it an act?'

Alice eyed me sourly. 'It's a very good act.'

'*Lucy* says that we have enough information to compromise several grown-ups in the People of White. *Purely* in order to get them to help us.'

'What information?'

Rosalind opened a small black book. 'On Monday, Siobhan at the *Harbour Inn* saw two of the younger women from the People of White wearing smears of pink lipstick. Her Dad had deliberately left some of her Mum's lipstick in their en-suite bathroom at the *Inn*.'

'Michael's very much on our side.'

Minnie frowned. 'That's OK as long as we have common interest with him. After that, he had better watch out.'

'Good. Spottie Mattie saw Serena Snow at the House Farm pick up a purple grape and eat it. At the Tystie Bay Hotel, Friedrich Frost was seen to write a letter to someone – presumably a female friend – on scented pink hotel notepaper. He put it in a white envelope to post, but Helena managed to take a photograph of him doing it. Two of the young men staying in Doytown ate some mushy peas with their cod and half-cooked white chips. Patsy Junior says that Paul Pristine also ate one mouthful. And...'

'Hold on.' I held up a hand. 'Why are you telling *me* all this?'

'We'll come to that. And here's the big one. We couldn't pin anything on Simeon Silver. But Minnie's Dad, Shining-son, wears boxer shorts with pink stripes.'

I held up a hand. 'I don't want to know that, thank you.'

Rosalind glanced at Minnie. The latter scowled. 'We'll take that one offline. He is my Dad, so I will blackmail him myself.'

One of the other girls was puzzled. 'How does he wash them without anyone seeing?'

I interrupted. 'For the sake of your Non-Aggression Pact, I suggest...'

'We'll move on.' Rosalind agreed reluctantly. She produced a black pen and scored out the last entry in her book. 'But now it's over to you, Timothy.'

'Eh?' I became uncomfortably aware that a frightening group of hard-faced youngsters were all staring unblinkingly at me. 'What's over to me?'

Rosalind handed me the small black book. 'It was *your* idea. And no-one will listen to us. Minnie can't blackmail her own grown-ups. We don't have the ear of anyone important enough. But you can lean on someone – maybe Paul Pristine – to get us our coloured chewing gum smuggled in.'

'Why on earth should I do that?'

Alice gave me the sort of look that she probably reserved otherwise for fledgling sparrows looking up at a hungry cat. 'Because if we can get a package of coloured chewing gum smuggled onto the island, it can arrive wrapped in something white to disguise it. Something that the spies at Port Doy will think is just a cover – and not a piece of clothing. Something that could, in fact, be unrecognisable as a *wedding dress.*'

■　■　■　■

On the grass in the sunshine behind her garden fence overlooking the valley, Jessica was appalled. 'I don't want my wedding dress wrapped around some *chewing gum.*'

'Have you any other suggestions?'

She thought hard. 'Not yet.' She sighed. 'But I certainly don't want it risked on the first consignment, at least. And it would be horribly squashed even then.'

We sat thinking. 'I don't suppose could take the lifeboat over to the Isle of Man?' I suggested. 'They surely wouldn't search the lifeboat.'

'That would be unethical, even if I could decide where the lifeboat went.'

'Or, what about someone whom the lifeboat has helped? Don't any of the small boat sailors owe you a favour?'

'That's an idea.' She sat thinking. 'There are one or two who I know might make a trip across. And I could have a chat to The Buoy.' The Buoy was the universal nickname of Brendan Todd, the Port Doy harbourmaster.

'Or what about anyone who sails *into* Port Doy occasionally?'

She brightened. 'Now I *do* know someone. There is one of the charter boat trip skippers who takes sea anglers and basking shark watchers out from Peel harbour on Man. He has dropped in at Port Doy a few times recently, because he has taken a fancy to a girl who works behind the bar of the *Harbour Inn*. I think his name is Charlie Anvil. But does that help? The People of White would certainly search anything he landed.'

We looked at each other. The same thought had clearly struck us both. '*If*, that is, he landed *there...*'

■ ■ ■ ■

On Thursday, it rained solidly, so Keith and I spent the day tidying up our stores. Jess and I spent Thursday evening doing wedding service planning with her mother and Uncle Wilfred. Keith and I spent Friday collecting litter across the Reserve and rescuing lost birdwatchers. At teatime, Jessica came round to Little Cottage and we pored over a map of the island. 'We had a lifeboat practice after the rain stopped,' she said. 'And I had a word with Seamus. He'll do anything he can to help us, except for taking the lifeboat somewhere unnecessarily. He says that he knows Charlie Anvil well and he thinks Charlie might even drop into the harbour this evening to see his girl.'

'Does he think Charlie could deliver a package to somewhere around the island?'

'I think he'd be game.'

'Then we need to decide where.'

Jessica started folding up the map. 'I don't think we should tell Charlie where. He will tell us where he could land. I think we should go down to the harbour to ask him ourselves.'

We set out and walked down slowly. As we passed through the bottom end of West Doy village, we saw Paul and Anna coming out of their bed-and-breakfast. They gave us shy smiles. 'Going anywhere interesting?'

'Come with us, if you have no meeting this evening. We're walking down to Port Doy.'

Jess and Anna walked ahead while I followed beside Paul. As I walked, I felt a hard shape in my shirt pocket. It was Rosalind's notebook. 'Paul?'

'Yes?'

'Is there any way around these prohibitions on food and clothing?'

'The food restrictions might not be so strict. But only if we could be persuaded that there was a critical nutritional reason for it...'

I scowled. 'Are you sure that your People of White are so pure themselves?'

He looked at me sharply. 'What are you suggesting?'

'I hear you ate a mouthful of mushy green peas. Does Simeon Silver know that? Supposing someone was to tell him?'

23 – In the Black Book

He stopped and stared at me. 'Ten out of ten for espionage,' he said. 'But I think you have us wrong. We make mistakes, like everyone. But we just try harder. If you are thinking of blackmail, think again.'

'Paul? There are things that really matter to me.'

He paused. 'You're referring to the wedding dress? I'm sorry but there is no chance on that in particular, I'm afraid. Simeon Silver has made that a very high priority issue. Every member of the People of White on the island has been ordered to watch out for that. There isn't a cat's chance of your smuggling any white clothing onto the island. Have you thought of a creamy-yellow dress?'

He saw my expression and shut up.

I stared him down. 'Do you really believe all this stuff, Paul? I have you marked down as the most human of them all.'

'The shining light of Johnson Shining...' He gazed ahead. 'Well, can *you* prove he is wrong?'

'The Bible says we are *all* sinners.'

He was suddenly bitter. 'Not in Johnson Shining's corrected Bible, it doesn't say that.' He looked up. 'I'm sorry we had to take your uncle's Bibles from the chapel. I regret that more than anything else we've done on the island.' Then he smiled. 'And I'd like to bet your uncle is already making plans for Bible smuggling. Don't bother to deny it. He'll fail, though.'

I changed the subject rapidly. 'Have you *read* the ordinary Bible?'

'No. We've not been allowed to since childhood.'

'Perhaps you might find yourself holding one, one day.'

He gave me a long glance, and then turned away. I could still hear his voice, softly. 'I might not object, at that.'

∎ ∎ ∎ ∎

At Port Doy, we left Paul and Anna, and walked round to the lifeboat. Jess was delighted to find Charlie Anvil already there, chatting to Seamus and Barney. He was a tall, slightly stooped

161

young man with a closely shaven head and the nut-brown skin of someone who spends his life in small boats. He was as cheerful as a daisy, and as obliging. 'Certainly I'll drop a package in for you. I always fall for blondes.'

Jessica smiled. 'Sorry, I'm already spoken for. When and where could you do it?'

'My blonde is in the *Inn*. Straight to the point, eh? When is the wedding?'

'A week on Saturday.'

He whistled. 'I think the weather will be OK. And the moon will help. It's nearly full.'

'Where would you land?'

'Any suggestions? A very quiet, sheltered cove.'

I had a thought. 'Do you know the cliffs south from Sound Point? And the coves?'

'Like the back of my hand.'

'Even by night? The cove with the two caves?'

'Yes.'

Jess looked at me. 'When is your second Storm Petrel hunt?'

'Keith is planning it for Saturday night.' We looked at Charlie. 'Could you do half past midnight, Saturday night?'

Charlie frowned. 'Do you really want to be on those cliffs at that time of night?'

'We'll be up there surveying birds. Storm Petrel nests.'

He was intrigued. 'Fascinating. And perfect. I'll confirm by phone on Saturday morning.'

I hesitated. 'Ah – is there any chance you could bring some chewing gum, as well?'

'What?'

■　■　■　■

We walked back along the quay and walked down onto one of the boat jetties to stroll between the moored yachts. I was enjoying the warm, delighted squeezes Jessica was giving me. We stopped to gaze across the water.

Paul and Anna had rented a dinghy from the harbour shop and were paddling around in the calm water between the jetties. 'Hi, folks.'

We continued to the end of the jetty, and then retraced our steps. We reached the ramp leading back up to the quay. A small trolley was following us as something was unloaded from one of the yachts, so I stepped to the edge of the ramp, nearly in the shadow of the quay above.

'Halt!' Without warning, three white-clad figures stepped in front of the trolley. 'Island baggage check.' To the newly arrived yachtsman's astonishment, they descended on his trolley. Before he could protest, they had already opened two boxes and were searching through them.

Jessica and I stared in anger. 'They shouldn't be allowed to do that,' I said. 'Just a minute…'

They turned round. As they did so, a familiar voice came down from heaven. 'Timothy! Perfect!'

I looked upward in astonishment. From almost directly over me on the quay above, my Uncle Wilfred's face was beaming down at me. As I watched, his expression changed into a huge grin.

Horrified, and restricted by Jessica and the trolley in front of me, I stepped back. Unfortunately, there was no ramp left. With a plaintive cry, I fell backwards into the harbour.

■　■　■　■

Paul and Anna were already dragging me onto their dinghy by the time every other time-waster around the harbour had gathered to gape and smile at me.

Jessica helped me out of the dinghy at the jetty. 'Did she push him, or was he trying to escape from her?' asked someone.

I was in a very bad mood indeed. As Jess found me a plastic sheet to keep me warm, I looked for someone to blame. Uncle Wilfred had vanished; the only people immediately in front of me were the three searchers in white. Behind them appeared Simeon Silver.

All my clothes were clinging to my body, including my shirt. Simeon reached out. 'You want to get rid of everything wet and cold. Especially *this…*' He reached out and plucked Rosalind's small black notebook from my top pocket. 'This is black. That's probably why you fell in. I'll take it and destroy it.' He opened it and started turning the sodden pages.

Before I could respond, Uncle Wilfred appeared next to him. 'Timothy? I'd brought Martha's car down. I had hoped you might be able to go to Man on this evening's ferry. But I suppose that's impossible now. Are you all right?'

I was about to reply when a startled exclamation came from Simeon Silver. His face was thunderous. 'Is this *your* notebook?'

'No, I said truthfully.

He stared at the page he had opened it at. 'Then where did it come from?'

Uncle Wilfred spoke up before I could reply. 'Timothy and Keith have been picking up litter all day. Is that a piece of litter, Timothy?'

For once, I blessed Wilfred's little socks. 'Er, yes. It seemed quite a nice piece of litter so I put it in my pocket rather than throw it away.'

'Is that true?' Simeon Silver scowled.

One of his acolytes supported us. 'I saw this man emptying several large bags of litter at the tip an hour ago.'

Simeon, still staring open-mouthed at the pages in shock, looked up, and gave me a very long, cold stare. 'Watch this man. Watch him like a hawk at all times.' He snapped his jaw shut and walked off without a word, followed by his team.

Uncle Wilfred looked at me. 'It seems you are under as much surveillance as I am, Timothy.' He scratched his chin. 'It will have to be someone else who drives our Bible car, I suppose. I wonder who that must be?'

■　■　■　■

In the *Harbour Inn*, Michael served me something colourless but powerful while his daughter Siobhan found me some dry clothes to borrow. An hour later I was feeling distinctly more cheerful when the *Bagpipe* arrived at the quay on her Friday evening run.

Shortly Angus came into the bar wearing a large smile. 'I hear you've been trying to drink the harbour dry. It's a good job you weren't in the dock when I steered the ferry in, Tim.'

'At least it saved me from an expedition of Uncle Wilfred's,' I said. 'He wanted me to take Martha's little car back with you, fill it with contraband and return with it tomorrow.'

'The car *is* on board now,' Angus nodded. 'He has put it on himself. I'll drive it off and back on the ferry at the other end. But I won't be able to drive it off when I get back on tomorrow's run. Your island guards would search it if I drove it off – or if Wilfred did.'

'Same here.' We looked at Jessica. She shook her head. 'I'm a marked woman too, since the meeting in the church hall.'

We strolled out onto the dock. To our surprise Alice was there, looking downcast. 'They found a consignment of chewing gum we had risked on the ferry. The Cabal and the Intriguers together are down *ten pounds*.'

Jessica consoled her little sister. 'What did they do with it?'

'Threw it into the harbour.'

'It's a pity it wasn't in there earlier.' Jessica grinned. 'Timothy could have dived and fetched it.'

'I heard about that.' Alice eyed me hopefully. 'I don't suppose…'

I did not deign to reply.

Alice sighed. 'Oh, by the way, can we have that black notebook of Rosalind's back?'

'Sorry. Simeon Silver has it.'

'*What*?' She was horrified. '*How*?'

'He saw it in my shirt pocket when they fished me out of the water. He confiscated it because it was black.'

'Did he look inside it?'

'Yes, but only at one page, because it was all soaked and stuck together.'

'What did he say?'

'He saw it was subversive. But my Uncle Wilfred and I convinced him that it was just some litter I had picked up, which could have belonged to anyone. You don't need to worry; he has no idea who has been spying on the Cult. None of your names were against the spy reports.'

Alice had turned red and was now white. 'But he still has it?'

'He'll probably read it all when it has dried out. But he already knows there are people on the island who are against the Cult; it won't tell him who they are.'

Alice was now purple. 'But ... but...' she gasped.

Jessica gave her a look of command. 'What's up, Alice? Tell!'

Alice gulped. 'That list of the top officers of the Intrigue that Minnie gave to Rosalind...'

'Rosalind left *that* in the book?'

'Yes, by mistake. It gives all their names!'

'Who are they?'

Alice gulped again. 'Mr. Silver will think *they* wrote the book. Minnie, her brother and two of the other Cult's children, and Spottie Mattie and her friend. If the Cult thinks their own children have been spying on them they will hurt them – the Cult can be rough on their kids. And Spottie Mattie is the niece of Graham Fytts – he'll crucify her, too. The Intrigue will be destroyed!'

I sniffed. 'The Intrigue are only your friends because you have been forced together in the fog of war.'

'Yes, but don't you *see?*' Alice was distressed. 'Minnie hasn't yet paid us the five pounds for her half of the lost chewing gum. Our Cabal can't possibly afford to be down *ten* pounds!'

Jessica was outraged. 'Your collaborators are in serious danger of heavy punishment, and you are worried about your pocket money? I'm appalled at you, Alice. But surely they wouldn't actually touch their children?'

Alice nodded. 'The Cult has secrets; and one of them is that Shining-son uses a leather belt on his kids. There may be others, too.'

We were shocked. 'You don't mean that? That's beyond the pale. We must get that information to someone who can do something with it.'

A new voice spoke behind us. 'Actually, you just have.' It was our *Manx Chronicle* friend Simon. And standing behind him were four more eager-looking figures like him, with more and bigger cameras than his.

24 – The Most Dangerous Man

Alice was pleading with us. 'You *must* help us get that black book back.'

One of the other journalists was quick off the mark. 'Does this black book contain *proof* that the People of White abuse their children?'

'No.'

He lost interest. 'We'll start sniffing for ourselves, then.' The other journalists walked away.

We looked after them. 'Simon, who are they?'

'Lifandoy is in the news at the moment. They are some of the big newspaper Press. This is a journalistic quiet period – the holiday silly season – and the Earl's disappearance and the Cult's arrival are both still very live stories.'

'Have they found the Earl's body yet?'

'Had you not heard that? No. No bodies at all. Divers went down to the plane, but the cabin was empty. But the Earl is now definitely thought to be dead.'

'And the People of White are here to stay.' We sighed.

'You can make it hard for them if you can prove they are child abusers.'

'Is parental punishment a crime?'

'With a leather belt, it is.' Jessica was angry.

'Well, so what.' I shrugged wearily. 'What could I do about it?'

My fiancée turned to me, holding her small sister by the hand. Together they gazed at me with wide eyes. Jessica's blonde tresses drifted across to trail over my arm. They glanced at each other, and nodded.

Jessica's voice was sweet, tremulous, and irresistible. 'If it would protect gentle vulnerable children, ones who are weeping themselves to sleep tonight…' A mental picture of Minnie's grim, ruthless face flashed across my mind, but I was too hypnotised to note the inconsistency. 'And if it would help dear Alice as well … *darling* Timothy, *are* you willing to break into Lifandoy House

Farm tonight and get the list of names back, before Simeon Silver can dry it out and read the names...?'

. . . .

'The first problem is, how can we get you away from your *followers*?' Alice was watching the two white-clad figures that were now trailing me everywhere I went. 'We need a distraction so that you can get to the farmhouse unseen after dark.'

Simon was excited. 'This will be a great story, Tim. I'll give you a stunning write-up when you succeed. A hero of the child protection campaign.'

Alice agreed. 'If he doesn't, do you charge for obituaries?'

Jessica rebuked her. 'I want a wedding announcement in the *Chronicle*, Alice, not a memorial one, thank you.'

I set my chin sternly. 'I have no intention of giving Graham Fytts the satisfaction of locking me up.'

Alice gazed at me with admiration. 'I really do believe that we will not be diluting our family blood very much by allowing you in. I didn't think you had it in you.' I did not have it in me, but it was impossible to say so when Jessica's wide eyes were still holding me in a trance.

Alice looked round. 'I have an *idea*. The harbour bus is about to leave. We'll catch it. Then as it starts moving you two men could walk behind it, immediately change jackets, and Simon can walk out again while Timothy jumps on at the last second.'

The plan seemed not impossible and Simon was happy to come up to West Doy later to swap our jackets back. We did as she said. As the bus pulled away, Alice looked out of the back window at the two puzzled white-clad figures staring after it. 'Absolute amateurs,' she sighed.

I gave her a hard look. '*Now* what?'

. . . .

When we met in the chapel garden shed, Rosalind produced a large, highly detailed plan. 'We explained their danger to Minnie and Spottie Mattie, so Mattie gave us this. This is a map of the farmhouse. Simeon Silver's room is at the top of the stairs. But hopefully he will have left the notebook drying on the boiler in the kitchen. Mattie will suggest that idea to him, if she can casually manage it. If not, you will have to sneak into his bedroom.'

Had it not been for Jessica's warm arm encircling my waist and her lips nuzzling my neck from time to time, I would have regained my sanity. As it was, I was led like a sheep to the slaughter through the gathering gloom by Jessica's soft hand, as we sneaked from Jessica's house along green paths, across the Burn by a rickety plank bridge known only to Alice and her friends, and through the tall cornfields to the farmhouse drive.

The farmhouse was in darkness. The People of White were known for their early-to-bed habits. I had no idea what Graham Fytts might do at night, but every light had gone out.

I muttered a protest. 'I can't just *walk* up to the farmhouse.'

'Be quiet, darling,' said Jessica. 'Rosalind and Alice know what they are doing. They have ways of visiting Spottie Mattie without any grown-ups knowing.'

'How can you be sure?'

'Because I taught them. I was friends with Mattie's big sister. Girls have secret ways that no boy ever learns about.'

'Hah.'

Spottie Mattie was waiting in the shrubbery. Like a ghost, she led us around the edge of the lawn in the shadows.

I protested again. 'Why can't *she* steal the list back?'

'Because this is a man's job, sweetest darling.'

We gathered in the black shade of a yew tree. Jessica gave me a gentle push. 'That's the back door over there, darling. Go up the corridor until you are opposite the stairs, and then turn right. We don't know if Simeon took Mattie's advice about the boiler, but if he did then the book should be on the boiler beside the left wall. If the book is *not* on it you will have to go up the stairs to the bedroom facing you.'

Like all doors on Lifandoy, the back farmhouse door was not locked. But it squeaked slightly as I opened it. I stopped dead, but there was no sound.

To my surprise, theft proved surprisingly easy. The kitchen door stood open and the black notebook was on the boiler. Its pages

170

were now partly dry, so as instructed I leafed through it, located the single loose sheet, transferred it to my pocket and replaced the book so that Simeon would suspect nothing. I crept out again, shut the door and was walking confidently across toward the shrubbery when the large white car suddenly swung round the corner of the house, illuminating me in its headlights.

Like a shocked rabbit, I froze; but the car was turning rapidly and swung into a parking place beside the back door.

Eight female hands suddenly reached out of the darkness, grabbed me by every protruding extremity and yanked me away. I landed in a rhododendron bush like a trussed chicken. As I crashed to a halt, I heard the car doors slam.

The voice of Graham Fytts sounded through the gloom. 'Was that a sheep?'

The second voice was Simeon Silver's 'I didn't see it. But what are we going to do about *him*?'

'Tom Fothergill?' Fytts sounded grim. 'He should have been put out to pasture years ago. Rest assured, the island is mine now. Things will go as I choose, and your cult can flourish unrestricted. I have in mind a very large piece of land that you can spread across at will.'

Had I not been face down with a mouth full of crunchy rhododendron leaves, I would have leapt up in fury. But three female forms were now sitting on me, holding me down.

'We will,' Simeon assured him. 'But it's more the population that worries me. They are becoming rebellious. We have already stopped a couple of attempts at smuggling non-white things onto the island.

Fytts' voice was low. 'This white thing is your business. But I'll keep them under control. Lifandoy is not governed by the same laws as the rest of the British Isles. Listen – not many people know this, but firearms regulations are more lax here.'

Simeon sounded shocked. 'I really don't think the People of White want to become involved in keeping control with guns.'

'Suit yourself,' said Graham. 'But I shall look out for myself. And if I find any smugglers myself, they had better look out.' He paused. 'Do you have any idea if any more smuggling is being planned?'

171

Silver was grim. 'That Darren Stocks bears watching. I'm sure he has an idea of bringing beer onto the island at night.'

Fytts snorted. 'Stocks is a mindless baboon. He couldn't organize a booze cruise between two breweries. No, the man you want to watch is that Timothy Corn. I rate him as the most dangerous man on the island.'

'He gave two of my men the slip at the Harbour this afternoon. He's certainly slippery.'

'I think he has…'

Graham's voice faded away as the back door closed. Immediately, I was picked up, and a gag was placed over my mouth to stop me protesting. Spottie Mattie disappeared like a ghost.

Like a prisoner, I was led by the other three at the run back into the cornfields, across the plank bridge and back up to the chapel garden shed. The gag was removed, a light was switched on and I saw my fiancée and two sisters-in-law-to-be gazing at me.

Alice leaned forward, extracted the sheet of paper from my pocket and sat back. As she stared at me, there was an expression on her face which I could not at first interpret. After a few seconds, I realized it was one I had never seen her use on me before: deep admiration.

'"The most dangerous man on Lifandoy,"' she quoted approvingly. It was plain that my street cred had reached an all-time high. Politely, Alice and Rosalind averted their gaze as Jessica leaned forward and kissed me. It was a *very* satisfying kiss.

25 – In it Together

On Saturday morning, Simon came up to West Doy to swap our jackets back. 'I love it!' He was delighted at my report. 'When can I publish it?'

'Would you not be sued? We may have prevented some child abuse, but we have no proof yet that it happens.'

'If I think it does, I'm willing to make insinuations,' he said. 'In my journalistic experience, there is no smoke with fire somewhere.'

He took some notes then headed off. As he was disappearing, Alice and Rosalind came down the street. They looked at me expectantly. 'Well?'

'Well what?'

'You have a reputation to maintain now.'

I eyed them coolly, and put forward one foot, taking the sort of pose I imagined a hero should hold.

Alice looked down. 'Why have you put your foot on a piece of chewing gum?'

Grimly, I scraped the slime off against the edge of the kerb. 'I didn't like the flavour of it.'

She gazed up at me. 'You are our only hope, now. Jessica says that you have arranged with Charlie Anvil to smuggle the wedding dress across tonight.'

'Yes, I'm phoning him in a few minutes to confirm it.'

They looked up at me beseechingly. '*Please?*'

I struck a pose again. 'You don't know what you are asking. You have no idea how difficult it could be.' This was true; it would not be difficult at all, since Charlie had already loaded the chewing gum into his boat for delivery, as I had requested earlier.

Uncertain at my intentions, they brightened a little then trudged away. I was just starting in the opposite direction when Uncle Wilfred appeared at his door. 'Timothy? I may have found someone who can drive the car off the ferry for me this afternoon.'

'Who's that?'

Uncle Wilfred hesitated. 'I'd better not say yet. But two friends had a very long chat to Martha and me, yesterday evening.'

173

I walked on. I was still feeling tired, but when Jessica came downstairs at her home she looked as fresh as a field of poppies. 'Timothy? Have you heard the news?'

'What news?'

'Not good, I'm afraid,' she said. 'The People of White have several white cars being delivered on the ferry this afternoon. They are setting up a fast response squad, to race to anywhere on the island where they think mischief is underway. Simeon Silver will lead it personally.'

I frowned. 'I may need to ring Charlie Anvil again, then. But I've just confirmed the arrangements for tonight's shipment: half past midnight in Two Cave Cove.'

'Is he bringing the chewing gum, too?'

'Yes. But don't tell the girls. I don't want them anywhere near.'

'I won't. But Alice has a bush telegraph *par excellence*; it's always possible she will find out something.'

We twined close. I looked at the back of the chapel. 'The long grass?'

'Not yet, lover boy. I'd like a long walk today. Do you fancy Raw Head?

We set off on a walk through the Lifandoy Reserve. It was an idyllic day. We climbed Raw Hill and gazed across toward Ireland. We sat on the cliffs and watched the last puffins of the year departing. We walked down to Irish Sands, took our shoes off and went for miles along the white shell-sand there, in Culla Bay, in Machair Bay and – ignoring the forbidding warning sign, in Crystal Bay.

We were sitting by the last when two figures came walking slowly along. It was Paul and Anna.

Paul looked at us with a smile. 'You shouldn't be here. We're delighted that you are.'

They lay beside us. 'Timothy,' said Paul.

'Yes.'

'I've been reading the Bible.'

We sat up. 'Do you mean, *our* Bible?'

He nodded. 'There is only one. Anna and I are thinking of leaving the Cult of White.'

174

'*What*? Is that an easy thing to do?'

'No.'

'Is it even a safe one?'

'Perhaps not. Certainly not on Lifandoy. We would have to escape the island, I think. Do you know any way of getting off Lifandoy other than by public transport?'

I looked at him. 'You're serious, aren't you? You're desperate, even. Why?'

'I'd appreciate an answer first.'

Jessica squeezed my hand. I knew what she was thinking. 'I have no boat to transport you with,' I said cautiously.

Suddenly, they seemed to shrink a little, as though I had punctured them a little and a hope they had been holding onto had leaked away. They looked so downcast that something strange happened to me. I felt a sudden warmth toward them. I glanced at Jessica. I was not entirely surprised to see a tear in the corner of one of her eyes. She nodded slowly.

I went on. 'But where there's a will there's a way.'

They turned to me slowly. Paul nodded. 'You *know* a way, don't you?' He bent his head. 'It will be hard to trust us, I know that. I was speaking to your Uncle Wilfred last night, and...'

'*Wilfred*?' Jessica nodded. 'I wondered if it might have been you.'

'He ... he ... prayed with us.' It was clearly something hard for Paul to say. 'We're sorry about what we have done to your beautiful island. I'm going to try and make recompense this afternoon.'

We looked at him. 'We'll be there. If we can speak to you afterwards, we'll help you.'

'*If* is a bigger word than it seems.' Paul's face was white.

Jess nodded. 'But God is a bigger God than we sometimes think Him.'

Paul looked at her. 'Is He?'

She returned the gaze. 'Paul, what did Wilfred say to you last night which had this effect on you?'

He hesitated. Anna spoke instead. 'Tim's Uncle Wilfred knows Jesus.'

Paul nodded. 'Our People of White has the idea that God is beautiful and pure and that Jesus joined Him and that we can join them. So we try to live more and more *perfect* lives.'

'And Wilfred showed you that He believes something different?'

'Wilfred knows Jesus in a way that neither I nor any of us has ever known Him.' Paul looked far across the sea. 'Your Uncle Wilfred knows Jesus as his Friend.'

■　■　■　■

The harbour was sunlit and full of life as the *S.S. Bagpipe* creamed into it. Jessica and I watched it. We had set off back toward the harbour, then had diverted up to walk around the walls of Doy Fort. Now the entire haven was laid out before us from our high view on the grassy foot of the fortress.

Two other figures had continued down the road we had left. Paul and Anna were already nearly down to the quay. As we watched, they reached the harbour edge and turned right toward the steamer pier. A large group of other white-clad figures were already waiting on the pier.

Jessica stared down at the two white figures. 'I think we should *pray*, Timothy. We can't help Paul physically in what he has made up his mind to do.'

I looked solemnly at her. 'If the other People of White stop him as he drives Martha's car off the ferry, and see the boxes of Bibles in the back, then there is no telling what they might do to him.'

She nodded. 'Let's sit on that seat just below. Only the Lord alone can help Paul now; and he has made up his mind that *He* will, if Jesus is who Wilfred has told Paul He is.'

We sat on the seat, with arms twined around each other. Jessica gazed across the bay. 'We've been here before, haven't we? This is a déjà vu moment for you and me. There's the South Rock that Angus mentioned without thinking during the famous affair of the "Nest".'

'And there's the Black Channel in front of it that you steered through during the matter of the "Orchid".'

176

'And there is the gangway where Whitey put his arm around Sanda Farn after Trog was killed trying to reach the "Falcons". So where are we now?'

'In darkness. We're chasing some 'Night Birds", I suppose. We're all chasing them; and Paul and Anna are in the greatest night of all.'

'Then let's pray for them.'

■　■　■　■

When Martha's little Mini rolled off the ferry some fifteen minutes later, we could see that there were two people in white in it. I had my birdwatching binoculars to my eyes, watching its every move. 'Anna's joined him, Jess. She's in the passenger seat.'

She had tears in her eyes. 'They have decided to sink or swim together. Both of them are risking everything. They're determined to be in it to the end. Dear God, help them!' We watched intently as the little Mini was surrounded by a crowd of other white-clad figures. The car boot was opened and slammed shut again. Then all the car doors were opened by those outside; one of the white figures inside started to emerge; and for a moment we thought the mob had taken control.

Then the figure, which was evidently Anna's, got back in. The doors closed and the little Mini drove away from the crowd in white.

By that time we had already jogged down to the start of the quay. As one or two of the white crowd turned to look at us, we slowed and walked as normally as we could around the haven.

The occupants of the Mini had seen us. They had pulled out of view into a narrow shady gap behind two vans at the front of Doy Garage. I could see the whites of Paul's eyes in the wing mirror as we approached.

The back of the car was piled high with boxes. One was visibly open, with the words 'Holy Bible' visible on several of the books inside. We stopped and Paul wound down his window. Both he and Anna were covered in sweat. He gave a half-smile. 'It seems your Uncle Wilfred is right, Tim. Their eyes were blinded, every one of them. They didn't see *anything*. Jesus really is our Friend.'

Then his face lit up in a huge grin. 'But what do we do *now*?'

'Drive up to West Doy,' I instructed him. 'To the chapel. We'll follow you in a little while, on the harbour bus. Wilfred will be waiting for you as well. Then we'll take you to our church.'

'What do you mean? I thought the chapel was your church? Some of the People will be there at your service tomorrow. Won't they simply confiscate your Bibles all over again?'

'Not unless they look underground.'

'What?'

26 - All in Black

Angus saw us waiting for the harbour bus as he came out of the harbourmaster's office, and strolled across. 'It seems that Paul Pristine has been doing a lot of thinking, he said. 'A great deal, in fact, for him to show that much courage.'

'He has. He had a long chat to Uncle Wilfred last night.'

Angus gave a broad smile. 'It's like *that*, is it? Well, well. I believe in God, now, as you know. But like Jane, I'm not sure I know a God who actually *does* things. Or at least, I didn't until now. I might have guessed Wilfred's faith was behind it.'

Then his face changed. 'I was chatting to a friend of mine. Charlie Anvil. He says he has promised to sneak in below Sound Point tonight with a wedding dress.' He looked concerned. 'It's a risk, you know.'

'Seamus is confident that Charlie will be safe around Sound Point even in the dark.'

'I think he will. But that's not what I meant. These People of White are becoming quite aggressive.' He paused. 'Tim. I'm going back over with the ferry now. But I'll drive over to Peel when I get back, and I'll come over tonight with Charlie in his boat. Jane is in Douglas now, so she might come with me.' Angus had a set expression. With his barrel chest and massive arms, he looked very much like someone who would be useful if there was a problem.

'You think there might be trouble? But how could the People of White know anything about Charlie's clandestine trip?'

'I don't suppose they do. But I just have a bad feeling about tonight.'

The ferry car deck doors were closing, so Angus headed back to his helmsman position. We were still waiting for the harbour bus when the ferry backed out. As it did so, Angus sounded its siren at a small launch driving erratically near its course.

I lifted my binoculars to my eyes. 'Oh *no*! That's Darren Stocks and his mates. They are in one of Ulric Ronaldson's sea-angling boats. They must have rented it from him; I can't see Ulric on board. What are they up to?'

Jessica and I turned to each other. '*Don't* tell me Darren and his mates are smuggling their booze over from Port Erin *tonight*?'

'I sincerely hope they don't try it at all,' she said. 'Charlie Anvil is a very safe pair of hands on a dark night. Darren Stocks – well, I think we'd better have a word with – oh, that's convenient. Here are Barney and Seamus. Seamus?'

The two lifeboat-men ambled over. Jessica pointed. 'Seamus? Do you fancy rescuing *them*?'

Seamus borrowed my binoculars then lowered them. 'I fancy sinking them. They're not the only ones, either.'

'What do you mean?'

'All of Ulric's boats have been rented out for tonight. It's such a calm night, you see. If Charlie Anvil is bringing your wedding dress across he may find the Sound of Doy positively crowded at midnight. Some other lads from Doytown appear to be planning to smuggle some colourful girlie magazines in from somewhere. The golf club doesn't like wearing white – they say they're not cricketers. The trout-fishing club claims that they can't catch anything on white trout flies. And I hear the latest Manchester United strip might feature in yet another brightly coloured cargo.' He sighed. 'I have a feeling that the lifeboat might well get a call out to rescue one or other of them. And Barney's wife is ill. I'm driving him and her up to the surgery now. Are you busy yet tonight, Jessica?'

'Not yet.'

'I'd be prepared for a lifeboat callout, if I were you. Probably up toward the Sound of Doy, that's where they are all planning to cross. Anyway, here's your bus.'

'Thanks, Seamus.' There seemed little we could say. 'We hope we don't see you later.'

■　■　■　■

At the chapel we found Paul, Anna, Uncle Wilfred and a smooth piece of grass, but no Bibles.

Paul had a grin as wide as any of Uncle Wilfred's. 'I had never realized how God's real work was going on beneath the

180

surface. I think it has been that way all of my life. Anna and I have just discovered what matters, in every way. Or rather, *Who* matters.'

Anna was even more excited. 'They *really* did not see all those Bibles! They actually looked at the boxes and just said that the back seat looked rather uncomfortable. I'll never forget that moment as long as I *live*. The power of prayer!'

Wilfred smiled. 'The power of *God* through prayer.'

'The Bibles are all safe underground, then?'

'Very.'

Uncle Wilfred beamed again. 'Have you time to join Paul and Anna at Big Cottage, Timothy? Martha is making oatcakes and cheese.'

'I just need a word with Keith first, Wilfred. Jessica can come with you and I will follow.'

Keith was busy at the Reserve Office with maps and plans. Bob, Jamie and John Khourei were all with him. 'What time are we leaving tonight, Keith?'

Keith gave me a stern look. 'I've been talking to Seamus. I understand you have arranged an extra attraction this evening.'

'Do you mind?'

He relaxed. 'Not for Jessica's wedding dress, no. As long as it's just Charlie, in his boat alone.'

I decided to say nothing incriminating. 'Er – there is one other thing.'

'Yes?'

'Do you know Paul Pristine and Anna?'

His expression darkened. 'I have no time for that twisted Cult.'

'Nor have they. They have decided to leave it.'

'*What*?' John Khourei was ecstatic. 'That's awesome news. But they will be in great danger when they make their decision known.'

'Not if we smuggle them off the island tonight.'

Keith's eyes narrowed. 'I see. So you want them to come up to Sound Point with us? I suppose so. But not if they are dressed in white. They would frighten every petrel that came within thirty yards of them.'

'I'll put them all in black.'

'I'll see you all at eleven-thirty, then. And this time, I will have my night vision binoculars and we will see if we can find a Leach's Petrel at Two Cave Cove.'

．　．　．　．

I left them still poring over maps and walked down the street. I was nearly at Wilfred's house when there was a loud hiss. I assumed that a couple of tom-cats were fighting until Alice's face appeared from behind a bush.

'Why are you hiding?'

'We think Simeon Silver overheard Spottie Mattie boasting. He's looking for us.'

'Why not for me and Jessica?'

'Mattie mentioned our names. We don't want to arouse the suspicions of any of the Cult tonight. Not until our chewing gum consignment is safe.'

'It will be.'

Rosalind's face emerged. 'We may decide to come up and collect it from the boat ourselves.'

'I'll tear you to shreds if I see you. Or at least, I'll tear up the pieces that Keith leaves. Keep *away* from those cliffs – for a whole host of reasons.'

'Yes, Timothy.' They nodded meekly and vanished from sight, leaving me fuming.

I addressed the bush they had vanished into. 'And if you come within a *mile* of Jessica's wedding dress, you will have *her* to answer to.' I felt that Jessica's fury would be a more efficient deterrent than mine. But the bush said nothing.

．　．　．　．

Uncle Wilfred had an expression of deep thought. 'What are you going to do now, Paul? You could be in real danger now.'

'It's all sorted, Wilfred,' I said. 'We're taking them up to Sound Point tonight when we go on our Storm Petrel survey. Charlie Anvil is delivering Jessica's wedding dress into Two Cave Cove at half past midnight and is taking Paul and Anna back with him. They will be off the island before the Cult can do a thing.'

He was amazed. 'Is there anything we can do?'

'Yes. You can keep them safe in here for three hours until we are ready to go. And you can dress them in the blackest old clothes you have.'

Paul was shocked. 'Yes, I suppose it had to happen.' He looked down at his pure white garments. 'It will take some getting used to. But I know now that no-one is this pristine inside.'

Aunt Martha was rummaging round in her knitting bag. 'What are you up to, Martha?' I asked.

She produced a huge ball of black wool. 'If I knit fast, they will both have black balaclava helmets by the time they leave.'

Anna laughed. 'I can knit, too.'

'Take these needles then, dear.'

Wilfred still had a dour look. 'You still aren't convinced, Wilfred?'

'The Cult is now patrolling all the island roads in those new white cars they have brought onto the island. I'm afraid you may have difficulty getting Paul and Anna up there safely without them being stopped. Unless...' Then he started to grin. 'Yes. I have an *idea*.'

27 – Ride on a Giant

Uncle Wilfred disappeared to the telephone. When he came back, he was still grinning. 'I thought so,' he said to no-one in particular.

I eyed him anxiously. 'So what is your idea, Wilfred?'

He waved dismissively. 'Oh, I was just speaking to Jack Dooley down at Ferry Garage. He has been looking for someone to do a driving job for him. He asked me this morning, but I was too busy.'

'Driving what? What sort of a driving job?'

'Killing two or three birds with one stone.' My uncle was trying to conceal his grin and failing.

Jessica leaned over to me. 'Do you think we ought to warn Paul and Anna?'

'Wilfred isn't going to tell us what he is planning. Why turn them into nervous wrecks now?'

Wilfred went hunting through his and Martha's wardrobes and eventually produced black trousers and jumpers that were not very much larger than Paul and Anna. 'I suggest you change at the last minute, just in case anyone from the Cult happens to come to the house during the evening. And here are a couple of warm jackets and waterproofs for the boat journey. I'd like those back, but just leave them with Charlie and he will send them back with Angus on the ferry later.'

Paul nodded. 'I think we also need to collect a few things from where we are staying.'

'That's a point,' said Wilfred. 'They will wonder later why their guests have not come home. We don't want them to phone the Cult asking where you are. Is it Mrs. Soss's B&B down at the bottom of the street that you are staying at?'

'Yes. We've paid her for another week but we don't want the money back.'

'Come with me. She's the sister-in-law of my old friend Tom. She'll play along with us if I explain.'

When they had gone, Jessica and I polished off the rest of Martha's oatcakes. Then I went back to Little Cottage to change my own clothes for ones suitable for a night expedition. Jessica came with me and inspected my wardrobe. She threw out several good pieces of clothing of which I was rather fond. 'I know a dog that will like to sleep on these,' she said. 'I'll start a more thorough revision of your wardrobe once we're married.'

When we reconvened in front of more oatcakes, Wilfred was missing. 'What have you done with him?'

Paul looked slightly bewildered. 'Your Uncle has gone down to Port Doy. He told us to go out through his back garden gate and down the alley, and to be ready waiting at the bottom of the village on this side of the burn bridge at eleven o'clock, standing in the shadows and carrying the step-ladder from his garden shed.'

■   ■   ■   ■

As before, Keith, John Khourei, Jamie, Bob and I crammed into Keith's Land Rover at eleven and set off for our second Storm Petrel survey. Jessica set off home for her bicycle; she had decided to head down to the harbour and be on hand at the lifeboat, in case a call came.

Keith came to a halt at the bottom of the street, where it joined the road across the West Burn and valley. 'What in the name of wonder is *that?*'

Driving up the road from Doytown was a vehicle so large that it hung over both sides of the road. Reversing hurriedly before it were two white cars full of white-suited figures. The two cars backed up a track and their occupants flagged the huge vehicle down. With a thunderous crunch of gears, it rolled to a halt.

'It's a digger. But what a *monster!*' Keith peered at it through the gloom. 'Look at those wheels! Hold on, I know where it's from. It's from Sound Hill Quarry. I saw it down at Harbour Garage – Jack Dooley at the Garage was doing some welding on it. Who on earth is driving it, and at this time of night?'

The white-suited figures leapt from their cars and surrounded it, except for two who saw us and came over to question us. Keith got out as they approached. 'I'm Keith Potts. This is our wildlife survey team, going on an official Lifandoy Reserve survey, looking for Storm Petrels. I've already spoken to Simeon Silver about it.'

The Cult members nodded. 'We know about you, Mr. Potts. We'd rather you looked for white birds, but you are free to go on your survey.'

'Thanks.' Keith put as much scorn into one word as he was able, but they were already turning away.

We all got out and walked down towards the immense digger. At the wheel, not very much to my surprise, was Uncle Wilfred. He was smiling and oozing with charm. 'Oh, I am *so* sorry,' he said to the search team. 'Did you have to back *all* the way up the road? We decided I should drive up at this time of night thinking that the road would be clear of all traffic.'

The leader of the white group peered up at him in astonishment. 'What on earth *is* this vehicle?'

'It's a caterpillar wheel loader from Sound Hill Quarry. The quarry manager drove it down to Harbour Garage so that some welding repairs could be done on it. I'm returning it to help them out, along with its trailer.'

The Cult members scattered to inspect the vehicle. It had a huge bucket, which was well above their heads. But the trailer was covered with tarpaulin. They lifted it off and peered into the darkness below.

The leader held up a hand. 'I'm sorry, but you must wait until we can find a torch to inspect the trailer.'

'Oh, would you like this one?' Beaming, Wilfred handed them his torch. They shone it all round the trailer. The leader of the group returned it. 'You are free to go, Mr. Corn.'

Wilfred gazed at their shiny white cars. 'I suggest you go first, just in case I get into the wrong gear. I wouldn't want to accidentally reverse over your new cars.'

The Cult members got into their cars with alacrity. Both cars turned and went down the road to Doytown, which was the only road open to them, as Wilfred had blocked the rest of the road.

We strolled up and greeted him. 'Are you *safe* driving this, Wilfred? It looks like a JCB, but its bucket is *huge*. It could have anything in it – I can't see into it from down here. It looks big enough to fit a double bed in it, though.'

'Precisely.' Uncle Wilfred grinned. 'I've put an old mattress of Jack's into it. All it needs now is two passengers, carried high above the view of any People of White inspection teams. If anyone stops me they will search the trailer again, assuming that any fugitives will be hiding under the tarpaulin there. If they ask about the bucket, then I will tell them it's locked and can't be lowered while I'm driving it on the road, which happens to be true. Paul and Anna will be high above their view.'

'But likely to be bounced right *out* of the bucket, if you go over a bump in the road?'

'Hmm. Perhaps they had better tie themselves in...' Uncle Wilfred looked at us. 'Do you want to go first up the road to Sound Hill?'

Keith nodded. 'We'll get out of your way.' We returned to the Land Rover. He turned onto the road down to the West Burn bridge and Wilfred followed.

As we reached the bridge, I tapped Keith on the shoulder. 'Hold on a minute, Keith. Just stop here, if you don't mind; I want to watch something.'

He obliged and I watched through the Land Rover's rear window as Wilfred halted the monster next to a clump of trees. Two figures in black emerged. They set up a step-ladder and climbed up into the bucket. Wilfred picked up the stepladder and put it into the trailer. Then he returned to his driver's cab.

He closed its door quietly. As he did so, I saw something else. 'Hey! Who's *that*?'

'What?' asked Keith.

'It looks like several more figures in black have just emerged – small ones. They've disappeared behind the trailer. They...'

At that moment Wilfred switched his main headlights on. '*Aaah*! Just a minute! I want to get out and see who it was that...'

Keith was in no mood to delay. 'I'm getting right out of the path of that *thing*,' he insisted. 'We're working. We have a job to do. And perhaps, a very rare bird to find.' He accelerated away. 'Under *no* circumstances am I staying stationary on a road when Wilfred Corn is grinning and driving a monster in my direction.'

187

■ ■ ■ ■

Wilfred and his juggernaut soon fell behind on the road. No other white cars stopped us, which was a good thing for them as well as us, since it was not obvious that when Wilfred caught up he would be able to stop in time.

We turned off the island road next to a small farm near Snaefell Bay and parked again on the track near the cliffs, this time directly above Two Cave Cove. There was very little wind and for a few minutes it was almost silent apart from the distant sound of the surf far below. Then Wilfred arrived. He juddered to a halt next to us. Keith was exasperated. 'Wilfred? Get that monstrosity up to the quarry! A noise like that will frighten every bird for miles.'

My uncle climbed down rapidly from his cab. He reached under the tarpaulin over the trailer, and pulled out the stepladder. He placed it up to the bucket and Paul and Anna climbed down. They looked rather green. Paul winced. 'I think we spent about ten per cent of that journey in mid-air. We rebounded every time the machine went over a bump. If we hadn't been tied down on that mattress we would be lying somewhere at the roadside.'

While they regained their balance, Wilfred put the stepladder back. As he did so, I noticed an odd noise from the trailer. I was turning to look when Keith spoke. 'Where do you want Paul and Anna, Tim? I don't want them in the way of our survey.'

I looked down towards the cover. 'I would suggest they walk down carefully and hide in one of the caves in case any intruders appear.'

Equipped with Wilfred's torch, Paul and Anna started to descend the long slope to the Cove. I was talking to Wilfred and watching them go when I thought I saw a movement in the corner of my eye. I turned, but all I could see was a field of odd-shaped rocks beyond the trailer.

28 - Gunshot

Uncle Wilfred returned to his cab and drove off up the hill to the quarry. Shortly he reappeared, walking back again. We were still looking at maps and listening to the first petrels that were starting to fly overhead. I looked up.

'Wilfred? How do you propose to get back to West Doy again? You'll have to wait a couple of hours and then squeeze in if you want to go back in our Land Rover.'

He shook his head. 'When I was at Harbour Garage I bumped into Gareth Jones from Snaefell Farm, just down at the road junction. His little muck spreader needs a hole patching. I also wanted to talk to him about renting a field for sheep from him. He's invited me for a late supper so I will go and have a chat to him. I'll drive his tractor and spreader down to Harbour Garage and then retrieve my car.'

'You'll be very late back.'

'Martha knows where I am. And frankly it's easier to drive the island roads in the early hours now, rather than answer all the foolish questions at the roadblocks the People of White operate during the day.'

Again, as Wilfred was talking I thought I saw a movement, this time on the path Paul and Anna had descended. But in the moonlight my eyes were probably playing tricks on me.

Before I could respond, Keith had called us to order. 'I can't hear anything from the hole where we heard that strange petrel calling last time. And I felt right into the hole, but it is empty: there's no chick or egg. So we'll head along the coast and repeat two more surveys like the last. Then we'll come back here and listen for different petrels again nearer the time when we heard that one before. That should get us back to the Cove nicely in time to meet Charlie Anvil motoring in, if he's on time.'

We set off and began two more of our ten-metre square surveys of the rocky slope which the stormies seemed to prefer. As twelve-thirty approached we returned to the car park above Two Cave Cove. To our alarm there were no less than five cars there in addition to our Land Rover. But none of them was white.

Keith was apoplectic. 'Who are all these night owls?' he demanded. He lifted his night vision binoculars to his eyes. 'I can see a *crowd* down in the Cove. And...' his voice rose two or three tones. 'I can see at least *four* boats coming in!' He continued his exclamations, in language that would have turned the air blue if it were not already black.

He threw his maps into the Land Rover and set off down the Cove path at a furious pace. The four of us followed, as fast as we dared.

■　■　■　■

Reaching the Cove, we found it full of moving shapes in the darkness, which seemed to want to evade our torches. I went to one of the caves. Paul and Anna were sitting on a flat rock, looking cold and rather puzzled. 'What's going on, Tim?'

'I don't know. There are strangers about, but they don't seem to be in white. You'd better come down to the beach and I'll signal to Charlie in his boat.'

We walked down to the shoreline. Behind me, I thought I heard a stone move in the second cave. But I wanted Charlie to land as soon as possible, so I started flashing the agreed signal to him. In a couple of minutes, his launch was sliding in beside some flat rocks.

'Charlie? It's me, Tim.' I grabbed a rope that was tossed toward me.

A torch flashed for a moment, showing his face. 'That's a relief. What's going on, Tim? There is a small flotilla out there. Who are all those night birds off Lifandoy? Who's in the other boats?'

'I'm afraid the word has got around that this would be a good place to land contraband tonight. I think they're all smugglers. Darren Stocks is one of them.'

'Actually, I don't think he is. I know Darren. I thought I heard his voice in a boat we saw further out. It was one that appeared to be stopped in the water. I don't know why. I thought it was drifting, and then it started off again.'

'It was heading around the far side of these rocks. There's no good landing there.' It was Angus's voice.

'Angus? I'm glad Charlie has company.'

'Jane is with me, too.' Another face lit up for a moment. 'Are Paul and Anna here?'

'Yes. Have you brought the wedding dress?'

'Wrapped up as if it were made of gold.' A flat package appeared; I took it reverently. John Khourei was standing behind me, so I passed it to him for safe keeping. He retreated back to the beach carrying it as if it were a crate of eggs.

Paul and Anna came forward in turn, and took Angus's arm as they stepped down into the boat. Charlie shone his torch to show them where to sit, and then turned back to me.

'And here's your chewing gum.'

'What?' Keith was now standing curiously behind me. 'You can drop that in the water.'

Suddenly, a tide of small figures swept past him. '*Hey*!' He slipped and sat down in a rock pool. The chewing gum box was lifted from the arms of a startled Charlie and vanished into the gloom as if it were a lost soul being snatched by dark spirits.

■　■　■　■

Then, all at once, several startling things happened in quick succession. The first was that a red hand-held distress flare seared into flame somewhere behind the rocks beyond us, from where we could hear breakers on a sharp reef. A cacophony of shouts came from the direction of the flare. 'That sounds like Darren's voice! He's close to the reef!'

The second was that a fleet of car headlights suddenly shone out from the car park above, shining high over the whole Cove. In the sudden glare, we could see that at least two of the cars were white. Several car doors slammed and many feet started clattering down the stony path toward us.

The third was that a searchlight suddenly shone toward the Cove from a vessel rapidly approaching the Cove from the south. 'That's got to be the lifeboat! Seamus must have brought her up here just in case.' The searchlight focused on the far side of the rocks behind us and the roar of the lifeboat's powerful engines echoed from the rocks across the Cove.

I dropped the rope. 'Charlie! Get Paul and Anna *out* of here, fast!'

'Not yet!' Angus leapt forward and held the rocks. 'I'm coming ashore. If there's trouble starting…'

Jane leapt forward too, a bag in her hand. 'And you might need a doctor!' Angus and I helped her ashore and he followed her onto the rocks. Charlie instantly swung his tiller over and his boat roared away, with Paul and Anna sitting stunned together.

The new lights showed that several boats had now pulled ashore on the beach. Various figures were unloading boxes and packages. They all froze, horrified by the stampede of newcomers down from above. A mass of white figures poured onto the beach, racing to grab the boats and the packages. One figure escaped their attention; I could see John Khourei creeping up the further slope, avoiding the path and taking advantage of the geographical knowledge we had gained while looking over the Cove earlier. Bob and Jamie were following him; Jamie's bulky Scots form provided a dark rearguard; it was clear that any attempt to steal Jessica's wedding dress would meet a furious Braveheart response.

High on the path, a darker figure was following the Cult's white legion down towards the beach. Meanwhile, from the distressed boat out of sight behind us, a white flare suddenly soared into the night sky. In its glare, I saw that the latecomer was Graham Fytts. He reached the beach and started in our direction. He pointed out to sea, towards Charlie's departing craft. '*That's* the boat we *should* stop!'

Four of the Cult heard him and leapt towards a boat close to us on the sand. A brief fight ensued and one of the boat's original occupants was punched and fell out of the boat. Two of the white figures climbed in and began trying to start the boat's motor.

Angus leapt down onto the sand and approached the boat. '*I* don't think so!' The other two in white were trying to push the boat into the surf. Angus brushed them aside like an irritated bear and reached in toward the two struggling with the motor, one of whom grappled with him.

I leapt down from the rocks and ran after him. 'Stop it! Dear Lord, help us! Angus – don't push them too far!' I came up behind

Angus and tried to push past him to stop him and the Cult members injuring each other.

■　■　■　■

For a moment, the other figures across the Cove paused at my shout. Then another sound stopped us all. Graham Fytts was approaching Angus and me. He lifted his arm. Just as he did so, Angus turned round, extended one huge hand and pressed down on my shoulder, forcing me to fall flat in front of him. There was a single sharp crack. I was looking at Graham as I heard it, and saw the jet of blue flame from the gun in his right hand. If Angus had not pushed me down, it would have been pointing at my head. As it was, it lanced over me. I heard a gasp from Angus above me.

Jane's scream pierced the night sky. The gunshot and the cream together shocked the whole struggling crowd into immobility. 'Angus!'

The massive short figure of the *Bagpipe's* helmsman began to topple. Angus crumpled slowly backward over the gunwale into the boat. Jane raced up, leapt in, dropped to his side, threw open her bag and started tearing away at his clothing. Around the boat, many figures, dark and white, stood suddenly silent.

29 – Good News

I leapt into the boat to join Jane. We pulled up his thick seaman's jersey and exposed the small hole above his heart. Jane grabbed a thick dressing and held it on tightly as the blood pumped into it, turning it red rapidly. 'Get me another! And another! And wrap him – keep him warm!'

Graham was standing beside the boat. 'Is it any good? I wasn't aiming at *him.*'

She ignored him. A tall figure stepped forward. It was Simeon Silver. Without a word he reached out and took the gun from Graham's hand. He gestured and two of the largest Cult members took Fytts fiercely by the arms.

Jane spoke, more to herself than anyone there. 'It's above the heart. If it hasn't hit a major vessel he has a chance. Get him to hospital *now.*'

'The lifeboat!' I leapt up. 'Where is she?' Several of the bystanders leapt up onto the rocks and started flailing their arms in the light of the searchlight shining near the reef beyond them.

The light swung round as the lifeboat surged forward into view, abandoning a boat and its occupants adrift behind it. It was calm enough to hear the shout. Seamus's stentorian voice sounded over the noise of the lifeboat's engines. '*What is it?*'

I bellowed back. 'Gunshot wound! Life or death!'

Someone got the engine of our boat started. The boat, with Angus, was steered out toward the searchlight. We came alongside. Several large figures leapt down and started to lift Angus, as Jane kept the dressings pressed hard onto the wound.

Jessica shouted down to me. 'Tim! What?'

'Fytts shot him. He was aiming at me. Angus saved me. Get Angus to Douglas Hospital *now!*'

'And leave you with Fytts?'

'Simeon Silver has him under arrest. *Go!*'

The lifeboat's engines suddenly raged. Leaving us rocking wildly, it roared round in an incredibly tight curve and set off out to sea, obviously under emergency full power. Angus might die or live; but he was in the safest hands he could possibly be in.

. . . .

As the lifeboat disappeared, voices became audible from the boat that it had stopped rescuing. Darren's was loudest among them. 'Hey! You can't leave us here! And we have twelve cases of beer on board.'

I turned to the two Cult members still in the boat with me. 'Just land me on the rocks, will you? Then take this boat out to them with a squad of your friends, throw all their beer overboard and then tow them in.' They nodded angrily.

I crossed the rocks and walked slowly back across the sand. I felt very old. Two new figures had appeared, those of Sergeant Farquhar and his constable, William Williams. 'We saw the cavalcade of cars and followed to make sure there was no trouble. But we were too late. Is Angus alive?'

'Jane MacEachern is doctoring him. She thinks he will probably make it.'

Farquhar had a very hard expression. 'There has never been a shooting on Lifandoy. Mr. Fytts is already in handcuffs. He will be in custody for a *very* long time. Now give me the names of all the witnesses.'

As he was writing them down, Simeon Silver came up. He eyed me uneasily. 'If we had known that Fytts might attempt to kill you, we would never have co-operated with him for a moment.'

'I don't doubt it. It never crossed my mind, either. I think Graham needs help as well as punishment.'

Simeon stared at me. 'We pride ourselves in the People of White on having the purest motives and hearts. You have put us to shame by saying that.'

I gazed around. 'Perhaps it's what we are inside, and what God sees us to be inside, that really matters. A lot of people just couldn't see that Jesus was God Himself from the beginning, merely by looking at a carpenter.' I gazed around. 'You'd better get back to your policing duties. There are lots of non-white things in sight.'

He nodded. 'There are. But I think that we of the People need to go back home and reflect on why we do what we do.'

He signalled and all the white figures started back up to their cars. On the beach, there was a solemn tidying up as some packages were carried up to the cars and others left in the boats regardless as the boats all slowly launched one by one and moved off.

When the last had gone, Keith and I stood still and just listened to the sound of the waves for a minute. Then we started up the path. Near the top, we met John, Jamie and Bob descending to look for us. They stopped and waited for us. 'The wedding dress is safe, Tim, if that matters.'

'I'm only interested in Angus until we hear good news.'

We all walked wearily up the slope. Then we stopped. From a small boulder pile to our right was sounding a curious noise.

Keith looked at us. 'That's the other petrel again.' He walked across to the boulders and located the dark crack from which the sound came. 'A hundred to one it's a Leach's Petrel.'

John Khourei knelt down and looked at the hole. 'I've never seen a Leach's Petrel.'

'It's like a Storm Petrel, with a white rump, but bigger and with a forked tail.'

'I know. And this is a Leach's? Not one of those black-rumped petrels you said you saw from the ferry?'

'You mean the Swinhoe's Storm Petrels, which nest on the Selvagens Islands off Madeira?' Keith laughed. 'They certainly don't nest in the British Isles.'

'No?'

'Not in a million years.' Keith reached forward and inserted his hand slowly into the crevice. 'I can feel an adult ... and a chick!' he said in astonishment. He moved his hand around very gently then removed his arm from the hole little by little. In his hand was an adult petrel rather larger than the Storm Petrels we had seen earlier. He turned it around and we shone a torch onto its tail. There was no trace of white at all. It was black all over.

'Not in a million years, you said? This is one of our *real* night birds off Lifandoy.'

■　■　■　■

Next morning, I found Alice chewing strawberry-flavoured gum and leaning on my hedge. She looked up worriedly. 'How's Angus Donald?'

'He's alive. We'll know better later. Where did you get that gum?'

'Need you ask?'

I scowled. 'Was it you in that trailer? But how on earth did you get it back here?'

'We don't reveal all of our methods.'

Someone was coming up the street. It was Simon. 'Tim? Have you heard the news?'

Simon's face did not look like one about to bring grave tidings. 'What news?' I added cautiously. 'About Angus?'

His face fell. 'I don't know anything more about that than you do. But I certainly haven't heard any bad news. No, I meant about the chewing gum.'

Alice and I both turned to look at him. '*What?*'

He looked down at Alice and her gum. 'Did you smuggle that onto the island, young lady? If so, you've done a great service to child protection.'

'I *have?*' For once – perhaps the only time ever – my sister-in-law-to-be was completely taken aback. 'How?'

'The children of the People of White have all acquired strawberry-flavoured chewing gum now. The daughter of Shining-son, Minnie, was chewing it at the Doy Hotel when her father saw her. He took off his leather belt and started to hit her. But Constable Williams was visiting the hotel on business. He called Sergeant Farquhar and they arrested Shining-son. Shining-son's wife is giving evidence against him and says he is a serial child beater. All the Press are down at the Doy Hotel…'

'Except you?'

He smiled. 'The story has missed my deadline. I'm only a weekly and the dailies have it already, so it will be old news by next week. My nose tells me there might be a different story in this direction.'

'That's just possible.' I looked down the road past Simon. A line of white cars was moving slowly toward us. 'If so, it will be in church at ten-thirty.'

■　■　■　■

West Doy chapel was bursting at the seams. Arriving late as usual, I was amazed to find virtually everyone in the village was there, plus many from Doytown. Entering through the main door at the rear corner of the building, I saw Jessica standing next to Seamus. I squeezed in beside her. Even from there I could see that a whole section of seating was filled with members of the People of White, with Simeon White, Serena Snow and Friedrich Frost at their head. All of them had grey faces. In front of them the chapel choir, with Rosalind and Alice at the front, gazed at them.

Uncle Wilfred walked up the aisle carrying a large stack of Bibles, handing one out for each row of seats. 'There are more to come.' They were his new Bibles; the Cult's version was nowhere to be seen.

Simeon stared as Wilfred handed one to him. 'Where did you get *these*?'

Uncle Wilfred smiled. 'Paul Pristine drove them off the ferry, in my wife's Mini.'

Simeon's jaw dropped. 'I was *there*. I looked into the Mini.'

'They were on the back seat, in boxes.'

'I looked straight at the back seat. There was *nothing* to be seen there.'

Wilfred nodded. 'Nothing, for those who did not *want* to see anything.'

Simeon took the offered copy with a shaking hand and opened it. He stared at it wordlessly. Wilfred handed out more Bibles, and then went to the front. 'Before our morning worship starts, you will all want to know about Angus. I heard from Jane three minutes ago. I'm delighted say that he is out of danger.'

30 – Forgiveness

There were gasps, one or two sobs, and a cheer. 'Praise the Lord!'

Wilfred picked up one of his new Bibles and opened it. 'This is a time for great reflection.' He lifted his head and examined the serried ranks of the People of White. 'I shall preach from the true Bible this morning. It may be that I will not be allowed to do so again, but you must hear the truth this once.'

He turned the pages. 'One of the problems with trying to live a flawless, perfect life is that we *cannot*. We are all sinners and have all fallen short of the glory of God.'

As he was speaking, I noticed the door of the chapel beside me open. Three figures slipped quietly inside and stood silently at the back, otherwise unseen. I did not turn round but from the corner of the eye something seemed familiar about the foremost of them.

'A second problem,' Wilfred continued, 'is that it makes us forget the reality of forgiveness. We forget God's forgiveness through the death of His only, eternal Son; *and* our own forgiveness of each other.'

'There are those who have taken Bibles from this church. There are those who have forced distorted Bibles on us. We forgive these people, though we cannot forget their acts or abide them. There are those who have carried out crimes against children, or even attempted to kill. We forgive these people, though we will fight to our last breath to prevent such crimes.'

'We forgive because we have been forgiven. We have been forgiven because we have a heavenly *Friend*. We have such a Friend not because we went looking for Him but because from the beginning of eternity He was looking for *us*, and came to prove it.

'Jesus, God's Son, is able to provide us with forgiveness because He is all that God ever was or will be – so He is *able*. And He is all that we are – so He is *willing*. And the third Person of God is as real as He is. Christians believe in God, the Three in One. If you do not, then I will ask you this: where is your Friend who will forgive you?'

Wilfred sighed. 'These words may fall on deaf ears, for the future of this island is not in my hands or in the hands of anyone who agrees with me.' He stared down the aisle at Simeon Silver. 'Is that not so?'

Simeon lifted his head. 'I can't help that,' he said quietly. 'Though I would almost *like* to. Our present situation is not one I would have chosen, or would continue with, if there was any alternative. But I can't do anything.'

'But *I* can.' A new voice spoke, quietly but firmly. It came from the back of the congregation, from the figure behind me who seemed familiar.

We all turned in surprise. A fairly small man moved along the rear of the congregation to the centre of the chapel and walked slowly up the aisle toward Wilfred. He was grey-haired, with a slight limp and a plaster across one side of his temple. An elegant-looking woman, and a fit-looking young man with a similarity to them both, followed him. As the small man's face came in sight of each row of seats in turn, the startled whispering grew.

Uncle Wilfred's eyebrows rose nearly to the top of his head. He was about to say something, but the small man stopped next to Simeon Silver and turned to look at him. 'Mr. Silver. I am interested to meet you. I am the Earl of Lifandoy.'

Simeon's jaw dropped. 'Which one?'

The Earl regarded him thoughtfully. 'I owe your people much for the care you have taken of my son Dominic. But that does not include Mr. Shining Senior. He is, I believe, now under arrest by the Canadian police for historic offences not dissimilar to those which his son is also likely to be charged with here. I will ensure that every possible force of law will be applied against him, so far as it is within my power.'

The Earl paused, gazing at Simeon. 'Had I arrived earlier and not heard the thoughtful words of my old friend Wilfred Corn, and the words with which you replied to him, I might also have applied such hostility to you. But forgiveness is a great gift, when possible.' He turned and walked forward.

Uncle Wilfred held out his hand. 'This is a *very* great surprise and pleasure, Richard. Where *have* you been?'

200

The Earl smiled. 'If by any chance you are ever forced to ditch in the Channel in a small plane, and then to float away in an inflatable dinghy when it sinks, try not to drop all your mobile phones in the sea. And certainly, try not to get rescued by a foreign merchant vessel which has no-one at all on board who speaks English, and which has a broken radio. It was an interesting voyage, but a tedious and very frustrating one. We arrived back from Montevideo in a chartered plane an hour ago.'

■　■　■　■

As we walked out of the chapel, I looked closely at the line of white cars. Every one of them, on examination, proved to be splattered with dirt and worse. 'Wilfred?' My uncle was standing near me. 'Why are all their cars dirty?'

My uncle grinned. 'I can't imagine. I drove past them last night with Gareth Jones's muck-spreader behind me. But I'm sure I had it switched off.'

Jessica was at my side. I took her right hand firmly while my uncle shook her left hand. 'Well done. I understand you were at the helm.'

The Earl and his wife appeared at Wilfred's side. 'We owe the lifeboat crew a great debt. It's a pity they weren't on hand to rescue *us*! And you have all played a good hand.'

'I'm sorry.' Jessica smiled. 'If you had called, we would have come.'

His wife took Jessica's left hand and looked at the ring on it. 'When is the wedding?'

'Next Saturday. Here.'

She laughed delightedly. 'Oh, *goodness*. Could we possibly come?'

'Of course.'

'Will you be dressed in white?'

'Yes. The wedding dress was smuggled in last night.'

The Earl was outraged. 'Because it was *white*? My dear, we have a great debt to repay to you.'

Uncle Wilfred smiled. 'From what I have heard, the entire island was indignant on Jessica's behalf. We are all very fond of her.'

'I shall see what we can do to help her wedding, in every way.' The Earl looked at Jess. 'Who will be presenting you as the bride? Your father was the lifeboat hero, Jessica, wasn't he? We miss him very greatly.'

Jess lowered her head for a moment. 'Yes. It doesn't matter. There is no one else.'

'If you need a friend, just ask me.'

She looked at him. 'I might just do that.'

Wilfred nodded. 'There is nothing more precious than a friend.'

■　■　■　■

The week before one's wedding is both the fastest and the slowest week of one's life. By Saturday morning I was terrified. I was standing just outside the chapel door, with one hand on Angus's wheelchair and one eye on the choir screeching at their choir practice inside, when it finally hit me.

'Angus? This is my last *hour* of freedom.'

'I'm glad for every hour, Tim. All of Wilfred's words came back to me on that lifeboat. I know how important it all is now, even more than before.'

I looked around for more sympathy. 'Hey, Simon. Good to see you. How did your scoop of the story of the Earl's return do?'

Our journalist friend was beaming. 'I scooped all the dailies through the agency, while they were all chasing the child abuse story' he said. 'An Earl back from the dead is as good a story as they come. And for the *Chronicle* this week, you're sure I can use the rare petrel story?'

'As long as you don't name any location on the island.'

'You don't think it will attract unwanted attention?'

'We won't be swamped with birdwatchers. They know they could never find the nest without our guidance, and we won't be giving that except possibly to a select few. But our all black birds may well benefit the island tourist business, now that birders know the *Bagpipe* crossing is the best one to watch for Swinhoe's Storm Petrels from.'

Simon nodded. 'And what about the People of White? Is it true the Cult is breaking up?'

'They've lost their prophet. We hope they will profit by their loss, certainly. Paul and Anna have left for good, and Paul has reverted to his old surname, from Pristine to Preston. Most of the People are returning to Canada. Friedrich Frost is going to set up a new charity to take over their hospital at Fourjohns, now as a purely medical operation. Dominic Lifandoy will stay there under their care, of course.'

Angus looked up. 'What about Simeon and Serena?'

'Simeon is devastated by how the Shinings were deceiving him with their child abuse, and by Fytts. He had no clue what was going on. And he now sees what their Cult did to the island in a very different light. He and Serena are thinking of staying on the island and trying to make some restitution. Did you know that they are married, by the way? Shining-son had forbidden any of the other Cult members from wearing rings. Serena is a trained nurse, so with the help of some of the Cult's money she is going to work with Jane to set up an on-call Minor Injury medical facility on the island, working alongside the island surgery, so that there would be a fast response medical team on hand if any incident like Angus's happened again.'

'And Simeon himself?'

'Uncle Wilfred has been promoted into Graham Fytts' position as House Farm manager. But he admits he's getting a little old for a major managerial post. Simeon has worked as a farm manager in Canada; he says he would be greatly honoured to work under Wilfred as a trainee to see whether he can learn enough about British farming to take a proper role. In any case, he and Serena will keep living at the House Farm for now. Graham Fytts himself, of course, is facing a life sentence for both attempted murder and grievous bodily harm with a firearm.'

Simon finished scribbling notes. 'Tim, your stories should be written in book form. You've had some amazing adventures.'

I laughed. 'One day, maybe. But here's my best man.'

Keith walked up and stood beside me. 'Is it time to frog-march you into the chapel?'

'Oh, can't I have a few more last minutes of freedom in the sunshine on the lawn?'

'That reminds me,' said Simon. 'I presume your underground church can be opened up now?' He looked across the lawn. 'Why is it still sealed? I thought Wilfred left it open after he brought up the Bibles he had hidden there.'

'We had to seal it up again. Didn't you hear? Darren Stocks and his mates came up to the chapel yesterday evening to see if I was under arrest. They were furious about their lost beer. But they had had too much white wine. The hole was open and Darren fell down it and was too drunk to get out. His friends left him and we hauled him out only an hour ago, blue with cold.'

'Serve him right for letting himself be trapped.'

'Hah. Should I be feeling trapped, too?'

'You're a willing victim.'

31 - Wedding

I turned round as the bridal march started and Jessica began walking up the aisle. Ahead of her, in fluffy pink dresses, were Rosalind and Alice. I was startled to see that Jessica's sisters were, in fact, genuinely female.

Rosalind's appearance caused the only untoward incident of the day, when pimply Julius, who was dressed in a tight, smart suit like his father the Factor, fainted clean away on seeing her. No-one fainted as Alice walked slowly along behind her, although several small boys went pale with shock as she passed them and they realized who she was.

Jessica – well, she was – *oh*, my oodles-of-oozing gorgeous sexy haze-of- loveliness *delightful* –and more. She whispered to me. 'Stand up straight, Timothy! If you lean like that toward me, you will fall over.'

We turned together and faced Uncle Wilfred. He cleared his throat. 'Dearly beloved, we are gathered here…' Shortly, he looked to one side. 'Who presents this woman to be married to this man?'

The Earl of Lifandoy, resplendent in full morning dress, stepped forward. 'I do,' he said clearly. 'And…' he looked over his shoulder at the whole congregation 'We *all* do.'

Wilfred had to wait for the cheers to subside before he could continue. 'In the presence of our Lord Jesus Christ…'

■　■　■　■

'You may kiss the bride…' As Uncle Wilfred stepped back, his face broke into a grin. As a connoisseur of grins of all levels, I judged that it was possibly the broadest and most dangerous one of his I had ever seen. But the congregation behind me, for once, did not duck or flinch at the sight of Wilfred's teeth. In fact, they returned it with increased power. Or I assume they did, for my eyes were focused at very short range on Jessica's alone.

As we walked down the aisle, smiling faces were everywhere. We took our time, acknowledging some of them.

At the front was Angus in his wheelchair, with Jane beside him. We grinned at the engagement ring on Jane's left hand. Further back were Paul and Anna. They looked down shyly then up again, sharing our smiles as another engagement ring, on Anna's hand, glittered in the light. Further back still were Simeon and Serena; we were delighted to see that John Khourei was standing firmly alongside them. Behind us, Keith was walking arm in arm with Jessica's mother, while Alice and Rosalind, with looks of awe on their faces, were walking hand in hand with the Earl.

Behind us – and around us, as we walked out into the sunshine, it seemed that all of the Isle of Lifandoy was present. They waited expectantly as Simon set up his camera; then they cheered like a football crowd as we kissed again.

■　　■　　■　　■

After the reception, we stepped into the Earl's own Rolls Royce, which carried us in serious style down to Port Doy. A small army of vehicles and bicycles followed us. The grand car rolled along the quay and stopped above the lifeboat. The lifeboat was decked out with bunting. I whispered to Jessica. 'It will be a colourful rescue if Seamus gets a call while we are on board!'

She whispered back. 'We can handle it.'

We descended to the deck. Suddenly, a small rocket shot over us. It was evidently a confetti rocket, not a distress flare. Seamus grumbled as lots of pretty little fragments fell all over his lifeboat. Everyone cheered.

With Uncle Wilfred, Alice and Jessica's mother at the front of the crowd, everyone cheered again as the lifeboat set out. Jessica had exchanged her wedding dress for a sleek blue outfit, which looked stunning with a yellow lifejacket over it. The lifeboat creamed out to sea.

We passed the South Rock at a safe distance. I held Jessica close as we stared at the black, grim stone. She nodded. 'Daddy is sharing today with us.'

'We've shared a *lot* together. We have lived through a lot. Now we can live through the rest together.' The Cape of Doy and the shell-white beaches of the Reserve gleamed in the late evening

206

westerly sun as we creamed slowly through the sparkling waves past them.

The Great Stack was just disappearing into the shadows as we approached Raw Head. We rounded the head and set off past Mourne Point along the coast. As Tystie Bay and its secret white sands appeared, the lifeboat slowed and began to turn.

■ ■ ■ ■

The picture window of the Tystie Bay Hotel's bridal suite faced straight out towards the setting sun. When we landed at the jetty, Seamus carried our cases across and gave them straight to John Davies at the hotel door. We followed him upstairs. He put them down and handed us the key. We closed the door softly behind him as he walked away, and locked it.

Jessica sat down at the dressing table. 'I *have* to do something with my hair. You can shower first.'

Before long, feeling fresh and clean, I was standing at the window, wearing just a warm hotel bathrobe, gazing out at the first stars of a perfect Isle of Lifandoy evening. I heard the shower stop running. There was the sound of a hair-dryer; then the door opened and I heard feet padding. Lips kissed the back of my neck. We gazed at the twilight together, only our fingertips touching.

'Marriage is a very strange thing,' she whispered.

'It is. According to Wilfred, it is an extension of eternity. Jesus Christ weds His Bride, the Church. And He does it always, *forever*. Our personal marriage is not merely human. It's not even merely a Christian marriage, which is one that involves all of our bodies, minds and spirits.'

She nodded. 'Our marriage has its reality *inside* His, as all real marriages do, even when we don't realize it.'

'What about those who never marry?'

'If they know Jesus, then they are inside His marriage just as much as we are. Even more so, I suspect.'

'Is marriage more real to them than us?'

'We'd better find out.'

My left hand took my wife's right one. I could feel her feeling my ring. We clasped our fingers together hungrily, savouring every moment.

'Jess? I've been meaning to ask you.'

'Ask me what?'

'You said that girls have secret ways that no boy ever learns about. *What* ways?'

She laughed. 'You're not a boy now, Tim. You're a man. The only thing that matters is that you're my husband from today. Even better, you're my *friend*.

'May I have your permission to learn?'

She laughed again. 'You are allowed to learn, now. As am I, about you.'

'What can a man learn, then?'

'Whatever you want, darling.' She smiled at the twilit sky. 'We can learn about everything that you, I and Jesus have been waiting quite a while for.'

We turned to look at each other. I reached my right hand gently round through her soft tresses, to feel the back of my heartbreakingly beautiful wife's femininely slender neck. I kissed it, then her lips. 'I think this is where things start to get funny and embarrassing for us both.'

She raised an eyebrow. 'Is that all?'

I winced. 'No. But it's not all one-sided. I've just realized what I've *done*.'

'What, married a woman?'

'Exactly.'

'Why are you *grinning*, then?'

'So are you.'

Jessica chuckled. 'But your grin is related to your Uncle Wilfred's.'

'You'd better watch out, then.'

■　■　■　■

Shortly, there was a faint creak from the bed. The picture window was now unobscured. Slowly the stars came out brighter and brighter, until God's own fires were as strange and joyous and glorious as ours.

THE END

Previously in the Lifandoy series:

A Nest on Lifandoy
An Orchid on Lifandoy
Falcons over Lifandoy

More details from www.hillintheway.co.uk